Magegift

Magegift

Scott Calver

Magegift Copyright 2019 by Scott Calver

All rights reserved, no part of this book may be reproduced in any form or by any electronic or mechanical means including information storage and retrieval systems, without permission in writing from the author. The only exception is by a reviewer, who may quote short excerpts in a review.

This book is a work of fiction, all characters and incidents are fictitious and products of the authors imagination. Any resemblance or similarity with any persons, living or dead or real-life events is entirely incidental.

Scott Calver

Printed in the United Kingdom

First Printing May 2019

Second Printing June 2019

ISBN-9781095956519

For Theresa and Jess, Cheryl and Russell.

Contents

Foreword		7-8
Introduction	the Seal	9-10
Chapter 1	The Funeral	11-17
Chapter 2	Hawkins	18-25
Chapter 3	Cairo	26-31
Chapter 4	The Summit	32-38
Chapter 5	Lines of Power	40-47
Chapter 6	The Pit	48-54
Chapter 7	The Will	55-61
Chapter 8	The Break in	62-79
Chapter 9	Nihilism and Fatalism	70-76
Chapter 10	Caught Red-handed	77-84
Chapter 11	The Yard	85-92
Chapter 12	Decipher This	93-101
Chapter 13	Behind You	102-109
Chapter 14	Politics, Politics, Politics	110-117
Chapter 15	The Runner	118-125
Chapter 16	Not Quite Yoga	126-133
Chapter 17	Rooftops	134-140
Chapter 18	The Second Seal	141-148
Chapter 19	Bonds Weaken, Arms Reach Through	149-155
Chapter 20	Black Winged Warning	156-163
Chapter 21	The Masons Deal	164-170
Chapter 22	The Book Reads Thus	171-177
Chapter 23	The Third Seal	178-185

Chapter 24	The Legions Gather	186-192
Chapter 25	Too Late	193-201
Chapter 26	The Discovery	202-208
Chapter 27	Dimensional Alignment	209-216
Chapter 28	The Car Accident	217-224
Chapter 29	Heveningham and the Angel	225-231
Chapter 30	The Drenched Blade	232-239
Chapter 31	The Ritual	240-247
Chapter 32	Better Never than Late	248-253
Chapter 33	The Imps Bargain	254-260
Chapter 34	The Hordes Arrive	261-266
Chapter 35	Mad Woman, Power Hungry Man	267-274
Chapter 36	Turncoats	275-281
Chapter 37	Blue Skies Above Suffolk	282-286

Foreword

Once when I was young and at school, I had said to one of my teachers that 'I was going to write a book.' I was only sixteen then, very naïve and I was sure that I knew better than anybody else. My teacher had said to me, 'What will you do whilst you write this book?'

My teacher was correct, I needed a job, so I took a job, working in a local factory. I made friends there, went out drinking and partying and soon, I had forgotten all about what I had wanted to do when 'I grew up!' Occasionally as the years went by, I had skirted with the idea and maybe got down ten or fifteen thousand words, but then I would run out of steam, another whim taking hold and I would forget about the writing.

I then suddenly found that I was getting into middle age and had taken the ever-popular vow to start ticking off the various things on my 'bucket list.'

to my shock I had still not written a book, I had a sports car, black belts in various martial arts, I had married my beautiful wife, had a successful job, but the one on the list that I realised had been there the longest still evaded me.

So, I am now writing a foreword after a lot of early mornings before I would get in my work van. Each morning writing a little more, getting closer to my target; completing my first novel. I must really thank my good friends and work colleagues, Layne and Jeff who have been reading the story I have weaved as I went along; who without, I do not think I would have completed this undertaking, they have allowed me to focus on writing for somebody else, preventing me from picking up on another thing to do.

I also would like to thank my wife Theresa for putting up with me getting up early every morning, the constant progress updates I would give her, I think I am lucky I have not been smothered in my sleep.

I have always loved telling stories, from a young age I have been interested in role-playing games, with a long-standing group of friends from school, this has developed in me an ability that I think I have to tell a story. I know there is a long list of stories I have from these games, all will be doctored, and hopefully some will be enjoyable reads for others in the future, worthy of becoming other stories and novels in their own right.

In short, I am really happy that I have discovered that I have the ability to complete this undertaking, that I have really enjoyed the whole enterprise and am already planning my second, and many more.

Lastly but certainly not least, I want to thank any and all who have decided to buy this book, I really hope you enjoy it and my way of story-telling, I am sure that I have a lot still to learn but I plan to improve as I continue in the next tale.

Introduction

The Seal

Have you ever wondered why sometimes you get to the top of the stairs, then when you reach for the light switch; you discover it is already on, or why sometimes as you approach the traffic lights, you think to yourself *'they are now going to change'* then they do? Some would call this luck, or karma maybe.

The truth is, magic is real; the world is tied together by trillions of strands of reality, at a molecular level and our minds can control them. Dimensions other than ours exist, some, where the rules of physics are stronger, others weaker, all are different. But the links exist, still the same. Energy and matter can cross these invisible boundaries with little or no effort at all.

Beings may inhabit some of these alternative dimensions; in history when these boundaries have overlapped with our own, portals can, and have appeared. The knowledge of these dimensional conjunctions has long been intertwined with our ancestors religious and esoteric belief systems, these boundaries and the way they interact with our own universe has allowed time and space to be distorted. It is our belief in the mutable quality of physics that is the key.

****

It was the last weeks of summer, hotter again than the year before, as it seemed the weather was breaking all the records each year now. There were no clouds today, just a bright sunlit sky that would be a devil to drive towards in a few hours' time. The woods were surrounded by farmland, wheat fields arranged in an orderly military style of rank and file. The occasional dog walker would skirt along the edge of the treeline but never venturing through, following a well-trod path, to the left, the woods continued with a palpable denseness which felt almost unnatural, like an indescribable closeness ebbing from within. The breeze seemed to sweep down the path no matter where the wind came from. An occasional crow call would echo through the woodland, disturbing the quiet with its deep throaty gurgling cacophony. The only people who would go within were the local teens who had nothing else to do other than to sit around making fires, high on acid, or smoking the latest seedless weed strand, listening to the current musical trends.

The undergrowth kept many secrets hidden below the brambles and ferns, old stones worn with time and shrouded in moss dwelt undisturbed; save for today, something was looking at these worn stones, searching among them. The quietness did not disturb it and the crows would not scare it away. The thing stood about two-foot-high, its skin was a dark grey complexion, lank and it held in several folds over the skinny frame, coarse black hairs protruded through from within. The diminutive beast kept its nose close to the ground snuffling about the stones and rocks, any watching would have had the feeling that the creature searched for something, almost like it wished to find a particular stone.

The search proved fruitful, the Gruul picked up the aeons long scent that defied time to go away The creatures warty, spindly, long clawed fingers felt along a flat edge, its nose close behind snuffling, the Gruul stopped and began to concentrate, focusing its mind upon the stone, willing to believe that the seal would open. Pushing upon the stone, it did not budge, The Gruul closed its eyes again, convincing itself that the portal would open. The Gruul then pushed forcibly upon the stone…. It still would not budge. The Gruul then considered the large flat worn stone, circular in shape, the moss had been disturbed where it had been pushed. 'I will need help.' The Gruul said to itself, the gravelly voice disturbed the quiet, 'I better go to the people from the path, they will help!'

The beast shuffled off, stopping briefly to look around one more time; wistfully, then it left.

Chapter 1

The Funeral

Craig Souter's mobile phone went off, chancing a look, it was his Grandma Liz, what did she want? Looking up from the computer screen on his call centre desk toward the LED caller display, situated at the end of the room, he had five minutes still before his break. Craig put his telephone on 'not ready' then quickly tapped in a text saying;

'I will call in 5mins! x'

He then touched the 'not ready' button again, immediately a customer came through, 'Hello my name is Craig, you are through to...'

The mobile went off again, alerting of an incoming message this time, Craig looked up, expecting to see his team leader shaking her head at him for the distraction. Picking up the mobile once more as he continued to talk to a lady wishing to purchase a boating holiday in north Norfolk, he read the text, the room seemed to slow down, the noise quietened he felt like he had physically shrunk; the text read;

'Craig you need to come to the hospital, your Grandfather has had a heart attack and he is on his way to James Paget Hospital xx'.

****

The sound of Auntie Mary sobbing at the back of the crematorium echoed all about the congregation room, the front was adorned with flowers straddling grandpa Bob's light brown coffin as it stood at the front, ready to pass into the furnace behind the curtain on its journey to the other side, the vicar stood there, his arms wresting upon the bible he had just been quoting from. Craig sat at the front next to his

Grandmother, she watched intently but no tears came, Craig felt the loss terribly, things would never be as they used to be.

Craig's grandparents were great, you could not ask for better. Craig's parents had worked away in the middle east, but his father's parents had stepped in and raised him throughout his young life, now they had fell out and didn't speak anymore. Craig remembered the game his Grandpa and he would play when in the car waiting at the traffic lights; predicting when the lights would change, Grandpa Bob had always won, or when the green man would change when waiting to cross a road upon foot, he had always won that one too.

'We are all gathered here today to wish Bob a fond farewell… '

The vicar went on with the eulogy taking Craig back to the sombre scene. He knew this would not have been what grandpa Bob would have wanted, but Grandpa no longer cared, Craig guessed. He thought back to the time his Grandfather had taught him 'the ways of old' as Grandpa had always called it. It always sounded funny, in no small part due to his broad Suffolk accent. But again, that was what made him such a great role model; patient, calm, funny and at times stubborn, the only person who was better in an argument or discussion than him was Grandma Liz.

'So now we have some words from Bobs son, Steven.' Continued the vicar, and with that announcement Craig's Uncle got up and walked toward the lectern and the vicar.

Craig's mind wandered off again as Uncle Steven began to talk, he thought back to that first time Grandpa Bob had shown him how the gift worked, how all those times he had not guessed, but had known the lights would change; he had made them change, It was at the age of sixteen, and with it came rules which he had been showing Craig throughout his life. Starting from an early age he had been convincing Craig that anything was possible, It had taken time but with practise the sixteen-year-old Craig had developed the rudiments to use his mind to its fullest, to affect the world around him, how the world is affected by all of us subconsciously; how belief is key and also the negative effects of carelessly using this power to affect the world.

'God, I miss him so much, he would always help, and now, now he has gone' continued Uncle Steven.

Craig smiled but he wanted to leave, the feeling of loss was oppressive, the symbols of religion; the coffin, words from the bible smattered all over the walls, it felt set up and he knew his Grandfather would have hated it. A confirmed atheist, Grandpa Bob would not have any truck with any religion, believing it all to be systems of fear and control. Well if there was a big man upstairs, Craig certainly did not wish to upset him. Craig's Grandfather had always warned against large congregations worshipping, as the group effect could easily empower an individual, like a priest for example, or maybe worse, it was all down to the will of the individual and the mass.

****

Half an hour later the congregation left the building, and headed to the wake, it was being held at Craig's uncles' home, located in the North Lowestoft suburbs, the home was large and spacious built in the early to mid-eighties of sturdy grey brick, a small porch with faux Greek pillars straddled over the front door. Upon entering the smell of freshly cooked bread crept through from the kitchen, the distinct impression was given by the sheer number of people inside the property of well-wishers of just how many lives Bob had touched; Craig had never realised just how popular his Grandpa Bob had been.

Continuing through, Craig reached the kitchen, inside he saw his cousin Cairo, she was a little older than Craig, fair of hair and slight of frame, she had been blessed with a pair of eyes that always lit the room whenever she entered it, they were now red rimmed and sore as if she had just wiped tears from them.

'Hi Cairo.' Craig said.

'Hi.' She replied with an obvious effort to keep composure.

'What a shit day, I'm going to miss him' Craig said,

'I know, we all will, I just didn't know how many people loved him, god, I think we even have the rotary club here, eating all of mums sausage rolls.' Cairo said as she pointed toward the living room where two well-dressed people neither of whom she knew, stood eating food from the buffet with a glass of wine in hand.

'So, when do you go back to Uni?' Craig asked,

'I'm here for the rest of the summer, I plan on catching up with some of my old school mates, we ought to go to the Tring some time', Cairo said.

The Triangle or Tring as it was often called was a small local tavern very popular with the youth culture in Lowestoft.

'Well what about now, too many suits around here for me.' Craig said.

Cairo looked at Craig with a thankful look in her eye and then said, 'I'll get my coat!'

Cairo left Craig in the kitchen and ran up the stairs, a few moments later she came down again with a worn brown leather jacket on, it suited her style 'You ready Craig, let's leave them to my Dads bad jokes and anecdotes about Grandpa Bob' Cairo said.

'Come on then, I'm right behind you', they both left through the back door and walked to the Triangle pub.

****

The Triangle tavern was a small family run pub in northern Lowestoft, it was only a ten-minute walk from Cairo's parent's home. The pub was separated into two distinct sections, a front bar and rear; the front bar was quite dark with a large wood fire that would be lit during the winter giving warmth when a customer entered, the walls were timber framed and all about them, adorned with beer mats from yesteryear, in the centre of the ceiling was a vintage cart wheel. In the summer months it would have barley, hops and summer flowers entwined about the wheel spokes, giving scents of the country. The bar was tucked into the far corner with just about enough space to serve three at a time during a busy period.

The back bar was decorated to appeal to the tavern's younger clientele, the central skylight gave a lighter feel instantly upon entering. The large pool table was always kept in good condition and was very popular, a jukebox hung upon the wall beside the long bar, six tall stools of an ergonomic design stood along the length of the bar and a sizable alcove was tucked away, near the pool table, two wooden topped tables, both metal legged allowed revellers a place to leave there drinks.

Craig and Cairo entered from the front door, and immediately turned right entering the front bar.

'I'll get the drinks, what do you want' Craig asked Cairo.

'I'll have a glass of red wine thanks'

Craig got to the bar in the corner as Cairo sat at the table nearest the fire, the bar manager walked through with a big smile upon his face.

'Hi Craig, no work today?' the bar manager said.

'No, it was my Grandfather's funeral, we've just escaped the wake.'

'I know what you mean, I hate funerals.'

His name was Jordan he had been a local at the Tring for a long time and recently he'd taken on the position as manager. Craig came over to the table placing the glass of wine in front of Cairo and sat down with his beer taking a sip as he did so. 'Good job we got out of there. God, Grandad would have hated it' Cairo said.

'I know, he would have wanted trumpets, loud music and a giant conga line, go out in style kind of thing'.

They laughed, 'you know I'm going to miss him though' Cairo said.

'Me too'

They went quiet for a moment, then Cairo's mobile phone went off, she looked down at it, to see who called.

'It's my mum, I'll take it outside' she said.

Pressing the receive button as she raised herself from the bench by the wall and she walked to the door.

'Hi mum, I'm with Craig, we went to the pub…'

she exited through the door talking on the phone, it left Craig time to withdraw into his thoughts, he took a deep draw from his beer and recalled good times with his Grandfather.

****

'When I was your age, I always asked myself what are we here for? What's my purpose? Is there an afterlife? These questions and hundreds more I kept coming back to, well I'm going to tell you what I think Craig, I think it is all connected.

Think of our universe as a raindrop falling through the sky to eventually splash upon the hard concrete of the street far below, everything inside the raindrop is connected and so life within goes on at a molecular level, but outside the raindrop is a whole world, unthinkably large in comparison to the individual raindrop and so, we do not think of it. The thing about a raindrop is that it never ever falls alone; no, they come from a cloud, in there are billions more, like a primordial soup continually creating more raindrops if you want. Well the thing about these other raindrops is they are just like other universes, making their way to their own individual demise upon the road below.'

Grandpa Bob loved to talk in metaphor it was his way.

He continued. *'It is these other raindrops where we would possibly find another reality that we could call heaven or hell I suppose, but the truth is there would be trillions of them falling from our own singular cloud, so there is so much more than just that, and each of these realities would have their own individual rules of physics depending upon what is in their own makeup. When it rains there is an increase in humidity, so to a greater or lesser degree the individual raindrops touch one another, from time to time we have overlaps, and some things can come across, bridge the gap as it were.... from time to time.'*

Craig had pondered at his Grandfathers words *'So when we use the gift, how does that matter?'* he had asked.

'Well each time you use your gift to affect reality, the edges of reality weaken a little, that is why you must be careful, the momentary weakness allows things from other realities to happen or come into being!'

Craig straight away had thought about monsters. *'Wow like monsters you mean?'*

Grandpa Bob looked at Craig. *'It's not funny Craig, but yes possibly, or other things could happen; it all depends upon what you are doing, and that is why you must only use your gift when it is truly needed. Craig as your power grows you will understand, the gift you have is so rare it is practically unique. I have chosen you because you have a grown-up head on you.'*

He continued after a brief pause. *'I mean you understand responsibility and will do the right thing when the time arrives.'*

****

Cairo came back, 'Hey you okay' she asked.

'yeah, I was just thinking about Grandpa'

Chapter 2

Hawkins and his Help

There is a large house called 'The Manor' it stands in the centre of Pakefield, it is a large square built townhouse, owned by a young man named Hawkins Abel Blessed. Twenty-eight years of age, he was born of a very privileged family and background. His parents had bought the Manor for him five years previous. Hawkins stood at five foot nine inches, powerfully built due in large part to long hours spent in the local gym. His parents were wealthy, upper class; his father was a peer in the house of lords in Parliament, his mother had died when he was young. He had spent most of his childhood away boarding, in a very prestigious public school, Hawkins was the heir to his father's fortune and so he lived an absolute life of luxury.

Dark of hair and broad shouldered, he sported a close shaven beard with a piercing stare, his eyes were a dark brown, his jaw was square, and his teeth were American white, he had inherited the family trait of a pointed, hooked nose. Hawkins father Lord Alfred Blessed had taught his son the special family gift, what they called 'the touch' it was the ability to affect things with your mind alike to that of Craig and he had nurtured it in no small part to the amount of time he found he had spare.

Often called to Surrey to look after the family affairs when his father was busy, Hawkins enjoyed the finer things in life that his privileged upbringing had endowed him with, however there was one family trait he had inherited that he had not been born with; the Gruul.

****

The Gruul had left the wood and headed back to town, towards its nest of sorts, it needed to get help and that help would come albeit unwittingly from the stupid human called Hawkins. Each night when

Hawkins would be sleeping the Gruul would enter his room and take some of his energy, leeching from him some of his very essence; breathing it in, concentrating on taking Hawkins energy. The Gruuls race could eat meat, they preferred meat, cats were a personal favourite. But sucking the lifeforce from a person was a boon they would not pass up; and besides, there were less scratches.

Some would call it a Goblin, some would say a devil or demon, others with forbidden knowledge might call the creature a breath-stealer, whatever you decided, it was an infernal being of feral countenance. Out of place on this planet, out of place with nature, it had come to Hawkins early in his life due to his father. The Gruul had been a pet of sorts of Hawkins father, but when Hawkins had been born and began to develop the touch the Gruul had found itself a "puppet", an individual it could gently influence as the child grew into a man. The Gruul had decided that Hawkins would help to weaken the barriers between the realities, and free its master who had been imprisoned so many years ago.

The Gruul would use invisibility to its exhaustion, if heavily garbed with a hood pulled over its head it could pass for a small child of around eight to ten, but the look was ludicrous, so the beast preferred to use the gift, or as it had always called it "magic", it was quite easy, as any around who actually saw the creature for what it really was would not easily believe a small monster of slough grey skin with long thick black hairs protruding from beneath its sallow hide, with long and sharp curled claws could truly exist. Thus, empowering its magic; to help in creating a still even more powerful effect.

It now crept into the house, through a small opening, like a cat flap, that the creature could open and close, tucked behind a number of potting plants by the front door. Listening in the hallway it could hear the sound of the television playing in the living room to the left, to the right was another room this was what the Gruul had claimed as its nest, all the rooms on the ground floor had expensive solid frosted glass doors, directly facing the front door at the far end of the hall was the downstairs toilet, with a large kitchen to the right of that. Beside the door to the right was a wide stairway which led upstairs to four bedrooms, a bathroom and a wide landing, of which all of these rooms branched from.

The Gruul slowly opened the door to the living room, it was very long with a table and six chairs at one end by the door, cupboards ran the full length of the facing wall, at the other end on the low cupboards was a large flat screen television of the latest design. Opposite this was a very large and luxurious sofa flanked by two expensive reclining chairs. Creeping in, the little monster noticed that there were three others in the room, useless meat-bags no doubt, it thought to itself, the Gruul hid behind the long sofa facing the television and listened to the conversation they were involved in.

'Hawkins your door just opened mate' Steve said.

Steve was Hawkins closest friend, they had been through school together, though Hawkins knew that Steve came from a family without the ties to the upper classes, he trusted him in no small part because he had always stuck by Hawkins, even when they had gotten into trouble, Steve had always been there.

'Yeah it's my ghost.' Hawkins replied.

'Shut up with your ghost crap again, you're always going on about that.' said Gabby.

Gabby was in her early twenties she was Hawkins on/off girlfriend, she was very pretty with a blonde bob, blue eyes and an athletic figure, she loved to run and swim, when she was younger, she had been on the county swimming team.

'Yeah, I would love to see it one day, your doors often open on their own, I reckon you have ropes or something?' said the third person in the room, his name was Cliff.

Cliff was a giant of a man and Hawkins primary gym partner. He was an easy-going person, he lived for the gym and playing rugby, if he wasn't doing either of these then the odds would be, he was talking about one or the other instead.

The Gruul listened from behind the sofa, the television was broadcasting the news; more bad news of suffering in this world.

Gruul cared not for that, its kind cared little for life or compassion, the creature wanted Hawkins alone that it may talk with him, subtly influence him, into going to the woods where the seal resided. For years the Gruul had known the general whereabouts of the three seals, but now the time was drawing near, they would need to be opened, before it was too late.

Maybe between them they could shift the seal so they would be able to go to the next other two. They were all located close by this was the last one's whereabouts the little monster had needed to find.

Once they were unlocked its master would be free, Hawkins didn't need to know about that though, nor about the reward the Gruul would get from its master for helping free him from his imprisonment.

Steve had gotten bored with the news on the television, it was all that Hawkins seemed to watch, they no longer got the collectible card games out, in ways Steve didn't mind this so much as Hawkins almost always drew that card which would win him the game when it seemed he was about to lose for sure. But even so, Hawkins had changed, he had become more morose and withdrawn of late; like a cover had been dropped over his feelings, dampening his very spirit.

'Hey, Hawkins, I've got a good idea.' Steve said.

They all looked at Steve.

'Go on.' Hawkins said.

'Let's all do a Ouija Board.' Steve grinned.

Hawkins was not prepared for this, he suspected that the Gruul had entered the room and didn't want the others discovering his secret friend, the Gruul too had heard, momentarily panicking. What should it do, the creature thought to itself, the Gruul knew it would be compelled to the summons? Then a thought entered the Gruuls vile mind, maybe if it were to show itself to these others, then they would help also, the keystone on the seal would easily shift if there were five attempting to free the keystone from its bindings.

'No, no not a chance.' Hawkins said.

'let my ghost sleep.' he said trying to discourage them from the Ouija board, but Gabby soon picked up.

'Yeah, come on Hawkins, don't be scared, it may want to tell you something, like the lottery numbers.' Gabby joked.

Cliff laughed nervously.

'I don't know, I don't really want to get involved in any of that, I'm with Hawkins.' Cliff said.

However, the other two were already in action.

'I'll get a wine glass' Gabby said as Steve was already on his knees by a set of draws beside the television.

'I know you've got a scrabble board in here somewhere.' he said.

'Hey guys, stop that, Gabby, we are not doing Ouija boards.' Hawkins pleaded.

'Found it.' Steve exclaimed as he took out the Scrabble game box, leaving the cupboard door open, he went to the table, Steve then upended the box on the table and proceeded to arrange the letters in a semi-circle, Gabby came in with a bottle of red wine in one hand and some glasses in the other.

'I've got a wine glass, so Hawkins cannot cheat by pushing it.' she said, smiling at Hawkins who was by now in freefall panic.

Hawkins then heard from the other side of where he was sitting a gentle yet gravelly whisper.

'Do it.' it was the Gruul and the creature obviously had something in mind, so Hawkins stood up.

'Alright then you win, let's see if we can contact the ghost.'

The Trio sat around the end of the long table, the lights had been turned down low; for effect, the scrabble board letters had been spread upon the table and the wine glass was surrounded by the letter tiles. All of them had one of their index fingers extended to the top of the glass.

'Is there anybody there?' Hawkins said.

Gabby giggled a little, 'shut up, be serious.' Steve admonished her.

'Sorry, I couldn't help it.' she said, Hawkins tried again.

'Is there anybody there?'

As Hawkins called out to the room, the Gruul could feel the summons upon its soul, luring its essence toward the glass, forcing its mind to the upturned drinking vessel. The feeling was akin to giving blood, the light-headedness and an almost palpable sensation of your own inner being leaving your body, uncontrollably the Gruul was forced to answer their summons.

Slowly the glass glided toward the yes answer on the table.

'Stop pushing the glass Steve.' Cliff said, a hint of fear in his voice.

'I'm not.' Steve replied.

'Shut up Cliff, I think we've got one.' Hawkins said.

'what is your name?' Hawkins asked, suspecting he already knew the answer, the glass glided to the first lettered tile,

'G.' they all said aloud together 'R, U, U, L.' they all exclaimed as more tiles were gradually indicated, one by one. The excitement taking over in the most part, aside from Cliff who looked around the room, worrying about what they were doing, hoping that Steve was pushing the glass with his finger.

'What do you want here?' Gabby asked.

The Gruul replied 'I live here.'

The glass moved very fast, she giggled again, this time it came out a little more forced.

'Hawkins knows me.' the glass spelled out, with this, they all looked at one another, a bit more worried.

'It knows your name, stop it Hawkins, stop moving the glass.' Cliff said.

Panic starting to set in, Hawkins lifted his finger from the glass.

'Fine you ask it a question, I won't even touch the glass.' Hawkins wasn't sure what would happen, he wasn't sure what the Gruul was up to, it was suddenly very worrying why the Gruul had wanted them to take part in this occult ritual.

'Can you cast any spells?' Steve asked.

'Don't ask anything like that' Cliff said, really scared now.

'Yes.' The glass spelled out slowly.

'Which one of you is pushing the glass, own up.'

Cliff begged, real fear and worry now in his voice, the glass started spelling a jumble of random letters, rotating faster and faster in the centre of the table, it then stopped abruptly.

'I can give you true power.' the glass spelled out.

'I think we should stop now.' begged Cliff.

'No, let us ask what it means?' Steve said.

Abruptly all the lights went off, there was not even the cold blue glow from the internet router connection. 'How did you do that?' Gabby asked.

She had asked Hawkins, but the three with their fingers upon the glass could feel it still moving, though none of them could see what it spelt. Hawkins went over to the light switch and clicked it several times, but nothing happened.

'Turn the lights back on.' Gabby said, and a moment later the lights winked on, bathing the room in dim light once more.

'Right I am going.' Cliff stated, getting up from his chair.

'wait.' Hawkins said.

'He wanted us here for a reason, he wanted to let you know about him!'

Hawkins continued, 'Let us find out what.'

'I am here.' came a gravelly voice from behind them.

Cliff dropped to the floor unconscious upon the diminutive creature's appearance at the end of the room, Gabby and Steve both involuntarily backed up toward the door 'What the actual fuck…' Gabby stammered out.

'It's okay, I told you I had a ghost, well, this is him its Gruul, he won't hurt you!'

The Gruul stepped closer, focusing its mind entirely upon the three cowering by the glass door.

'I want you to help me, do not fear me!' the Gruul said in its gravelly voice. Slowly the fear left them, held in thrall by the diminutive little creature's gaze. Cliff started and slowly came to, the signs of fear affecting him only moments earlier gone, the glamour caused by the Gruul had taken hold upon them completely, Hawkins was amazed.

'How did you do that Gruul, if I had attempted that they would not have believed, I mean it would have failed.'

The Gruul studied Hawkins, it then said.

'The magic worked because they were waiting for something to happen, they expected something to happen, your parlour games and my appearance, made the stage for me to cast easier.'

'Why though?' asked Hawkins.

'I need you and your friends help, I need help with a ritual, I need to open the three seals!' the Gruul said.

Chapter 3

Cairo

Cairo had grown up with her family in the suburbs of Lowestoft, she had always been very close to her family and was studious at school. Eventually she had left for the University of Sheffield, where she studied cinematography, she had a brother called Greg and her parents were Steven and Mary. Her father worked as a bus driver and her mum; Mary had worked at the local paintbrush factory. Cairo's brother had moved to London with his Fiancée and got a job in the City. It was good as she had somewhere to stay in London if ever, she went to the big city; and they didn't fight any more due to the distance between them. Since then whenever she had come back to Lowestoft, she would hunt out her Cousin Craig, the two had grown close and she had found they could always relate to one another.

Cairo was Quite tall standing at five foot ten inches with a slight frame, her hair was fair, straight and shoulder length, neatly trimmed. Cairo always smelled fresh and clean, she preferred baggy jumpers in colours of pale pastel which she would match with a pair of faded blue jeans, she always lifted a room when she entered as she had an exuberance and a latent kind of energy that made people smile and induced them to action. Her skin was smooth, the only marks upon her face, a dimple upon either cheek, it seemed to exist only for the purpose of accentuating her smile which was cute and slightly crooked. She was blessed with a long sensual neck which gave her an appearance to the casual beholder of someone taller and more sophisticated than she really was.

She was back from Sheffield; it was near the end of the summer holidays and she would be going back soon. Grandad Bob's funeral had been quite tough, Mum and Dad were going about trying to act like everything was normal, it was infuriating. Cairo just wanted to get out, but it was hard, she knew that her Dad had taken it really hard and Cairo's Mum had always got on very well with Grandad Bob as well. It had been good to get to the pub with Craig, she decided she would call him later tonight to go for another drink. As

Cairo went through the hall towards the stairs, she saw the postman dropping the mail through the letter box, a few letters dropped to the floor, Cairo thought nothing more of it and skipped up the stairs toward her old bedroom.

She laid upon her bed, listening to some nineties rock music, it was the Smashing Pumpkins, a band she had heard many times playing on the jukebox at the triangle, she liked it and so had bought it on audio download for her phone. She had pulled out one of her study books and was researching George Lucas's style of movie directing, then there was a gentle knock on her bedroom door.

'Come in.' She said.

the door opened, and Cairo's Mother's head appeared, she was holding a letter.

'You got a letter darling.'

Getting onto all fours and crawling to the end of her bed Cairo retrieved the letter, she crawled back to the head of the bed.

'Thanks Mum.' she said as she read the address, it was typed, she guessed it was probably a bill or official letter of some description, but in this instance, there was no markings from any bank, car insurance company or the like.

'I'm just putting the kettle on, would you like a cup of Tea?' Cairo's mother asked as she retreated out of the room.

'No thanks Mum, I'm okay.' Cairo said as she opened the letter without looking up.

Her mother closed the room door softly behind her, again trying to be as inoffensive as possible and not upset anyone, due in no small part to the recent loss of Cairo's Grandfather. Cairo had had, as many other teenagers had a period in her later teens when her and her mother would not see eye to eye. But since she had gone to Sheffield University, Cairo had matured quickly; though not completely. Coming back now she appreciated her time here and enjoyed her parents' company, now she had her independence she felt when she came home, she was given a respect that she was comfortable with; which she had not been given as a youngster.

Reaching over to the sideboard table she took a pen and with it tore open the top of the letter, inside was a hand-written note and a small key. Cairo was intrigued. Emptying the key into her hand she turned it over and examined it, cold to the touch, about an inch and a half long and made of a dull grey metal which had been gold-plated long ago. The grey alloy now clearly showed through; it would have been beautiful once, long ago. It was the kind of key that would unlock a music box or maybe some kind of small keep-safe box, putting the key on her bed-side table, she began to read the letter that had been sent.

To my dearest Granddaughter Cairo

My dear Cairo, I can still remember when you were but a pretty face staring out at me with your beautiful blue eyes all those years ago.

As then, still to today I always find my day lightened when I think upon you and how you have grown into a beautiful young woman. I have always been proud of how you; your brother and Craig have gotten along in life; I know that you will all lead amazing lives filled with excitement and hopefully fulfilment too.

Because I have written to you it means that I am no longer here and so it is important that you do something for me. I have enclosed a key with this letter, it unlocks a jewellery box that is in my bedroom at home, inside the box is a very old map, please retrieve it and keep it safe, the map is written in a strange foreign language but do not worry about that, just keep it safe. All will become clear later, one more thing do not let anyone see you retrieve it.

All my Love

Grandpa

Cairo folded the letter and placed it on the side near to the key, getting up Cairo paused, then involuntarily picked up the letter and key opened the bottom of her piggy bank and slid them in, then re-sealed the piggy bank with the plastic circular stopper. Putting it back on her book shelf, she slipped on some trainers grasped her old backpack, then left the room and went downstairs. Grabbing her old brown leather coat that was hanging near the front door, Cairo left without saying goodbye to her parents.

****

It was a fifteen-minute walk to Cairo's grand-parents. They all lived in the old part of Lowestoft, north of the mouth of the river Waveney, the buildings here had primarily been built for the fishing crews and fisher wives of old, built at the turn of the twentieth century. The roads were all narrow with plenty of back alleys, which had been intertwined through the backstreets. If you wanted to stay out of view going from one place to another, this area of the town was the place to do it. Due to the implied importance of the letter, Cairo decided to use as many of the back alleys as possible. As she made her way to her Grandfather's, she felt like someone was watching her or looking for her. As she crossed a street where four children played in the street, she eyed them, it felt that they all stopped and watched her, paranoia? She decided it was and continued. Still the feeling remained, following her on every step, as she dived down the next alleyway, it seemed to her mind that even the cats watched her moving towards her destination. Ready to inform any who asked of her whereabouts like some living closed-circuit surveillance system. She forcibly put the thoughts out of her mind. Crossed another road then turned down the cul-de-sac towards her grand-parents and Craig's home.

Cars had been crammed down one side of the road, the parking was always abominable on this street, some children played a game involving a ball and the curbs on either side of the road. She went to the front door and rang the doorbell. White and wooden framed, the door was showing extreme signs of wear; the paint was cracked and had flaked away in numerous locations, revealing the old grey wood of a very old weathered doorframe, it looked like it had not been painted in the last twenty-five years. Moments later Cairo's Nanny, Liz came to the door, she fumbled with the lock, then finally the door opened.

'Hi Nan.' Cairo said.

'Oh, hello dear, good to see you, come in, come in.' she said and with that Cairo followed her Grandmother inside.

Cairo's Nan Liz stood at four feet ten inches high, though she always walked with a hunch and so seemed even shorter. She was plump in a matronly way, her hair was white and thin on her head and she still wore it in a sixties fashion, the same for her glasses. criss-crossing lines showed her age to be well into her nineties. Her eyes were kind, they were blessed in colour with a delicate blue which seemed pure and innocent.

Cairo sat in the living room, it was narrow with the front door opening into it, there was another door on the opposite wall which led to the dining room, kitchen and stairs up to the two bedrooms above. The walls were decorated with pictures of the extended family through the last twenty to thirty years and the walls were a faded peach colour. There was a small worn leather sofa along the wall facing the Television and a leather armchair in front of the window, the centre of the room was taken up by a low oval wooden table. Cairo's nan had a television quiz show on the at the moment, the sound was up far too loud for the small room and was very distracting, Cairo's Nan came in to the living room, she had a tray with two cups, a teapot and a small plate of biscuits, she sat down on the sofa and placed the tray on the oval table.

'Help yourself dear.'

'Thanks nan.' Cairo replied as she took a biscuit from the plate.

'Glad you popped in; I didn't get to speak to you the other day at the funeral.' Cairo's Nan said.

'I had to get out of there, sorry Nan.'

'It's ok dear, I understand.' Her nan was very understanding in the way that all people who had lived during the second world war could be, an ability to lock their own feelings away enough to give the next generation a chance to grieve.

'God, I'm sorry Nan, I'm being so selfish how must you feel?' Cairo asked suddenly feeling very foolish for what she had just said.

'Oh, I'm bearing up, don't worry about me, I'm ok, you mustn't worry about a geriatric like me!'

But Cairo could now see the glint in her eye, the tears that were being held back, again that spirit that the war generation had developed to be able to put on a brave face so that others could cope with grief, a selfless giving love. Cairo got up and sat next to her Nan and embraced her, burying her head into her Nan's shoulder they both began to cry. The moment slowly passed and as the time moved on, they talked about Cairo's Grand-father and his life, it turned a light on in the back of Grandma Liz's mind.

'Oh, you've reminded me of something, your Granddad said that all of the grand-kids could have a look around and take something that would remind you of him, you know, before the will.'

They finished the plate of biscuits and the pot of tea. Next to the tray was a box of old photographs which Grandma Liz had retrieved, the pair had looked through them, they had had a laugh, and had a cry. As Cairo was about to leave, she got up and said 'If its ok with you Nan, I'll have a look around for something to remind me of Granddad.

'Ok dear, I'm going to feed the cat.' Cairo went upstairs and wandered into her grand-parents' bedroom, it was compact and cluttered with one window that looked down onto the front street below. There was a double bed that took most of the space within the room, a long set of clothes cabinets ran down one side of the room, a dresser table with a mirror beside one side of the bed and the rest of the room was taken up with boxes filled with odds and ends, baskets with clothes, and all over was clutter, showing a full life lived. But sure enough, almost like it had been left there for Cairo to find, stood a faded jewellery box, quite small, rectangular and made of brass above which a faded paper wrap seemed to show pictures of the earth as if drawn before the America's had been discovered. It sat proudly upon a plastic box filled with books. Hurriedly she took it, it was light to lift, almost like there was nothing inside, the box looked familiar, almost like she remembered it from when she was very young, retrieving the key from her pocket she slipped it in the lock, it fit perfectly. She took the key back out and placed the jewellery box in her backpack then went back downstairs, at the bottom of the stairs stood Cairo's Grandmother.

'Did you find anything you liked dear?' she asked,

Cairo said, 'Yes, can you remember that old jewellery box?'

'Yes, I remember, he said he remembered when you were very young you used to keep some plastic jewellery in there, Bob always said it reminded him of you!'

Chapter 4

The Summit

A wide-open room in the highest hall of power in the United Kingdom; the Houses of Parliament. The room was to host several influential people from around the Country, the host paced around the room, a glass of Napoleon brandy in his hand, he waited and considered the way he would deliver his meeting.

The rooms walls were all ornately decorated with finely carved wood panelling, paintings of influential people from British politics throughout the ages, hung upon walls, at a central point the paintings switched to Photographs of more recent prominent figures of the British Politico. The lighting in the room was bright, the shadows had evaded the centre of the room and had been pushed back to the very edges of the wide space. Hiding behind expensive antique chairs or peeking out from underneath tables. A large fireplace with a low fire made the rooms few shadows dance, above the fireplace hung a large painting of Her Royal Highness; Queen Elizabeth the second. There was a long low oval table made of Oak in the centre of the room. About it were six comfortable red Leather armchairs each aged but also well cared for throughout their long lifetime.

Lord Blessed was a large man in his late seventies, he was almost totally bald with a pair of piercing brown eyes and a pointed nose, from the side he looked almost hawk like. He would always wear a tailored Savile row suit of grey or blue. In his youth he had been head-strong and confident. He was unimaginably rich; his father had been a peer and he had made the most of his money on the financial markets. His mother had taught him how to use the gift when he was young, and he had used the gift; to exhaustion at times. Eventually resorting to manipulating shares and the money markets to increase his personal family wealth. He had two children, Hawkins and Isabella, he had taught his son the gift, but Isabella had left for Italy a number of years earlier his only real contact with her was a receipt for her expenditure each month whether expensive clothes or another sports car, he paid for it all. His wife had died over twenty years ago due to an aggressive Cancer when the children had been young.

The door opened, and a porter entered.

'A Mr David Smith is here Lord Blessed.' he said.

'Show him in please.' Lord Blessed said, a moment later, in came a slim gentleman in his late fifties, he wore an expensive black tailored Gucci suit. He had dark brown hair with matching thick eyebrows, he walked swiftly with a smoothness of motion that belied his age, he sat down and looked at Lord Blessed.

David Smith had long been an influential member of the Freemasons, high up in its echelons and circles of mystery and hugely influential. He had a way of being able to make things happen, a word here or a threat of a leaked photo there, the pair went back a long way. Lord Blessed and David Smith had met in the early eighties, Mr Smith was new to the masons and Lord Blessed offered to help him financially if he could influence various people within the organisation.

'Good evening Lord Blessed.' he said.

'Oh, please David dispense with the titles, we've known one another for years my friend.' Lord Blessed said,

'Well, I would if it didn't get under your skin so much Alfred.' David said, 'So, who else is to be here?' He asked.

'The Honourable Victoria Slattery, Marcus Humboldt, the Witch Sydora,' Lord Blessed briefly paused before announcing the last name, 'and the Nihilist.'

'The Nihilist, I can understand Sydora, but the Nihilist?' David said astounded.

'What is it all about, I don't like the sound of whatever you have cooked up.' There was a knock at the door interrupting David mid-flow, it cooled the rising tension that was already building up within the room.

'Come in.' The porters head appeared once more,

'Lord Blessed, your other guests have arrived' the porter announced again in his standard subdued tone.

'Please show them all in, thank you.' Lord Blessed said.

Moments later the porter once again opened the door and the other guests filed into the ornate room.

Dr Marcus Humboldt was a Historian, specialising in Occult studies, he was overweight, he drank and smoked heavily and could be thought of as a man determined to prove the truth of magic in the world, he wore a brown woollen jumper and a pair of jeans.

The Honourable Victoria Slattery was the newly elected Member of Parliament for Waveney. She had stood for the Conservative party, and had come from a local family with money, ambitious was an understatement. Of athletic build, she owed Lord Blessed for helping to finance her political campaign which had led to her successfully taking the parliamentary seat.

Sydora was an imposing person, her force of will was palpable, very slim she looked like she could easily snap, her features gaunt and withdrawn, yet she was beautiful in an otherworldly way. She usually wore a purple long dress that made her look mysterious and extremely eccentric. Her dark blue eyes were surrounded by long eyelashes and she always wore her black hair loose, its length easily came down to the small of her back. It was very hard to judge her age, to look at her you would say she was in her early thirties, but Lord Blessed new she was closer to fifty.

The reason she had been invited was due to her connection to the left-hand path; it was an Occult group with its direct heritage going back to the times before the Roman empire, some would call the Left-hand path black magic, Sydora preferred the Left-hand path though as almost no-one had ever heard of it.

The last to enter was the man known only as 'The Nihilist', nobody knew his real name, nobody knew where he had come from or what political affiliations he had. Tall; standing over six feet with chiselled features, shaven headed and with cold green eyes, he was imposing. It was known that he was an amazing martial artist, and a great shot, yet there were no records of him serving in any army. He would often be found at some pigeon shoot or a charity dinner, but nobody knew why he was there. It was just accepted that he held power over influential people, and this got him closer to whatever purposes he steered towards. It was rumoured that many prominent politicians, lords and ladies had had careers ruined upon the blackmail of this man's endeavours, their goals shattered. Though none gathered here liked him, they all were interested in maybe discovering a little more about this man that seemed a total enigma to the circles they lived and moved around within.

'Ladies and Gentlemen, I thank you all for your time,' Lord Blessed began, 'I've gathered you all here today, to garner help, my son has recently discovered something that I know several of you will find rather interesting and, I should say there is something in this find for each of us.' Lord Blessed said.

'What could you have for me?' asked Dr Humboldt.

'I believe you are always searching for signs of true magic; I think if you are prepared to help me, then you may find yourself closer to your goal.' Lord Blessed replied.

Sydora looked at the Doctor, she smiled warmly at him, he turned his attention back to Lord Blessed.

'So, what do you want from me?' the Dr asked.

The Nihilist looked over toward Lord Blessed also, unlike all the others he had remained standing, almost seeming uninterested in the conversation. Lord Blessed, walked over to a glass decanter and proceeded to pour another glass of Brandy.

'If you will just let me finish Dr Humboldt; I want your knowledge,' Lord Blessed paused then added, 'more specifically your expert knowledge on a rather unique ancient text which has recently came into my keeping.' Sydora's eyes lit up at the mention of ancient texts.

'I for one am listening.' she said.

'And what do you want with me?' asked Victoria.

'My dear, you already owe me anyway, but I need people I can trust, and I know you are somebody I can rely on.' Lord Blessed emphasized the last sentence it felt to all gathered that it was almost a threat. 'Victoria, there is I believe a will to be read out very soon of one of your constituents?' Victoria looked at Lord Blessed.

'I would imagine so; people die every single day' she said.

'But none that spring to mind.' Lord Blessed looked at her.

'Really Miss Slattery, you disappoint me, there is only one of your constituents that would ever interest me, and from what I have heard, he has recently died!'

This did not seem important to any gathered there, they all looked at one another, perplexed by the inferred importance of one person dying in Waveney and why it would be so important to draw these folks to the centre of power of the United Kingdom. All that is, apart from the only person other than Lord Blessed that was not seated in the room, the Nihilist, he just leaned against the wood panelled wall with his arms crossed, watching the others.

'No, the person now passed that I refer to is a member of an unaffiliated organisation, more specifically, it is diametrically opposed to yours, Sydora.' Lord Blessed said.

She gave him an even look which was devoid of emotion, 'His name is Robert Souter, or Bob Souter as most call him,' his voice had begun to rise, 'and he has been a thorn in my side for many a year now, well the old buffoon has died, and I want what is rightfully mine!' Lord Blessed had raised his voice with passion.

The Lord's outburst left an awkward silence in the room. Eventually the Nihilist broke the still.

'Now, now, no need to burst a blood vessel.'

The Nihilist walked quietly over to the Brandy decanter and poured himself a glass.

'I can get whatever you think is yours, Lord Blessed.' the Lord turned and looked over towards him.

'No, you cannot, not alone anyway, my son lives there, but he is head-strong, no, I want you to go Sydora.'

Sydora eyed him curiously.

'Tell me more Alfred, I'm interested as I said, but I want assurances and just what I get myself into; tell me about the book.' she said.

'Yes, the book. The book in question is a grimoire, it is of a magical lineage reaching far back into the mists of time, a copy of an early work of Honorius of Thebes I have been told by reliable sources.'

Both Sydora and Dr Humboldt's interest had been piqued,

'You have it here?' asked Dr Humboldt.

'No, it is currently on its way here as we speak, I anticipate it being here by this evening or tomorrow morning at the latest.'

'But, what does a centuries old book and a dead man have to do with all of us?' David asked.

'That is the million-dollar question David, a little bit of the history of Honorius can be given by Dr Humboldt.'

Lord Blessed looked over to Dr Humboldt.

He began, 'Honorius of Thebes is an interesting figure in Occult history, purported to have been the Pope Honorius third, an Italian born Pope of the twelfth and thirteenth century anno domini, but he could also have been a person alive a long time before that. He is rumoured to have penned various occult books.'

'What book?' Sydora interrupted,

'A precursor to, THE BOOK!' Lord Blessed answered,

'The Red Dragon?' asked Dr Humboldt 'I don't believe it; the only copy is said to be in the archives of the Vatican.'

'This is not The Red Dragon Dr Humboldt, it is a precursor as I said,' Lord Blessed continued, 'according to my sources, and trust me, they are very reliable indeed, Honorius relates to a figure who predates even Jesus Christ, and lived about the time of Alexander the Great.

All gathered there listened attentively, except the Nihilist, he seemed only interested in his glass of Brandy, of which he drank from frequently in small sips, studying all of the attendees at the meeting.

'From the formation of the Right-hand path to this very day there has been a custodian of a key to unlock the book we now have, and this gentleman that has died was, that custodian.'

'But how do you know?' there members are all sworn to secrecy!' Sydora asked,

'I know because he was the reason, I was not that custodian and he was also the reason I was expelled from the Right-hand path!'

Sydora watched Lord Blessed, 'Oh, Lord Blessed, you would never have liked following the Right-hand path, all that abiding by the rules, no misusing your gift, and all that jazz.'

Dr Humboldt sat uncomfortably, looking at all the others gathered here, he felt like he was in quicksand, sinking out of his depth, unable to reach a branch.

'Respectfully, I do not see how I can help you Lord Blessed.'

'I think you will be far more helpful than you believe, and as I said earlier, I have proof of magic, proof that you have desperately been searching for all your life.'

'There will be a will reading in three days, in Miss Slattery's constituency, I want you Sydora, and the Nihilist to go with Victoria and retrieve an ornate key and a parchment that help us decipher the secrets of this Grimoire.'

The two looked at one another, Sydora looked at the Nihilist, with a slight look of contempt, the Nihilist, looked at Sydora with a look of confidence and strong purpose, they nodded to one another.

'And I would like you Dr Humboldt to stay here with me in London to help decipher the book when Sydora returns with the parchment, of course I will pay you well and have you stay in the very best hotel in Mayfair that can be found.'

Chapter 5

Lines of Power

The Gruul took Hawkins and his friends to the first seal, the creature had the group drive out into the local countryside; to the place it had been before. The car had approached from the A146 Norwich road turning left down a narrow twisting and kinking road just outside of Lowestoft.

They stopped by a cottage, parking on the grassy verge, on the opposite size of the road They got out and then followed a dirt path beside the cottage that snaked into the back garden and continued around the edge of a large field. The sky was a light grey with no signs of the sun making any appearance in the near future, darker clouds that promised rain hung low in the sky and the bird song was subdued. Two crows advised of the approach of these foreigners to all other crows in the area; to this corner of the earth.

The group followed the Gruul toward a small wooden foot bridge at the end of the field it was no more than two ancient planks spanning an irrigation ditch. The track led into Mutford wood, which spread across the local area, behind cornfields and farms. A breeze whipped the leaves into action, they attempted to break free from the trees, unsuccessfully, now even the two crows stopped their cawing warnings and flew off.

Going across the bridge the small wood took on a deathly quiet, the only sound was that of the breeze through the trees that occasionally broke the still. The path was just cleared dirt, either side of which was covered by a blanket of ivy with large patches of blue bells penetrating through from the earth below, or low ferns and wiry bramble bushes. They continued into the woods until the path forked, the Gruul turned its head and said

'Left here.' as it turned and took the left fork, Cliff looked around.

'These trees are old.' looking at the oaks that had grown in this area over the years.

'We are nearly there, be quiet, and hurry.' the Gruul said without stopping, they all followed.

'I don't know about your friend Hawkins.' Gabby said, still worried by the events of the other night at Hawkins home.

'You will get used to him, he's quite nice really, well I think it's a he anyway, I mean Gruul it sounds sought of male doesn't it.' Hawkins said.

'Well I guess.' Gabby replied nervously.

Up ahead the Gruul stopped, the beast waited for them to catch up and then pointed into the bushes 'In here.' it croaked in its gravelly voice.

The wind had gotten up, moving the boughs, it whistled and howled through the trees. The whole area was subdued, devoid of any life beat. Only the sound of those two crows could be made out warning others that there were intruders about, they had come back.

Pushing through the undergrowth was a trial that neither Hawkins or any of his friends relished, it felt like the bracken bushes and thorny ground cover would fight them for every step, unlike the Gruul that could slip through easily due to its diminutive stature. Fighting their way through the group finally entered a grove of sorts. They had won entrance to the secluded area, cloaked from outside view by years of wild untended undergrowth and Surrounded by ancient trees with branches reaching in like twisted gnarled fingers; grasping. They all fell silent as they had entered, one by one. Looking around they all beheld the enormous moss and lichen covered circular slab of stone, there were some strands of ivy running across the centre with dark green leaves, and bunches of stinging nettles that surrounded the circular stone stood to attention. Eagerly awaiting any who would come too close, there was an eerie stillness that had settled on the area.

'We are here.' The Gruul said.

The Gruul pointed to the slab.

'What do you want us to do?' Hawkins asked.

'Will the Seal to open…' Gruul croaked, 'and believe it!'

They all looked at the stone slab,

'You what, how will it open, you are nuts.' Cliff said.

The Gruul looked at Cliff, yellow eyes beading into Cliff's mind, the beast focused on squeezing Cliffs brain, compressing it like it was in a vice.

'Aarrggh.' Cliff dropped to his knees, his hands reaching to his head, gripping either side of his skull by the temples, as wave after wave of pain swept through it.

'Make it stop, aaarrrggghhh. Make it stop.' Cliff cried.

'Please stop, please stop, please!' Gabby begged the Gruul to cease Cliff's suffering.

The Gruul turned away from Cliff he was now reeling around in the dirt, with its attention broken, the agony abruptly ceased inside Cliff's head.

He rolled over, looking at the monster as it slunk closer to the stone slab, the pain in his head now gone, just a memory; a very painful memory.

'It's a monster Hawkins, it's a monster!' Cliff declared as he slowly lifted himself off the ground. He thought of running, but soon realised the creature could easily do the same thing again, or worse. He wanted to stamp on it, punch it and kick it, he was confident that he could break the little creature in two, he was at least two and a half times the size of the Gruul.

The group walked toward the slab; Cliff was wary of the Gruul but did as he was asked as well.

'Stand over there, you stand there, you there.' The Gruul ordered them into positions around the moss-covered slab, they all obeyed, subdued by the offensive display, once in position the Gruul explained what he wanted them to do.

'You will all think that the seal will open.' They all listened, to the Gruuls demand. Concentrating on the circular slab the Gruul took the lead, focusing its entire being on the slab opening, Gabby, Cliff and Steve, not sure exactly what the Gruul wanted them to do just stood there, puzzled. Hawkins did as what had been requested, harnessing his thoughts alongside the Gruul's own.

It did not budge an inch, the Gruul stopped, Hawkins ceased as well, looking at the others, Hawkins said, 'look, we have to think it will open, it's that simple' Steve stated, 'It's not going to move, are you mad?'

The Gruul looked at Steve, 'The next time I have to force you, the pain will be terminal!'

'Eh, let's just try.' Cliff said with resignation, they all focused on the seal again, willing the circular slab to open, forcing their minds against it.

The sudden flapping of a crow coming down to land on a branch close by distracted Gabby, looking round.

'Hello there.' she said, it eyed here curiously, it was large with a beautiful lustrous black plumage, turning its head and seeing the others, its eyes stopped when they fell on the Gruul.

'Mmmaaaawwwkkkk, mmmmmaaaawwwwkkk' the crow burst into a cacophony and launched itself toward the diminutive beast taking flight once more.

'Kill it, quick!' the Gruul croaked laconically, turning to face the oncoming bird.

The crow swept low, lifting its talons at the last moment, scratching at the Gruul's face, the Gruul, swung its vicious claws in a wide arc but the crow was far more agile and swept past, attempting to escape.

'Kill it, kill the bird!' The Gruul repeated as the bird broke away, the black bird deftly shot by Cliff who flinched away. And the bird was gone.

'Wow that was weird.' Steve said,

'Yeah, weird.' repeated Cliff,

'Hurry, this changes things, we must hurry.' The Gruul croaked, as it ushered the rest back into position around the large slab, then they all as one, resumed; concentrating once more upon the slab.

Long moments went by and nothing happened.

'Keep concentrating.' Hawkins said as he could see Gabby about to look at him and probably laugh, then, a low grinding sound began to emerge from the stone, the noise of stone on stone; rubbing, the noise created was an unnatural one; eerie and unwholesome.

'It is opening!' Steve said

'Keep Focus!' the Gruul demanded without looking up, its arms outstretched, pushing the air as if it would help, and still the millstone sounds echoed out from below the slab.

'Its opening, look.' They all watched as the slab rotated slightly, the noise a long onerous and loud grinding noise, then, abruptly it ceased, and the slab dropped on one side, a dreadful smell emanated from below, a smell of stagnant water and methane as dark water quickly filled the crater where once the stone slab had been, creating a dark pond with a stone slab protruding from one side. The grinding echo retreated through the woods, like it had finally been freed from imprisonment below the slab.

'The first seal is broken; we must open the others.' The Gruul slowly croaked to the three of them.

'There are two more.'

Gabby looked at them all apprehensively then said, 'what about my work, I cannot gallivant around the country or wherever playing with big stones!'

'You have no choice.' the Gruul croaked once more.

'Like you could stop us all.' Cliff said, the Gruul turned to face Cliff; a sneer crept across the creature's face. Cliff realised what was about to happen again, he ran towards the little monster, closing the ground around the newly formed pond in moments, rising his leg in an explosive kick, direct into the stomach of the Gruul, blasting the beast back. The Gruul collided violently with a large oak tree several feet behind on the edge of the secluded grove, the Gruul then slumped to the ground at the base of the tree.

Cliff turned lifting his arms and flexing his biceps, a large grin upon his face. Confidence had returned to him after the creature had tortured him from within his own skull. 'Come on, let's get out of here.' Cliff said, 'I'll kill it.'

The others looked at him, 'What have you done?' Hawkins said, 'that was Gruul.'

'You saw what he did to me, I couldn't let him get away with that.'

'Hurry then.' Steve said, 'cos if he gets back up, he is going to be really pissed!'

As they talked, they had failed to notice that the Gruul, had slowly been getting up from the moss-covered ground. Looking intently at Cliff who was looking away towards his friends, bragging, due to his conquest of a seemingly smaller and weaker opponent that had bested him. The Gruul reached towards Cliff, focusing its demonic mind toward the large human before it, forcing all of the malice it could muster to assert itself aggressively in a malignant fashion upon the goliath before it.

'Burn!' were the only words that the Gruul uttered in its feral, guttural speech.

With those words flames burst into being upon Cliff, instantly igniting his clothing, he had only mere moments to realise the voice, followed by the comprehension of what was now transpiring. Then he felt the torturous pain as the flames, searing hot, licked about, scorching and burning, covering his body, 'aaaaiiiigyyyeee!'

Cliff screamed in agony once more, this time the scream was of a higher, more horrific pitch than before. The smell of burning clothes, hair and cooking meat quickly permeated throughout the clearing. Cliff turned, he had become a living conflagration, he ran towards the dark pond, and launched himself into the air, hitting the water with a high-pitched slap. With the pain, he struggled to keep his head above the water, the flames would not succumb to the water however, they just continued to burn and to scorch. Cliff struggled to stop the flames, but they would not be doused, continually he screamed all the time.

The others could only watch in terror as their friend had been murdered by this infernal beast.

'Stop it.' Hawkins and Gabby said together, Steve stood still, stunned by what had just transpired.

'It is too late for him, he will sink below and die, but a sacrifice was required!' The Gruul explained matter-of-factly.

The screaming trailed off, Cliffs lifeless body sank slowly, like his body had been dragged down from below.

'What are we going to do?' Hawkins said, an element of fear in his voice. He knew that the Gruul was not natural, but he had never seen this side of the creature before.

'You will all help me; I will make you all powerful!' Gruul croaked at length.

'Where is his body?' Steve asked, looking into the pond, it could not be seen, just a few lonely bubbles lazily made their way from far below, to burst on the surface.

'Cliff is gone!' was all the Gruul said.

'Fuck, fuck, fuck, fuck,' Gabby said, 'what the fuck has just happened?'

Gabby was scared as were they all, she knew that the beast could obviously do the same thing to any of them, what had Hawkins gotten them into. She was trapped, she understood that; quickly realising that the only thing to do was to go along with this creature for now, maybe there would be a chance to get away at a later point.

Steve was scared too, he had not expected any of this and since the Ouija board last night his world had dramatically been turned upside down, now his friend Cliff had been murdered, but this thing had promised power, what did that mean, a small part of Steve was secretly almost exhilarated by the thought of what this power was that the Gruul had alluded to. Could he be able to set things on fire just by using his mind?

Hawkins looked into the water, he could not see the bottom, he could not see a body. Nothing could be seen within the depths, not even bubbles now, just a gentle ripple that was slowly wearing itself out, disturbed water returning to a flat mirror-like surface once more.

'Right, we've got to think fast. There's no body, should we go in and get it out?' Hawkins asked all the others.

The Gruul said 'If you enter that water you will never come back out!' with a manner of finality in the croaking, broken voice.

'What about when he came here,' Steve asked, 'did anybody know he was coming to yours?'.

'No, he came from the Gym, he was on his bike, so we should be ok.'

'I think we should leave then.' Gabby said.

Quickly and quietly they left the wooded area, followed the side of the field and got back into the car. They went back to Lowestoft, nobody talked on the way home, the Gruul was in the passenger footwell, seemingly asleep, though all doubted this was the case. The silence made the return journey feel twice as long as it would normally have been. The car arrived at the manor; Hawkins's home. The Gruul ushered them all inside, it followed them in and with no more than a thought, closed the door behind everyone. Grinning evilly, the Gruul thought to itself.

'The   first   steps   had   finally   been   taken.'

Chapter 6

The Pit

In the darkest depths of the vast cavern complex all that could be heard was the sound of dripping water, a constant dripping. Walking for miles through the winding black tunnel and that was all that could be heard.

Drip, drip, drip, drip, drip, drip.

The tunnel gradually opened up into a gargantuan cavern it was a cave of immense proportions, so large that an entire city could easily fit inside, with space on all sides to spare and that is exactly what had happened. Those trapped here had been industrious, mining the stone, then they had wrought dwellings to survive, and to wait. All within the city waited, bidding upon their master and waiting for the time to arrive when their saviour would open the seals that they could leave the prison they had found themselves within.

Occasionally a person would find their way here by accident in dreams, people from earths and other realities. But they would never awaken, their souls taken here, if captured, would never be freed, never escape. The souls and minds instead would be devoured by the hordes that resided here, something for the base legions of a great and terrible lord who had been imprisoned here several millennia ago.

His forces had been stood ready, eagerly waiting for their freedom to come; so that they may continue their war upon the earth once more. Any sounds which echoed would cause a wild stir of excitement and crazed delirium as they prepared to usher forth onto the Earths reality, to slay, kill and destroy again, but each time the noises heard would turn out to be something innocuous and the pity would fall like a blanket over the unhappy denizens of malicious intent.

Drip, drip, drip, drip, drip, drip.

The only one who never gave up on the wait, forever patient, brooding was the dark master here himself; sat upon his great throne made of cold iron, he sat there almost human to look at in countenance, but for his great height of eight feet and the black bat-like wings upon his back. His facial features were beautiful to behold, the look of a regal prince, his black hair was shoulder length and fell in tight curls, eyes that were cruel looked out from the Adonis-like head, the jaw was square and untouched by facial hair, he was named in black books as one of the great Dukes of Hell.

Beside him laid his faithful mount, the creatures long tail curled around the throne, its enormous head resting upon the rocky ground, the beast's wings were so large that to open its span fully it could easily cloak a large area in dark shadow. With four great legs, each the size of an aged oak tree's trunk the dragon-like beast would have sure and sturdy footing. Each leg ended in malicious claws set like daggers each easily six inches long.

Its hide was covered in hardened scales, like a lizard's, only oversized and of immense proportions. The monsters head was a terror to behold, it was crowned with several horns. Its mouth was bedecked with multiple rows of vicious teeth, two canines that were wickedly curved, protruding from the creature's ghastly maw.

Imprisoned here in an age long past, the vile horde waited for their agent to free them that they may continue once more the slaughter and tyranny that they had originally came to the earth to sow, so very long ago.

Any who found themselves here would endure slow painful torture, exhausting, back-breaking slave labour and a slow terrible death, such was the whims of the miserable beasts that had been trapped here, for them reason was to hurt and destroy, maim and smash. Delight they only found in the suffering of others and of all its different kinds.

Drip, drip, drip......

The sound of the dripping water had ceased, all the creatures that could crowded and jostled into their infernal master's great stone throne room, until there was no space within, those that could not squeeze in, crowded at the doors; jostling to see. They watched and waited to see and hear his proclamation; what this could mean.

'It has begun, the Gruul has opened the first seal.' declared the foul king Ashtoreth from his imposing stone throne.

He raised his voice and announced to all his feral kin.

'We must prepare, sharpen your weapons and poison your blades, our time of terror approaches once more,'

The Great hall was filled with shouts, jeers and miserable screams of vile delight.

A few moments later three demonic beasts entered, they wore mail armour with crude swords upon their hips, they dragged in a burnt and blackened corpse. They forced their way through to the Dark Lord's Throne, laying the body at their master's feet, they then all lowered down to one knee and lowered their heads.

'We found this in an outlying tunnel master.' one growled 'We do not know where it came from?'

'It looks like it was once human, but its dead now!' another sneered.

'Feed, my friends, feed upon this boon!' Ashtoreth boomed, his voice filling the rocky hall, it slowly trailed away, echoing through the tunnels.

The three stood and dragged the charred prize toward a brazier, a large obese creature stumbled forward, a greasy, blood-stained apron hung loosely on its fat belly. It had beady yellow eyes that were small and hawkish, it held a large, dirty cleaver in one hand and a serrated fillet knife in the other, not a viler caricature of a cook could you find. With a slovenly grin the cook beast expertly started to butcher the charred remains of Cliff, chuckling happily to itself as it did so.

It was not long before a large crowd had gathered, a cacophony erupted with it, hustling in upon the butcher, squabbling for choice cuts of the blackened and burnt human flesh. The Demon lord watched with grim satisfaction, he knew the body signified a seal had been broken, two more and the ritual to open his dimensional prison could begin, already the link between this prison and the Earth's reality would begin to weaken, causing cracks to show, leaks. He would soon be able to help his agents subtly from here as the protections were removed.

****

The Dark Prince thought back to many millennia ago, to the time he had nearly taken the earth for himself, he had been thwarted by humans then.

His forces had been arrayed in a long line, sharp and spiteful spears bristling all along the front, his bestial cavalry upon the right flank. Across the grassy plain stood the enemy, the leader at the fore in front of a long orderly line of pike men, their weapons catching and flicking the sun towards the Demon lord's host provocatively. The Islanders army as Ashtoreth's kind called these humans had anchored their right flank upon the wide snaking river, matching his cavalry stood the Islander cavalry facing upon the human left flank, behind which led to the Dogger lands.

Ashtoreth knew the ground by the river was boggy and unsuitable for combat, his thrust would be through the centre by echelons starting with his leftmost units and gradually launching across the whole front, until his entire force was engaged, his plan was to send the initial attack as close as possible to the river, pinning the enemy in stages, preventing them from aiding one another as his force closed the distance. A distant cry echoed across the field, 'Archers.'

With the order, soldiers from the opposing army slipped to the front in a long loose formation, skirmishers. Soon the Islander's arrows would fall upon his army, Ashtoreth had Javelin armed warriors, but was outmatched for range; it was time to advance.

'Captain Baylaris, give the command to advance.'

Captain Baylaris was a large dark-skinned beast, wide of jaw with two fearsome seven-inch curved tusks. Dressed in dark mail and blackened leather armour, the demonic captain lifted its cleaver-like weapon and bellowed Ashtoreth's command, 'Left flank advance in echelons!'

The left side of the demonic horde started toward the Islander army, after fifty yards the tusked captain Baylaris commanded once more,

'Centre advance in echelons!'

The centre mass filed past the Captain and their dread master, slowly they marched by, Ashtoreth urged his winged mount to take to the air, the creature beat its immense wings, faster and faster, it began to run; great thunderous steps, beating its wings faster and faster, running quicker until with a mighty effort the monster took to the air, clumsily at first the creature pushed itself up into the sky until it could soar high above the two opposing forces.

Below Ashtoreth, the command reached him upon his mount, 'Right flank, advance in echelons!' and with that command the final third began to advance toward the Islander lines, as they did, the left flank had moved to within range of the Islander archers.

'Loose.' shouted an Islander marshal, with the command, a thousand black shafted arrows darkened the sky below the dark lord. As the monstrous line advanced, they left behind many dead and dying troops, pierced with grisly arrow wounds. Ashtoreth realised the Islander's had spell casters; they had used rituals to imbue their weaponry with the power to easily kill demon-kind.

'Loose and retreat.' Came the command again, and once more the sky filled with black arrows, more gaps appeared in the demonic lines. The centre would be within range soon, even as the skirmishers near the river began the retreat to the relative safety behind the Islander phalanx.

'Loose!'

Another officer clearly shouted aloud, then the demonic centre came under missile attack from the Islander army. This continued for three more volleys, each time scores of dead and dying were left upon the ground behind the advancing mass.

'Javelin's.' came a shout from within the advancing demonic lines and upon the command, hundreds of three foot short spears were hurled toward the Islander phalanx, gaps appeared in the human lines as a javelin here and there penetrated beyond the pike and shield defence, other men in the rear ranks quickly moved into the vacant spaces taking position and setting pike once again and keeping the formation tight.

From behind the Islander lines a torrent of arrows launched high into the air, followed quickly by another, and another, each volley brought with it a score of fresh demonic casualties.

Then the two sides clashed the shorter spears of the demonic forces resulted in them taking terrible casualties, but they outnumbered the Islander's ten-fold, the monstrous wave crashed onto the phalanx with the terrible and loud sounds of metal on metal, shattered shield and the screams of the dying.

On the right flank the last force to move was the bestial cavalry, the infernal mounts were a terror to behold, wherever they went upon the battlefield, they would bring suffering and death with them, those who ran were trampled, those who stood were slaughtered. The Islander cavalry had begun an advance of its own, at a slow trot toward the cantering monstrous cavalry making ground the two living masses closed upon each other.

The opposing forces cavalries collided, immense impetus from both sides inflicted massive casualties upon each other, horse's high-pitched cries of agony and the sound of the demonic mounts filled the air, the slaughter was cruel and terrible, and it was complete. Wherever the dark lord looked from far up above, his forces were engaged his cavalry had devastated the Islander cavalry and the survivors fled from the field, decimated. His infantry had not bent or broke the phalanx however, and this had cost Ashtoreth's horde dear. But he had lured the Islander's to battle here for a reason, and now he would unleash his trap.

The Evil lord dropped from the sky on his draconic mount plummeting toward the rear of Islander line, as he dived, a great horn was blown, a signal to those hidden within the muddy waters of the river, rising from the banks rushed another demonic legion, hacking and slaying into the rear of the Islander armies right flank, and the line began to break, small pockets at first fleeing the deadly beasts that wrought death from the boggy river banks upon all who came near, but then these pockets widened to long swathes of the line in retreat, then in it developed into a full rout. Ashtoreth saw his victory, he would soon rule this world, he would soon turn this world into a place of terror and woe.

With victory so close at hand he had plunged all in to finish the army of Atlantis, playing his final card to win the game. The Islanders had however out witted the great and terrible dark lord Ashtoreth. They had played him, they had judged he would 'go all in, they knew he would roll the die, one more time!'

They had been correct, he had, and it was then they had enacted a powerful ritual, trapping the demonic prince and all his legions with him. The ground began to crumble and collapse, pulling all down into the ground, he fell with his hordes deep within the belly of the earth, buried forever and sealed for eternity.

****

but it would not be so now, occasionally he had gleaned information from those hapless enough to have found themselves in this infernal subterranean prison, gaps in reality had trapped these poor souls to a fate worse than death as the infernal have ways of gaining pleasure from others misery, and they are the masters of keeping someone or something alive for as long as possible while maintaining as much pain as could be mustered. The few agents he had who had escaped the trap an age before had worked tirelessly to try to free him and his legions. To Ashtoreth; it was now apparent that the Gruul was close to freeing him from the eternity sentence handed down all those centuries before by the Islander's, by the Atlanteans.

Chapter 7

The Will

The room was crowded; filled, it turned out that Grandpa Bob had arranged for the will to be read in a local hall. The building stood very near to the paintbrush factory where Cairo's mother worked, on a very narrow street near the family home. Like so many buildings in the old part of Lowestoft this street had been built long ago to house the herring fishing vessel crews of yesteryear.

The hall was in the shadow of the only high rise building in Lowestoft, a fifteen-story cross shaped block with painted white and blue walls up to the very top. From the roof of the high-rise building, In the distance the other two primary landmarks in Lowestoft could clearly be seen. Looking across from the North Sea coast was a massive three bladed Wind Turbine, its name was Gulliver and once had been the largest turbine of its kind in Europe. Looking west from the rooftop you could clearly see the tall, pointed Verdigris green spire of St Margaret's church upon a hill about a kilometre inland, it sat upon the largest hill north of the river Waveney.

The Hall was called St Peters hall, inside there had been about one hundred chairs laid out in lines facing a table at the front. People milled about. It had filled up today, in fact it was packed. All the family were there, the whole extended family, all that is apart from Bob's son Paul, he would not come. Many invites had indeed been sent out, but there was many here who none of the family knew at all, they were complete strangers and where they had come from that was a mystery as well, but they had invites and had been allowed in.

Craig had spoken to some of the people gathered, accepting words of consolation like his Grandmother and all of the closest of Bob's relatives. Asking one group how they knew Bob; a kind hearted and warm faced lady in her sixties, she wore a burgundy woollen shawl and a brown flower-patterned dress. She sat beside a tall gentleman, he was balding and wore a gold rimmed pair of spectacles, it gave him a serious demeanour. They said they had come from Cambridge and had known Bob from his days in the army.

Another couple had come from Essex, they remembered Liz but she couldn't place them, they were in their forties, and had an air of the professional business type people, the woman wore a navy pencil skirt and white shirt, the man wore a high fashion suit with a green silk tie, the condolences were sincere though and for that all the family just accepted that Grandpa Bob had not only lit up their own lives, but obviously many others besides. Later Craig found Cairo, he sat down beside her.

'Have you heard from your Dad yet?' she asked,

'Not yet, funny I would have thought he would have come home?' he said,

'I guess some rifts go deep.'

Cairo reached over and held Craig's hand, she looked in his eyes, she knew of the family difficulties, and did not push it any further. She looked over at the gathering as still more people came in.

'I'm surprised, there wasn't this many at the wake?' she said.

'I know what you mean, crazy, isn't it?' Craig replied.

'Is that Matt over there? It is I'm going over to see him.'

Cairo then got up and walked around the chairs towards Matt who was sat and waving furiously on the far side of the room. Craig watched as Cairo walked across the room, as she went, his eyes following her they then paused as they locked eyes with a tall stranger in the room. The man stood next to a woman dressed in a purple suede dress, she looked like she was in her late thirties, the man looked to be in his late forties; he was dressed in a nice suit, but both seemed out of place in the room, Craig had a "funny feeling" about the pair, the man stared back, Craig broke the gaze, worried all of a sudden but not sure exactly why. Hastily he looked back over to Cairo as she had reached Matt on the far wall, they were in a tight hug, then released and started talking with one another.

Concentrating, believing he can hear across the noise and clamour within the wide hall, Craig focused all his attention on Cairo and Matt; steadily the clarity of his hearing got finer and finer, like his hearing was by remote, he then picked up what they talked about.

'I hope you are ok.' Matt said,

'Holding up, you know, it's pretty shit though really. Why are you here anyway?'

'I don't know, I mean I didn't really know your grandfather, but I got an invite, so here I am, I just figured you or Craig had something to do with it?'

'No, not to my knowledge, I mean, why would we invite you, nothing personal Matt, you know I love you mate, but it's a will reading, I guess I just didn't know he had so much to give?'

Craig using his gift decided to sweep the area, how many other people didn't know why they were here? Sure enough, various pockets of people were discussing why they had gotten an invite, obviously not wishing to miss out, they had turned up. He got up and walked over to a couple in their fifties whom he did not recognise. The gentleman was over-weight by a couple of stones, his wife was of an average build, her skin of a dark nut-brown complexion, as if too much time had been spent in the sun, he walked over and politely asked.

'Hello there, I'm glad you could make it, did you know my Grandfather well?'

'Oh, I'm sorry for your loss, well no, we didn't know him personally, but figured he may be a rich distant relative, so here we are.'

'We can leave if you would wish?' The lady said.

'No, you are alright, you are here now, you never know, he may have included you in his will. But trust me, we are not rich.'

Craig looked over the gathering once more, the influx of people entering the room had almost totally ceased now, there was a lot of low murmuring background noise. As he gazed across the hall, he spotted that once again, the two strange characters by the wall were looking towards him, Craig decided he would go over and ask them why they were here, he started moving slowly along the row of filled seats towards the pair. Halfway there the doors closed, echoing through the hall.

'Good afternoon everyone, If I could have your attention!' Announced a dark-skinned woman with a black, larger than life perm and spectacles. The room quietened, Craig decided he would speak to them later, he retreated to his chair where Cairo and he had sat, moments later Cairo and Matt had joined him.

As the will reading began Craig drifted off, thinking of times when his Grandfather and he had shared times again, all the little life lessons that had been shared, at the time none of them had seemed very important, but now he was gone, they all seemed to make sense.

****

'Do you believe in God Craig?'

'Well, yes, I guess Grandpa.'

'Why' Bob asked the sixteen-year-old Craig, whilst they were fishing one day, they had gone to the river Waveney, as it meandered around the town and village of Bungay and Ditchingham.

'It's what they say to do, isn't it?' Craig replied.

'My thoughts Craig is there may be a God, but he very probably does not care about you, or even know of your existence. I may be wrong so you will have to find your own answer, but I find it more likely that there is no Godlike figurehead, more we are a very, very small part of a bigger creature!'

Craig remembered that he had felt perplexed. *'When I die Craig, do not mourn for me!'*

'Why do you say that?' Craig asked.

'I'm going to die before you, your Grandmother will too, but I don't want you to mourn. Miss me yes, please miss me, but try not to cry, as I do not believe I will truly be gone, more like I will have returned to the millions of other living souls making this reality and all the others besides, work.'

Craig was totally lost at this point.

'What do you mean, other realities, like heaven and Hell?'

'I think there may be numerous alternate realities that we could class as a Heaven or a Hell, I would also imagine that some people when they die would go to these, but if they did then I would imagine also that they would be there for a reason, in some form that did not think of that place as a Heaven or a Hell!'

'Wow Grandpa, just when I think you cannot get any deeper, you find even more depths in the mind to fathom!'

'It's just my belief Craig, I will not force it upon you, your belief is personal, if people's beliefs were kept that way, we would have had a lot less wars that's for sure!'

'I believe that a soul is not connected to the body, more it is a symbiotic that uses a body as a host if you like.'

'Oh well at least I understand something you have said Grandpa!'

'That's good; What?' Grandpa Bob asked

'Your nuts!' Craig replied.

They both laughed.

****

'And to my Grand-son I leave the total sum five thousand pounds, my fishing tackle, my Omega Sea master watch, all the contents of my personal safe and a one quarter share in my house, to be shared as already stated with my wife Liz.'

The Executor read aloud to those there, Craig felt lots of eyes turn and stare his way, he felt his face suddenly aflush with colour, he dipped his head. Then he felt a gentle touch on his left arm, it was Cairo.

'It's alright Craig, he wanted you to have these, don't feel guilty.'

Slowly he lifted his head, looked over toward his Nan, she was looking back his way, she smiled, he did likewise. Straight away he could feel the natural colour beginning to return to his cheeks. He also noticed in the corner of his eye, the two strange individuals leaving in a hurry, he did not know who they were, he did not know why they were here, Craig felt that they seemed to be out of place, like they were trespassing. Craig wanted to follow the pair, to see what they were up to, and where they would go next, but he could not leave, not just after he had been bequeathed so much, what would that look like and so he stayed, and he listened.

'To my Grand-daughter Cairo I leave a sum of six thousand pounds and my Renault Clio car.'

The Executor announced, Matt leaned over Craig and said to Cairo.

'Beers are on you tonight then!' he winked at Craig as he retreated to his seat, Craig smiled then looked at Cairo, she had that knowing look in her eye, it was no secret that Matt fancied Cairo, he always had, but he had never raised the courage to take their friendship any further.

The will-reading continued for about another thirty minutes, all members of the family had been bequeathed moneys and something that would have been personal to them, some of the closest people to Bob had been bequeathed a token item or two, James the hippy who lived next door had been left all of Bob's tomato grow bags, the two had gotten on well together, often spending time talking about gardening. At the end of the reading most gathered there had been bequeathed nothing. People began to talk, causing a stir, why had they been invited, and not been required, some there said it was a mystery at best, others called it an insult to the deceased. The close relatives and friends gathered round to try to discover what had transpired, why had so many letters gone out, Craig, wondering again about the mysterious pair who had left shortly after the will had begun to be read had an idea.

'Has anybody here got a copy of their invite?' he called out to the crowd. A lady came forward with her husband, here I have, she fished a letter out of her purse.

It was addressed to her but reading the invite fully, at the bottom was a signature that was not Craig's Grand-father's.

'Cairo, something's going on, somebody wanted all these people here for a reason, and I think I know who it is. Did you notice that strange couple stood by the far wall, they left soon after the reading had begun, just after the announcement of what Grandpa had left me in fact?'

'No, I think I saw some people leave but I wasn't really thinking about it that much to be honest.' She replied.

'Well I did, and I think they wanted us still here after the reading had finished!'

'But why?' she asked.

'I'll tell you later, we've got to go and find them!'

Chapter 8

The Break In

It took about another hour of organising and managing the unhappy crowd at the will reading before Cairo and Craig could get away from the hall. Matt came along too, Grand-ma Liz had gone with Cairo's Mother and Father.

'Where are we going?' Cairo asked.

'Back to mine and Nan's, I have a bad feeling about the couple who left, we must hurry!'

It wasn't far from the Hall to Craig's home, just a few streets away, but if Craig was right in his assumption then they needed to be quick. After four or five minutes they got to the end of the street, they headed down the long narrow road, cars were parked all along the left-hand side, the road was cramped, the buildings gave the impression that they almost leaned in towards you as you made your way to the end. Like the very houses themselves looked down on the three as they hurried to the end of the street.

They arrived at the front door, Craig produced the key from his pocket and slipped it quickly into the lock, turned it and they all entered the property. They saw immediately the state of the place; it was in an absolute shamble. There had been a break-in, the floor was a mess, all the wall hangings had been knocked down, the ornaments upon the fireplace were scattered over the floor and the mirror had been smashed.

'Shit check through and upstairs. Matt, check the kitchen I have a feeling I know where they have been and want to see if it has been touched!'

Matt and Craig headed through to the kitchen, Craig continued to the back door and went into the garden, heading for his Grandfathers shed. The kitchen was in much the same state, all the cupboards were open, packets of cereal and bags of rice lay strewn upon the floor.

'They've been up here too, I guess they must have found what they were after!' Cairo shouted from upstairs.

Craig arrived at the shed in the back garden, inside the place was much the same; like inside the house, but Craig's eyes were drawn to the open digital safe upon the work top.

Looking at the open safe, inside were some papers, they looked like someone had been investigating them. Unfortunately, he did not know what was in there in the first place. Craig closed the door as he left, rubbing his chin, deep in thought as to what to do, or where to go next?

Inside the kitchen, Craig found the other two, discussing what they had found.

'I don't know what they were after Craig, but it wasn't your watch!' Cairo said as she raised her left hand holding the Omega timepiece.

She passed it to Craig, he took it, and put the watch on.

'It's going to need a link taken out!' Craig said.

'Yeah, your Nan's purse is on the floor, but it looks like it hasn't been touched either. Very strange,' added Matt.

'I've been thinking, there are no signs of entry either here or at the shed, so I imagine whatever they wanted was in the safe, it's been opened but I do not know how; it's a digital lock?'

I think we should tidy this place up, whoever did this wanted it to look like a break-in, but there is more to it than that!' Craig said.

Over the next two hours the three of them got the house back into a presentable shape, Craig tidied the living room, Matt, the kitchen and Cairo went upstairs and sorted out her Grand-mothers room. They decided between them they would leave Craig's room. The only real issue they had was the broken mirror, it was old and would not be able to be replaced.

When they had all finished their respective parts of the property, they gathered in the living room.

'Right we are all done, apart from the mirror, what's the story?' Matt asked.

'I reckon we say we were messing around with a ball or something and knocked it down, then say we will pay for it, you know, for the damage!' Cairo said.

'There is another way I think guys?' Craig said.

'Somehow I think it has something to do with everything that has happened today.'

Craig stopped and paused, Cairo and Matt looked at him questioningly.

'What do you mean? Do you know the people that did this?' Cairo asked.

'No, but there is something about Grandpa that you do not know, no one knew really, and I think that is why there was so many people at the will reading,' he continued, 'and I think that is why this break-in took place too.'

Cairo and Matt were intrigued. 'Go on.' Cairo said.

'Right, first this is going to sound crazy, so if you laugh, I am going to understand, but I'm going to tell you anyway!'

'Go on then, spit it out.' Matt said.

'Well, erm,' Craig stuttered a moment then said, 'Grandpa had a special gift, like a magic sought of thing!'

There was a pause, then Matt started laughing, Cairo said 'That's not even funny Craig, what are you talking about, you and your Nan's home has just been broken into and you are running on crap about magic!'

'I can prove it!' Craig said, Matt was still laughing.

'Go on then!' Cairo said.

Craig took a deep breath; relaxing, he knew with two people in the room who did not believe it in his gift, it would be harder to make his ability work, far harder to use the magic. 'Concentrating his mind on the mirror, Craig wanted it to be repaired, willed it to repair, forcing with his mind the material to fuse back together.

'What are you doing Craig?' Cairo asked, Matt had finally stopped laughing and was watching with interest now.

'Yeah Craig you do look funny.' Matt said, the mirror was still in two pieces, the fragments laid next to one another. 'Ok, let's do this another way, both of you just go into the back garden for a moment, when you come back the mirror will be in one piece.'

'Craig are you ok? I'm thinking we should call an ambulance or something.'

'Hurry up, go into the garden!' Ushering them out Craig already knew that he would not be able to mend the mirror, their belief that the gift would not work would prevent him from being successful, but he had an idea.

Outside in the back garden, Cairo and Matt stood by the greenhouse, inside was a row of tomato plants, with several bunches of over-ripened fruit hanging from them, since Bob had passed away, no one had thought to tend to the Greenhouse.

'What is he up to?' Matt said as he slipped his vape machine from his pocket.

'I don't know, he and Grandad were very close, I'm worried for him!' she said.

'We'll give him five minutes, then go in and call an ambulance.' Matt winked at Cairo, she smiled.

'But I do think we better keep an eye on him, I mean mending mirrors with magic and shit like that?' Cairo shrugged and raised her arms in a manner of resignation.

'Guys.' Craig said as he walked out of the kitchen door into the back garden.

'Given up have you Craig, its ok, we understand, you and your Grandfather were really close.' Matt said, exhaling a massive vapour cloud.

'Not quite, look behind you!' Craig said, they both turned, then with utter shock and awe they both stepped back, behind them, a hose was writhing in the air untouched by anyone's hand, meandering around with a life of its own, one end wrapped around the back gate, the other, slithered between both Cairo and Matt, until it reached Craig.

'See guys, it's because you don't believe that I could mend it with my mind, that the mirror would not mend itself, help me, both of you just think that after seeing this, that I am able to repair the mirror.'

They looked at each other, 'Ok, we'll try.'

With that they all went back into the living room, stood about the mirror, and waiting for Craig to complete his miracle, he began. Once more focusing his mind on repairing the mirror, forcing it back together, he urged it to mend, through clenched teeth he said to Cairo and Matt, 'Force the mirror to mend, think that it will mend!'

Then the two pieces slowly began to move, gently sliding together until they touched and then fused, mending with a seamless connection.

'Wow it mended itself!' Cairo said, total disbelief in her voice, 'did we do that?' She asked, Matt fell back into the armchair, just staring at the mirror.

'Pick it up, check it.' Craig said, Matt did so, 'It's totally fused, not even a faint make mark where the parts came together! Fucking hell, that's amazing, were rich!'

Cairo stood, still in absolute disbelief; she just could not fathom what she had just witnessed.

'Is this some trick Craig?' She asked, hoping it was, reaching for the mirror to inspect it for herself.

'No, sorry Cairo, but no, any way we have something to do, we need to find out who staged the break-in? I'm going to warn you though; I think they may have knowledge of how to use the gift too!'

'Is this dangerous?' Matt asked

'I don't know, but I want to find out what they are up to?'

'Where do we start, I mean, where could they have gone, how are we going to find out?' Cairo stated.

'Yeah where do we start?' Matt asked.

****

The pair had slipped to the back gate unnoticed, the sky was overcast, shrouding them from prying eyes above, those clouds threatened rain at any point. They had left the will-reading at the mention of a safe, getting into a dark blue BMW 3 series, and heading directly back towards the deceased's property. The back gate was unlocked so they had entered and then gone to the back door. Sydora focused her mind on the lock, willing it to open.

Click!

And they were in, she looked triumphantly at the Nihilist, he looked at her unimpressed.

'Parlour tricks, my dear,' he said, he knew this annoyed her, but he just couldn't help himself.

'Okay, you make it look like a burglary, I'll find the safe.'

The Nihilist headed straight for the living room, he produced a small wooden cosh and a pair of leather gloves from his trench coat, he slipped on the gloves, then immediately and forcefully smashed the mirror, shattering it into two, he tossed it on the floor, then kicked over the low table. Sweeping his arm along the mantlepiece, ornaments fell like raindrops onto, and all about the hearth, scattering onto the increasingly cluttered floor. The Nihilist left the living room and went upstairs to continue plundering the house.

Outside Sydora had knelt in a niche between the three different coloured bins and the greenhouse, she had taken a small trowel from the glass outbuilding, she placed it on the ground, then slipped a brown leather pouch out from a hidden pocket upon her waist. She drew several small bones from inside the drawstring bag, the bones were worn from usage and age, there were many dark stains upon them, some quite fresh, others faded through time, they may well have been human knuckle bones, but now smoothed with time it was hard to really tell. She cast them onto the paving slab in front of her, scanned over them a moment, focusing her mind, Sydora then slowly took an ornate knife of about two inches in length from another hidden pouch, she made a small incision on her left index finger. The knife was incredibly sharp, and parted the skin instantly, blood began to run from the tiny wound, she let a few small drops of blood fall onto and over the bones.

Thaumaturgy, or blood magic; it was a forbidden magical practice of the left-hand path, it was so dangerous because the use of blood within the magical practise would often induce dangerous beings to come to your summons. at lower levels it could be used as a highly affective divination, at higher levels of skill, it could be used to compel dangerous beasts to do your bidding. The blood increased the power of the magic due to the personal sacrifice made, however the beings you dealt with could be very dangerous if not controlled; in short, they came because of the promise of blood.

She watched the signs laid within the blood and bones in front of her, discerning any message that may come through, waiting patiently, listening intently, forcing her mind to listen through the barriers of reality, believing something would sense the sign and come to her aid. Minutes went by until, she felt an exhilarating sensation start in the small of her back, rising till her head tingled; she had made contact.

Emptying her mind of thoughts, she was left only with the answers that had entered her from an external, alien source. Abruptly she opened her eyes, stood and headed over to the shed door, raising a hand to it once more she induced the lock to open. It did so, the door swung open, inside she could see the signs of a well-loved personal space, Bob's 'Man-cave'. She walked in and spotted the safe almost immediately, nestled on a lower shelf at the rear of the wooden building, she walked over to it, gave it a slight kick, it moved easily. Putting on the gloves that the Nihilist had given her in the BMW before they had arrived at the building, she then lifted it up onto the worksurface. Sydora then settled her mind for a third time, concentrating upon the digital codes, it was a simple four-digit affair, and in seconds a mechanical sound of the mechanism unlocking came from within. Swiftly she opened the safe and took out everything inside, some paper written notes, a set of spare keys for the house and various other locks, and a roll parchment in a zip-lock bag, she took the bag, then looked at the keys, stopped and looked inside the safe once more. Feeling inside, for a secret compartment but it was now empty.

The Nihilist came to the shed door, 'Have you got what we came for?'

'Not all of it, I've got the ritual' She replied, 'But the key, it's not here.'

'Well it's too late now. We better go!'

Chapter 9

Nihilism and Fatalism

Two days before the Will reading.

Sydora and the Nihilist had left London by train with Miss Slattery, Lord Blessed had addressed the pair after the summit, giving them precise instructions. Tickets had already been purchased for two rooms at the Victoria hotel.

The hotel overlooked Lowestoft's south beach. Lord Blessed gave the Nihilist the keys to a blue BMW that would be waiting for them in the train station car park, when they arrived on the east coast.

He had also said that he wanted Sydora and the Nihilist to be available to help Miss Slattery if she should require their assistance in any way. Travelling north towards Suffolk, they journeyed by train having to change at Ipswich, then it was direct from there till they arrived in Lowestoft.

The journey had been uneventful, none of the trio really wanted to be with each other, and so they all sat in silence, barely saying a word to one another for three and a half hours. Sydora read a classic Charles Dickens novel, Victoria had taken up most of the table space as she focused on some paperwork. The Nihilist just gazed out of the window at the fields and little villages as they went by, trying to take in everything, possibly for later use, even taking note of the number of deer in a field as the train swiftly went by or what the graffiti said and that type of car rotting away behind a house near to the bridge close to Halesworth.

The Nihilist sat in an expensive suit it was dark slate grey, and made by Paul Smith, contoured down the sides, he wore a white shirt beneath with a blue tie, it gave the impression of a successful business man, he had an old weathered trench coat that was folded beside him, and he had brought with him an oversized case about four feet in length.

He thought back to the remit Lord Blessed had given them, get an old parchment and a key, the parchment would make it possible to decipher the old book that Lord Blessed would soon have in his possession, the key, what could that be for? He didn't know. Then bring them both back to him as quickly as possible. They had invites to the will-reading, apparently so did a lot of other people, it was the perfect cover to get inside the deceased's house. Pretty straight forward, he thought to himself, it was what he liked about working for Lord Blessed, no questions about who he was or where he came from it was just, job, pay and goodbye.

The Nihilist had worked for him several times, usually it was just cleaning up the mess someone else had made, but occasionally it could get interesting, blackmail, extortion, murder, it mattered little to him.

Sydora wondered at the possibilities of this book, though Lord Blessed was not a member of her organisation, he had very close ties, a practitioner of magic like herself, though he called it 'the touch' she had helped him develop his abilities in return for very generous donations and financial aids, they were on good terms.

She did not like the Nihilist, everybody who knew of him, knew that he could be a cold-blooded murderer, all who knew him could only guess at what his motives might truly be. A few years ago, she had had a close run in with this enigmatic character, she still did not know who had been pulling the strings. She went as far as to attempt an augury to discover his motives, but the augury would not work.

Sydora had worn a fine ankle length dress in her favourite shade of purple, she wore a black leather jacket, her long black hair had been combed back and clipped at the sides. She wore an inverted five-pointed star brooch of silver, within the central pentagon of the pentangle was a symbol of a left hand.

The train had arrived in Lowestoft in the mid-afternoon, all the passengers aboard alighted the carriage, going their separate ways. Sydora and the Nihilist headed for the exit closest to the car park, Miss Slattery headed for the ticket building.

'Don't you want a lift?' The Nihilist asked.

'No, I've got to go to my office in town first, I'll catch up with both of you after you've gotten the items Lord Blessed is after. Bye for now!'

She turned and walked into the Ticket building, the other two looked at each other then continued towards the car park.

'What a bitch!' Sydora stated as they left the station platform, 'Were obviously riffraff that she does not wish to be seen with!'

'Well at least we get to see the quality of the rooms that Lord Blessed has laid on for us a bit quicker.' The Nihilist added optimistically.

He did not seem to be at all perturbed by the flippant attitude of the minister towards the pair of them. He pressed the unlock button on the car keys that Lord Blessed had given them, the lights of a Blue BMW parked fifty feet away flicked on twice with a low audible bleep.

'Sydora my dear, your chariot awaits.' They walked to the expensive German coupe, opening the passenger door and getting in whilst The Nihilist opened the boot and put in both their cases.

'At least we are travelling in style.' She said as the Nihilist opened the driver side door. The pair then drove off towards their hotel.

****

After the break-in the pair had fled to the blue BMW parked in a small enclosed car park on the other side of Katwijk Way, it was one of the main arterial roads of Lowestoft which ran alongside the town centre. They quickly got into the blue car and decided to drive straight back to the Hotel. They would then call Lord Blessed to determine the next course of action.

A rainstorm rolled in from the North Sea, a steady grey, heavy drizzle; it reduced vision and the roads of Lowestoft quickly slowed to little more than a crawl as they always would when any form of outside influence affected the traffic system. The pair again, didn't speak; instead he, drove, and she just looked out of the window, wondering where the Key would be, it was not on the set in the Safe, it may be in that house, but she figured the two would have been together, why would they not be?

They were stopped by a build-up of traffic at the Bascule bridge; the bridge was up as a large standby ship returned to port. Returning from a month-long vigil, idly watching at the legs of a gas rig somewhere far out in the North Sea.

'Any ideas?' The Nihilist asked as he cut the engine.

'I'm not sure right now, I'm surprised that the key was not located in the same place as the parchment?'

He looked at her, wondering if she had a plan, her eyes were mirror-like and gave nothing away, no signs of panic, no signs of assurance. The bridge began to lower, he restarted the engine, moments later they were moving once more.

They arrived at the Hotel ten minutes later, going inside they, both went to the bar area, taking a seat and discussing their next move.

'I think we should try some other members of the family, what about Bob's sons?' The Nihilist asked.

'That was my first thought, but one of them wasn't at the will reading, I have a feeling he and his father were not on talking terms.' She replied.

'What about the other one.' The Nihilist said.

A well-dressed barman came over with two drinks, interrupting the Nihilist; Bourbon for the Nihilist and a vodka and tonic for Sydora, 'Thank you!' She said to the barman, he smiled, 'Your welcome.' The barman replied.

'What about the other side of the family, I think it is our only available option for now.' The Nihilist asked again

'Ok, do they live in this area?'

'I think so, but we better find out exactly where from Vicky.'

Sydora produced a mobile phone, she called Victoria Slattery,

'Hi Vicky, it's Sydora.,

'Oh hi, do you have it?'

'No, we need you to get us an address!'

****

The two continued to drink for the rest of the afternoon, watching the grey clouds out to sea as they lashed rain and still yet more rain upon the British coastal town, the seagulls circled playfully in the winds as they caught the strong up draughts caused by the cliffs that the hotel was built upon. They waited at the hotel for the rest of that day. Victoria had gotten back to Sydora with the details at seven the following evening.

'Interesting, Bob's other son lives close by Bob's home, we can go there and hopefully get things moving forward.'

'I wonder, what about Lord Blessed's son, could we use him?'

'I find it interesting that he has not used him in the first place, because he lives here, it cannot be a coincidence.'

'Maybe we should split up, I could check out his son, you go and find this key.'

'You know Nihilist that isn't what we are supposed to be doing, but it may be worth finding out a bit more of Lord Blessed's motivations for involving us and not Hawkins.'

She thought about his idea, if they split up, they could cover more ground and if it was possible to get help from Hawkins then they would have more hands and someone who knew the area as well, but why had Blessed not advised using his son? He may have just not thought about it? Not likely, he would have thought long and hard about it. It then dawned upon her, maybe Hawkins was already helping them in some other form or manner, she decided that was the most plausible reason.

'Yes, I think you may be onto something, Lord Blessed is too far away to stop us, and we can cover more ground with another pair of feet running about.' She said, 'I will need the car though as they live the other end of the town.'

The two, left the bar area a little later, the rain had picked up, they agreed to have dinner at seven then go out once more upon their separate objectives. Sydora would drive the Nihilist to Hawkins home in Pakefield, she would then go to Bob's sons' home; Steve's house to try and find the key. They ate together, Sydora had a salad dish, the Nihilist had the fish with capers, the dinner was very enjoyable, but not fine dining, afterwards, they left heading south. The rain had increased in severity lashing down upon the Suffolk streets, without any sign of abating what-so-ever.

The blue BMW drew up in the bus stop around the corner to the Manor, the Nihilist got out, he leaned over,

'Don't wait up.' He said with a cheeky grin, he wore a long, hooded, brown coat and he quickly pulled the hood up to help keep the rain off of his bald head.

She looked at him with the mirror orb eyes and replied, 'You are getting the seat wet!' she gave a hint of a half-smile upon her lips in response, he closed the door and walked briskly through the rain toward the front door. Sydora sped off, crossing over to Stradbroke road and heading toward the relief road that cut through the centre of the town.

The Nihilist arrived at the door, inside there was signs of life, a light was on downstairs in the room to the left of the front door and there was a light on in another part of the house in an upstairs window. He rang the doorbell, then hunched in as close to the door as possible to avoid some of the effects of the lashing rain. A few moments later someone could be seen making their way towards the door from inside, they came to and opened the door, 'Hello, can I help you?' A young man asked.

'Hello, it is Hawkins I am going to guess?'

'Yes, who are you?'

'I was hoping you may be able to help me, I am working for your father, you can call me the Nihilist, I need your help!'

'Well I will need to give my father a call, but I am really quite busy at the moment, so I do not know how I can be of any help?'

The Nihilist huddled inside the front door as Hawkins proceeded to call his father.

'Hi Dad, there is a guy calling himself the Nihilist or something like that, at the door, is he working for you, he says he is? And how does he know my name?'

The Nihilist could not make out any of Lord Blessed's replies, he just waited for the young man to return and let him get out of the rain.

'I guess you had better come in.' Hawkins said, the Nihilist entered.

'Go through there, my girlfriend Gabby will get you a drink and the guy's name is Steve, oh, and my father asked you to give him a call. He seemed pretty pissed that you have turned up here!'

Chapter 10

Caught Red-handed

Sydora had driven over the bridge from the southern side. The blue car threw up spray as it carved through the driving rain, until it finally pulled up at the far end of the street where Cairo's parents lived. The wipers hectically shifted the water from the windscreen. Sydora watched patiently, deciding to monitor what is happening. She turned on the radio. After about forty-five minutes the front door opened and out came the daughter Cairo, Sydora had noticed her at the Will reading, she allowed the young woman to walk past, then just before Cairo exited the road, Sydora turned the car and followed very slowly, waiting at each junction for Cairo to exit the street, then she would catch up; careful not to let her get to far away.

Cairo arrived at the Triangle tavern at about eight-thirty in the evening, she had walked fast due to the rain, it was the birthday of one of Cairo's friends that meant there would be a fair few in for a weekday evening. She went inside, it was warm, and the familiar smells crept towards her, loud music floated from the back bar, it was Chris Cornell, almost immediately she had been recognised by some friends and called over, with welcoming hugs, and kisses Cairo made her way through the gathering in the popular local tavern.

Jordan stood there, he smiled at Cairo as he took some money from another customer, 'What are you having?' He asked, leaning over to her.

'Gin and slim-line Tonic please, is the birthday girl in yet?'

Jordan pointed past the pool table, there was a gathering of eight or nine people clustered close by, making a nuisance of themselves as two young men attempted to squeeze past whilst playing a game of pool. Jordan took a glass and filled it with a shot of Gin, he then reached down and grasped a bottle of slim-line tonic, then proceeded to fill the glass with ice; and finally, a slice of lime. 'There you are Cairo, that'll be four-fifty.' She passed him a five-pound note and waited for her change, a few moments later a tan skinned man came over, he had black shoulder length dread-locks, wore glasses, moustache and chin beard, he was a Triangle tavern local celebrity in the way that long time drinking locals always become microcosm personalities, his nickname was Plug, he was in his mid-forties.

'How are ya Cairo, give me a hug.' He said, leaning in, he was dressed in his workwear so had probably already been in here for a number of hours. 'Hi, Plug, I'm ok, apart from the obvious, she returned his hug, patting him gently on the back, they retreated from one another a couple of steps. Jordan lent over, 'Cairo, your change.'

'Oh, thanks Jordan.,

She took her change and allowed Plug to lead her to the birthday girl, behind the pool table.

****

Exiting the BMW, Sydora quickly opened her Black and white polka dot umbrella and walked to the front door. Before entering the front door to the tavern her senses were already under assault from the noises and smells from within.

'And I thought the pub trade was dying.' She thought to herself.

She shook off her umbrella then went inside. Looking to her right; into the front bar she could see two people sat in there talking and laughing, but neither was Cairo, so she continued onwards toward the back bar and where all of the commotion came from. A person sat on the benches closest the open door into the back bar, he looked at her as she came towards the doorway. She walked past the young man and up to the bar, waiting as others were being served. She scanned the long room; it was very busy, and it took her a few moments to identify just where Cairo had sat down.

'Hi, what would you like?' The barman asked; Jordan had finished serving another customer and was waiting for Sydora to order a drink.

'Oh, sorry, I was, err, can I have a double Vodka please.'

'Yeah, sure.'

Jordan started preparing her drink, Sydora turned back and watched Cairo and her friends, a few moments more went by and then Jordan came back with her vodka.

'Thank you.' She said as she passed Jordan a ten-pound note. Two revellers were singing away next to her, Plug was slinging friendly abuse and banter at the pair, they just sang louder drowning him out with their rowdy chorus. It was quite annoying to Sydora, but all those in close vicinity found it very amusing. unaccustomed to back-street taverns, filled with locals from the working class, Sydora felt a little like a fish out of water. The circles she was used to frequent in, would look down and sneer at this establishment. A place where they were not welcome or wanted. She moved away from the bar as a dance trance track began to kick in, some groups within the bar started jumping about, like they were being agitated by the music and jolted into action by some unseen voltage the electro music carried.

The witch made her way to the alcove then sat herself down in the secluded and sheltered spot, just a few feet from where Cairo and her friends were talking and giggling with one another. It was set back from the pool table with two low tables. A number of small stools divided the tables from the pool table, all around the walls of the alcove, a comfortable padded bench was attached to the wall. A group of four people already sat in the alcove around one of the tables, two women and two men, they were all in their late forties, well dressed compared to most who were in the tavern and currently in mid-discussion about the best quotes and scenes from the Monty-Python movies.

'Hello, is anybody sitting here?' She asked as she sat at the second table in the alcove.

'No, you are fine, just watch out for Plug, a woman by herself: he may well come over and ingratiate himself upon you.' Warned one of the four sat in the alcove.

Though he was sat down, it was clearly obvious he was very tall, he had short dark hair and a styled moustache and wore a fashionable waistcoat. Sydora relaxed, put her drink down in front of her then sat back into the chair, focusing her mind on listening to the conversation just outside the alcove. With nobody around concentrating upon her. All who were here, were in various states of inebriation, she could easily conduct any simple magics, and so could suppress all of the surrounding noise to listen perfectly to Cairo and her friends.

The group discussed the weekend, and some day out coming up that they were excited about in Norwich. They all looked forward to it and that was evident in the way they enthusiastically talked about it. who was going and where to meet up? There had been a bus that would be picking them all up from one of the young ladies' homes. Sydora decided there was not much more information she would be able to glean here, so, instead she would gather her things and see if she could find a way of getting inside Cairo's parent's home to search for this key.

Then a drunken dread-locked individual staggered into a chair, around the table she had sat at; it was Plug, the very person that she had been warned about. Bumping into her table, her drink was sent towards Sydora, she watched, almost in slow motion as the drink fell from the edge of the table, to fall and land in her lap, ejecting its contents all over Sydora's legs. She rose, her long dress drenched through to her legs.

'You stupid, bloody idiot!' she stated, too loud.

all those sat and stood close by, stopped and looked over at her. Jordan was already on his way over with a cloth and an apology, the four gathered in the alcove were moving to help. The pool players stopped and stood out of the way. Cairo and her friends had stopped their chatter and looked at Sydora, Cairo recognised the purple clad witch sat in the alcove. Almost instantly she picked up on Craig's words about the strange couple at the will-reading, it was one of them, she was sure, though it had not registered at the time, this woman was definitely there. Cairo had thought nothing of her at the time, but after the other goings on, it all started to fall into place.

She turned to her friends. 'Look I've just realised, I've got to go!' after the shenanigans the other night, Cairo suddenly felt vulnerable, though she was here with friends, she began thinking home would be far safer.

'Oh, you have only just got here.' Said Rebecca, her friend whose birthday it was. 'I know, looking at Sydora, she then started to think about whether or not Craig was correct in his assumption that the people who had staged the break-in may well have the same kind of powers he had shown himself to have.

Sydora, took the cloth from Jordan and started to mop her dress, removing the worst of the liquid from her lap. She then realised what she was doing, looking up she saw a number of people still looking at her, including Cairo, with realisation upon her face, Sydora quickly figured that she had been recognised by Cairo. Carefully she tried not to look at Cairo, but it looked like Cairo was putting her jacket on and preparing to leave. Sydora decided to act as though she had no recognition of Cairo and go to the toilet to dry her dress, she rose and wandered past the bar, Plug was still apologising as she went by, she ignored him.

Cairo was not completely sure whether this woman dressed in purple had recognised her or not, but she thought that there had been a momentary flicker of comprehension? She could not be sure and so decided to say her farewells and leave as quickly as possible. Pulling her mobile phone out of her pocket, then she text Craig.

Hi Craig, think I have been followed can you and matt pick me up at the triangle!! X

She went out of the back door, so she would not need to walk past the lady's toilets where it looked like the woman in purple had went, she had decided to wait outside under the rain cover with the smokers. It was still raining quite heavily, there was only a couple of other people outside, all tucked in together under the Perspex overhang that kept the rain from falling upon the benches outside. Her mobile pinged, alerting her to an incoming message. She read it.

Ok Cairo, we will be there in 5! X

'Hi, Cairo, just got here?' It was American Nick, he had been a local here for many years, he was friendly and always approachable; ready to help with a problem if he could.

'Hi Nick, yeah but I'm going to be going off again, Matt and Craig are picking me up and we are all having a meal.' She lied.

She stood there waiting, worrying, and hoping that Craig would hurry, each second dragged on slowly, time seemed to lurch forward clumsily, she could not help but to check the time on her phone apprehensively, watching the seconds slip by.

Inside the toilet, Sydora went to one of the cubicles. Once inside, she sat down on the seat, focused her mind upon her dress, and with an irresistible force, mentally squeezed the vodka drink from her dress. She decided she would use a ritual once more to determine where the key had gone, if she could contact any kind of entity, it would let her know where to start searching, she knew that already she had overused her magic since getting to Lowestoft. She knew also that to keep using it this much could get very dangerous, but she felt there was no choice, so she retrieved her pouch of knuckle-bones, upending the bag she let the bones drop out onto the dirty toilet floor and then taking out her small knife again, and then she made a small cut upon her hand once again. Spilling a small amount of her blood upon the scattered bones in front of her, then she slowly Drifted off into a trance, she failed to hear the people who had entered the toilet and chatted about how much they were looking forward to the weekend as they reapplied make-up and she didn't hear the girl enter the other cubicle, arrange a line of cocaine and snort it from the white cistern behind the toilet. She instead had thrown her conscious into another plane of existence and contacted another reality. Delved into minds of madness that for a price would tell secrets. Beckoned some nameless horror to help find a key, to show her the last moments of the key before Bob had died.

After long minutes she opened her eyes again.

So, Cairo had the key.

She was closer than she thought, getting up and retrieving her bones from the floor. She placed them back in the pouch, unlocked the cubicle and quickly left.

She pulled her phone and called the Nihilist.

'Meet me at the lock up I'm going to bring you the key!'

****

Craig and Matt had been watching a movie around Matt's, it was a classic sci-fi movie that they had seen a hundred times or more. But they always had time to watch it one more time as it was a favourite; and with pizza too it was always a good night. Then Cairo had Text. When the message had come through. Craig read it to Matt and the pair had hastily gotten ready.

'She could be in danger.' Craig had said.

And so, the pair had gotten ready as quickly as they could and got into Matt's little Black Ford Fiesta and were now on their way. There was not too much traffic, but they had to get from the south side of town to the north, and that could be quite a drive if the traffic had built up at the bridges.

'Hurry Matt, she could be in danger.' Craig said as Matt drove, he was agitated and worried.

'I'm already doing forty, if we see a copper we are going to get pulled for sure!'

'I don't care, just get there.' Frustrated, Craig sat back, feeling helpless. They were in luck; the bridge was not busy, and they crossed the it quickly.

'Not far now, we'll go on Battery Green road, it'll be quicker, as long as we don't catch a light.'

By now, Craig's worries had infected Matt and he was hitting fifty miles per hour, they swept past the old magistrate's court and the police station, up Artillery way, then stopped at the roundabout to let a blue BMW go round, it went through the area lit by the Fiesta's headlights, Craig clearly saw Sydora.

'Shit, Matt we are too late, that's her, that's the woman, follow that Beamer!'

They were too late!

Chapter 11

The Yard

Craig and Matt followed the blue car south into the back roads outside Lowestoft. It was heading south and east towards the little hamlet of Hulver. They had driven for about twenty minutes; the rain had ceased, and the clouds had begun to break up, the full moon occasionally peered through gaps within the clouds.

'You are driving too close to them.' Craig said to Matt.

'I've got to see what way they go, the roads, round here are very twisty, they could turn off anywhere.'

They continued following the car as it sped through the hamlet, it almost hit a pair of Telecoms vans parked by a pole as two engineers worked around it, working overtime. One who was elevating a hoist arm gave the blue car a middle finger salute whilst shouting expletives. It did not stop, instead just continued off down the twisting road. Matt slowed as he arrived at the two parked vans, indicated then went around. He received an approving nod from one of the engineers as he went by, carefully. They then picked up their pace once more, there was no traffic on the narrow back roads, and the street lighting was inadequate, it helped Craig and Matt following the blue car, as they were able to drive further back. Keeping an eye on the BMW's headlight beams, they were clearly illuminating vast swathes of the road further ahead.

The blue car abruptly turned right up a sloped side road; the pair drove up to the road sign a couple of moments later.

'Up there on the right. Sotterley road they turned up there Matt.' Craig said.

'I know, I saw where they went, Craig.'

They followed; turning left, slowly up the road, then they continued, there was no street lighting at all. But up ahead on the back road they could see the full beams, flickering through a small wood on the left then the lights winked out.

'They've stopped, pull over here on the left.'

Matt did as Craig said, slowing the black Ford to a stop. He cut the engines. They got out and crept forward around the bend just ahead. There was not much light, but the moon did give enough illumination to see by; when the clouds would briefly part, bathing everything in a soft pale blue light. They could hear a woman talking to a man, but they were too far away to make out what was being said. Around the corner there was a wide blue gate, Craig and Matt then crept back away from the gates.

Craig said, 'I think we should cut through these woods; I think they are on the other side, behind the blue gate.'

'I don't know, Craig, shouldn't we just call the police, I mean we know where they are now.'

'Ok, you wait here by the car, if I am not back in ten minutes, call the police and get out of here, but I'm going to see what is going on!'

With that Craig, went to the low wire fence and quickly climbed over it, he then drifted into the shadows, leaving Matt stood by his car, Matt watched Craig leave, then he got into the driver's seat, and waited.

****

Sydora had determined trickery would be the best way to catch Cairo, getting into the BMW, she drove around to the side of the Triangle tavern, focusing her thoughts on Cairo and her car, she concentrated on the car looking familiar to Cairo, so she would recognise it; allowing Cairo's hopes and anxieties to help Sydora get within snatching distance. She pulled the BMW up near the tavern, then slowed and hit the horn, a quick blast then a few moments later Cairo was making her way over. How easy it is to manipulate an unaware mind, Sydora had thought as she got closer. She had opened the back door.

'Hi, ……' Cairo had stopped mid-sentence as she realised that the person in the driving seat was not her friend but the mysterious woman who wore purple from inside the tavern.

Before she could back away from the car, Sydora pronounced in a compelling manner.

'Sleep.' As she did Cairo slumped forward; she fell into the car. Sound asleep before she had even hit the rear seats. Sydora got out and closed the door hurriedly, then got back in the driver's side and drove away, she had gotten her.

The journey she made was by sat nav, once out of Lowestoft the back roads twisted and wound about the countryside. She had to focus on the sat nav as she went, she did not know where she was and there was no street lighting to speak of. She received a message via text, which she read as she drove, it was from the Nihilist, it read.

At lock-up now, I have Hawkins and his friends.

She dropped the mobile phone onto the passenger seat beside her, then paid attention once more to the satellite navigation and where it told her to go, until finally upon the small screen she could see the green line she had been following was at an end, just a few hundred meters up this dark back road, then a right for a couple of hundred of meters then turn in on the left, and follow a track.

As the blue BMW got Sydora and Cairo to the destination, she saw the Nihilist and a younger gentleman stood by an open blue gate. Sydora drove in and they quickly closed the gate, she then sped down the dirt track, trees on the left and right, until she eventually arrived in a clearing with three small outbuildings. One had a light on inside, and a large shed, which was filled with rusted farm machinery. She stopped the car by the outbuilding with a light on inside, as she did so, the other two came walking into the clearing from the gate.

They got to the car, then together they all entered the outbuilding which had a light on inside, half-dragging the unconscious Cairo along with them.

****

Craig stealthily crept through the low bushes in the woodland, keeping as quiet as he possibly could; stooping, he slowly approached the small building complex. The BMW was parked outside the only building which had any lights on. He continued towards it, all three of the buildings were portable chalet buildings, rectangular in shape with two windows on the long wall and a single window at either end, there was also a long open sided lean-to filled with industrial farming machinery and a rusted tractor. Craig crept into the clearing, getting past the shed he could hear speech, he neared the window, and peaked through at a gap in the curtain by the edge of the window pane; trying to see what was going on.

Inside he saw Cairo, slumped in a chair, being tied up by two men. The first was the man from the will-reading, the other he had never seen before, and the woman wearing purple. Craig inclined away from the window, forcing his breathing to calm down, taking deep breaths. He didn't know what he could do, he thought to call the police, retrieving his mobile from his pocket he immediately could see that he had no mobile signal, he did not want Cairo to get hurt by these people, whoever they were. So, he decided to listen and watch to see if he could get any more information, then he slowly leaned back in toward the window.

Cairo came back to consciousness, she felt like she had just awoken, refreshed, taking a moment to come to her senses, she realised that she was bound to a chair in strange surroundings that she did not recognise. Looking about she then saw the three people sat with her, the woman in purple was there, a tall gentleman in a suit who she thought may have been with her at the Will reading and a third, younger man whom she did not recognise at all.

'Who are you? What am I doing here? Don't hurt me.' She pleaded.

'Hello, its Cairo isn't it.' The suited man said, 'We are after something that we believe you have.' He said, 'Sorry I am being rude, I am the Nihilist, this here is Sydora and sat over there is Hawkins, we are after a small key that you have recently been given by your late Grandfather.'

'I don't know what you mean, he didn't give me anything.' She lied.

'I thought that was what you would say. Let me tell you about why they call me the Nihilist. Cairo, do you know what a Nihilist is?' He paused, waiting for her reply.

'Not really.' She said.

'A Nihilist does not believe in anything, they, or I believe that there is a futility to all life, you could say like life is meaningless.'

'So, what does that have to do with me and this key, you are after?'

'Well, I for instance have no qualms or compunctions about dealing with situations, any way that is necessary to get a successful conclusion. And I mean ANY way necessary!'

'I could kill you, easily, it would not bother me at all. It's not that I am evil, more that I accept that we will all die, the timing or manner is inconsequential!'

'Please don't hurt me, I've done nothing wrong.' Cairo begged once more, miserably this time as it dawned upon her that this man may very well be serious.

'No problem. Just give us the key, and you can go, it is as simple as that. Now where is it.'

She looked at them all, gathered, they all stared back, eager, waiting for her response.

'Come on Cairo, you don't want to be here with us, just give us the key and we will let you go.' Sydora said, her words were soothing, hypnotising.

'You will let me go, honestly.' Cairo asked, hopeful.

'Of course, we will, we are not monster's after all.' Sydora replied.

There was something in Sydora's tone that worried Cairo, an almost ominous threat; unspoken, a threat of the horror she would perhaps be prepared to undertake to get her way or take what she wanted, but it was almost musical as well, she wanted to believe it, hypnotic.

After a brief pause Cairo resignedly said 'Ok, I have it in the pocket of my jacket.'

Hawkins walked past her, then started rifling the pockets of her jacket that she still wore, she felt violated and helpless.

'I have it, it's here!' Hawkins said.

He rummaged inside the left side pocket for a couple of moments till he produced the ornate key.

'Excellent, pass it to me.' Sydora said, Hawkins did as she requested, passing the small key.

'We will go back to Blessed. Nihilist; deal with her!' Sydora said those words with a finality that hit Cairo across the face, fear took hold of her and she began to panic.

'But you said that you wouldn't hurt me if I told you where it was; the key I mean. I won't tell anyone, I promise, please do not hurt me!' Cairo struggled to escape the bonds, but the blue nylon rope that she had been tied with was too strong.

'You can deal with her any way you see fit, I am going with Hawkins, you will have to find your own way back.'

With that Sydora and Hawkins left the outbuilding, got into the BMW, the engine then started, and they drove out of the yard.

'Well, Cairo, what are we going to do with you?'

'You can let me go, I won't tell anybody, about it, nobody has to know.'

'I have a reputation to uphold, so that I am afraid, is the only thing I definitely cannot do, but I will tell you this, I will make it painless.'

****

Craig had listened to the interrogation as it went on, powerless to help his cousin, then Sydora and Hawkins had left, he quickly ducked out of sight behind the outbuilding filled with machinery, Sydora and Hawkins then sped away, only when he saw the beams of their car's lights disappear from view did he go back to the window. Hopefully now there was something that he could do.

Inside, the Nihilist was stood about five feet from Cairo, he was holding a long knife; its blade was slightly curved, and it looked incredibly sharp.

'I will make it quick so please do not worry.' Cairo struggled in futility against the strong nylon bonds.

'No please!' She begged one more time, knowing now that it was too late.

He approached her, lifting the knife, she could see the wicked looking blade clearly now, his eyes were devoid of emotion; just a cold uncaring stare, he took the knife to Cairo's throat.

Craig, outside saw what was now transpiring; as the Nihilist approached Cairo with the knife raised. He focused with a tremendous effort to save Cairo, he struggled to erase images of her throat being sliced open and instead just concentrate upon how hot the handle of that dreadful dagger was. The Nihilist raised it toward her throat, he had reached her now, hotter and hotter, he thought, it was so hard to believe with all of the pressure of what failure would entail. But he had no choice, he thought his head would explode with the tension that had built up inside his own skull.

The Nihilist took the knife to her throat.

'I'm sorry Cairo I have my orders!' He said, then he started to draw the blade across her throat with expert precision, she felt the dagger sting as it opened the skin.

Then the Nihilist dropped the blade with a scream, it hit the wooden floor with a thud. Grasping his hand that had held the dagger, he wringed it. Examining his hand; there were bright pink marks where he had been burnt. With an effort Cairo kicked out at the Nihilist's shin, striking clean, he fell, she struggled against the bonds, but they still wouldn't give, then the door burst open.

Craig somehow had found her. She thought with absolute relief,

Craig had found her and with two steps, he had cleared the distance to the Nihilist then delivered a powerful kick to the side of the Nihilist's head, and the Nihilist ceased moving.

'Help me Craig I cannot get free.' Craig rushed over to the nylon bonds and untied them.

'Come on, Matt's outside, we have got to get out of here!'

****

From across the yard, two beady eyes peered through the bushes. Nestled into a dense thorn bush was the Gruul, it watched the pair flee the yard, considering what was happening, the thing had snuck a lift to see what was transpiring with Hawkins and the Nihilist. The Gruul knew that Hawkins and his father were not aware of its true intentions; the Gruul knew they were not aware of the Demon prince, the Gruul knew that they were not aware of Ashtoreth!

Chapter 12

Decipher This

Hawkins drove with Sydora back to His home in Lowestoft, it was late and Sydora wanted to be on her way to London as soon as possible. The sky was still clear of clouds, myriad stars dotted clearly for all to see. The light pollution could not extinguish them all, and the moon gave all surfaces a soft cold blue aura.

'We can wait till the morning and get a train, what is a few hours anyway?' Hawkins asked.

'Everything, a few hours are everything, there is much more going on than you know about Hawkins, your father has need of every second, your inheritance could depend upon it.'

'Well, why would he have me and Gruul chasing around the countryside, and Cliff dying and all that shit, for what? I thought Gruul was nice, in a funny sort of way.' Hawkins began sobbing.

'What did you say?' Sydora asked, 'Cliff died, Gruul killed him.'

'No, not that, Gruul, who is Gruul? What is Gruul?' She pressed him further.

'He's; I don't actually know, some kind of Imp or something, I don't know maybe a Goblin?' Hawkins stammered through the tears that now came for his friend.

'And he has been helping you and your father? How long has he been helping you?'

'Well, he has been my little friend since I was really young, and I think he was with Dad before me.'

'What did you do when your friend died? What were you up to?'

Hawkins explained the details of the day in the woods with the Gruul, Sydora listened, taking in all the information.

Was it related to the grimoire?

'I will need to talk to your little friend.' She said.

'No problem, he is at home, I will get him before we leave tomorrow.' Hawkins said, unaware that the Gruul had followed the Nihilist.

'We are going tonight. You will get him before we leave tonight.' Sydora forcefully corrected him.

Since Hawkins had gotten back with the Gruul two days ago, it seemed that His little friend had changed in demeanour, Gruul was no longer the nice little imp thing that was happy to skulk in the garden, or read books that were infinitely boring, and playfully moving things with its mind, it had developed a very serious attitude; demanding and unforgiving. Now Sydora wanted to speak to Gruul, how could that little whelp help her? Only Steve had not, apparently been affected by the actions of Gruul and by Cliff's demise. When they had gotten back, he had pestered Gruul to teach him to use 'black magic.' Gabby was on the verge of a breakdown, she was afraid to get away, but Hawkins was well aware that she knew that she must.

They arrived at about midnight and went straight inside; Steve and Gabby were still there.

'Hi Hawkins, it's a bit late buddy' Steve said coming out of the glass living room door as they entered the house.

'Hi Steve, this is Sydora. Is Gabby and Gruul here?' Hawkins asked.

'Gabby is asleep upstairs; I have not seen Gruul since you left.' Steve was clearly very taken with Sydora as he could not take his eyes off her, his sight had been drawn to her, like a light metallic pin to a magnet.

She enjoyed the attention very much, an old trick she used whenever she met new people, a simple glamour that would make her pleasing to the eye, subtle changes, imperceptible to the eye, yet on a primal level they were very effective. They entered Hawkins home.

'I'm going to London with Sydora, I don't know when I will be back?'

'You will be back tomorrow sometime!' Sydora added, she now returned the appreciating looks that Steve gave her, he turned his eyes away, in obvious submission.

'Get Gruul.' She said. Hawkins went into the Gruuls room, it was empty, 'Gruul, where are you, this woman wants to speak to you.' He loudly called, but there was no answer, the Gruul was not there. Coming back into the living room, to find Sydora and Steve talking, it seemed that Steve was eager to learn about magic and had correctly assumed that Sydora could use the touch and he was hounding her to show him some technique; to teach him.

'He is not here.' Hawkins said, Sydora stood. 'Then get ready, we are off to London.' She then turned back to Steve.

'It's been a pleasure Steve, we can talk a bit more when I get back, I look forward to it.' She said with a look, that would keep Steve awaiting; eagerly.

'I'm looking forward to it Sydora.' He smiled.

They left the manor, after having a light meal consisting of nothing more than sandwiches a packet of crisps, an apple each and a warm drink. The pair took the Blue three Series Beamer again, filling the petrol tank at the large supermarket in Gisleham on the southern outskirts of Lowestoft, they then sped down the A12 to London.

'Where was your little friend then?'

'I don't know, he didn't seem interested when your friend the Nihilist turned up, why is he called the Nihilist anyway?'

'He is a fixer, his world views are just that, he is a Nihilist, he does whatever needs to be done, without a care, nobody knows his past, and trust me people have tried to find it out, but he is cold-blooded in his ways, and that is very useful to your father.'

'I do not like him.' She added.

'No, he certainly does have a way about him, anyway what is this thing my Dad has been after that you got off that poor woman?'

Hawkins thought, god she is dead now too; this is really serious, all his life he hadn't had to worry about anything, the money was always there, no need to work. Occasionally his father had forced him to donate some money to a charity, but other than that life had been a simple act of going through the motions, nothing more. He told himself his father would not have him snivelling over these events and the collateral it had occurred, just think of them as he would the pigeons he had shot from the sky at a recent local shoot.

'It is a key, her Grandfather had given it to her, it unlocks a book that your father has taken ownership of, I have a parchment which was kept in another locale. That will tell us when to read the ritual that your father will use to gather an enormous wealth, he wants us all to invoke it together; I guess your included in that now too.'

'Just us, or has my father got more people? You know I have not seen my father in months.'

'There are more Magi, I can call a gathering of the path, I have a feeling that the time is near for this ritual, and we must decipher the ritual before we miss out on the correct time for the convocation.'

****

One day after the summit at the Houses of Parliament, a red and yellow delivery van had stopped outside a prestigious Chelsea address. The house was a three-story end terrace, painted white and light blue, there was a low black spiked fence at the front. Parking on this street was almost always an impossibility and so the delivery driver left his van engine running, got out and hurried to the door, the parcel was very heavy for its size, ringing the bell he waited briefly until a large portly man came to the door.

'Hello there.' He said in a very well-spoken manner.

'A parcel sir, can I have a signature please.' The delivery man asked as he passed a hand-held device to Lord Blessed.

He signed it with his stiff, jagged signature and said goodbye, then went through to the lounge, eager to open the book, and look at the history that proved the existence of Atlantis.

'Doctor Humboldt, it has arrived.' He shouted excitedly, up the stairs, a few moments later the professor came down the stairs, hurrying. He had with him an old worn leather attaché case. The contents were threatening to burst out, fighting the loop and hook that prevented all of his precious paperwork from escape. He wore some blue faded jeans, and a white and brown check shirt.

'Oh, good I cannot wait, to look inside.' He scrambled down the last few steps and caught up with Lord Blessed as he walked into the kitchen with the book. It was still in the plain brown box it had arrived in, proudly stamped in bold red print upon the packaging, the words 'Fragile'.

Lord Blessed placed the box upon the table and quickly cut the box open with an impatience to reveal the book that had been covered in a bubble wrap protective covering inside. Lord Blessed cut away at this with a pair of scissors, revealing a polished metal cover, it looked like the cover was made from bronze, in the very centre of the book was a small keyhole, and a bar that ran vertically out of the locking mechanism, top to bottom. The bar prevented the book from being opened without the key, this would need to be unlocked to allow safe access to this fabulously rare piece of pre-history. The edges of the pages could be seen, they were made of some metal as well; it looked like they had been made from silver.

'The Manual seems to be made from Bronze and silver, this has made the book resistant to damage, it should be easy to translate.' Dr Humboldt said.

'Not so fast Professor, I believe that you will find the book is written in a language you have never seen before.'

'Sumerian, yes, it's probably Sumerian.' The Professor replied with finality.

'I'm afraid it is definitely not Sumerian, or Akkadian, but predates them. This; Professor, this is your chance to become somebody very important in the world of archaeology.' Professor Humboldt looked at the book, touching the cold Bronze cover, stroking the locking mechanism with care.

'It is beautiful isn't it, yes it really is exquisite.' There was an eager tone in his voice, as he wanted to read the pages now, like he could not wait.

'Can we open it? Without the key I mean?' He asked.

'No, not yet. Patience Dr Humboldt, Sydora and the Nihilist are now retrieving it. They should be here soon, the pages are silver, the lock probably conceals a canister of some kind of corrosive substance that will damage the pages within if tampered with.'

****

The blue BMW arrived at Lord Blessed's Chelsea home at about 03:30AM, three days after the summit. The waiting, for Professor Humboldt; had been excruciating. His eagerness was almost palpable, like a child who has just come to understand that Christmas meant they would receive presents. Sydora and Hawkins went in as Hawkins had a key to the front door.

'Wake your father, be quick.' Sydora said.

'But he hates being awoken.' Hawkins replied.

'He will want to get up, give him this!' she passed him the precious key.

Hawkins went upstairs, Sydora wandered through to the kitchen, switching on the kettle, she took four cups from a nearby stand. She noticed the heavy bronze grimoire set upon the table, as it had been when it had arrived a couple of days ago. Two minutes went by and the kettle was noisily boiling away. Sydora did not notice, her attention was fully absorbed upon the metal book, then Hawkins followed by his father dressed in an expensive silk dressing gown and brown leather slippers walked into the kitchen.

'Hawkins make the coffee.' Lord Blessed said.

'Good to see you Sydora, but you are late!' Lord blessed said, 'What went wrong.'

'The key and parchment were not located together, and we ran into some resistance, I have left the Nihilist to clean up the loose ends.' She said.

The Professor came down a little later, he had speedily dressed. 'This is my son, Hawkins.' Lord Blessed announced. 'Hello, pleased to meet you, I am Dr Humboldt.' Hawkins nodded.

'This is what we have all been waiting for.' As Lord Blessed slipped the key into the locking mechanism and turned it slowly. There was a gentle click, the bar moved slightly, Lord Blessed slid the bar from the mechanism and set it aside.

All gathered there watched as he gingerly turned the front cover, it opened easily, and inside was a silver metal page, with symbols of an unknown language stamped upon it.

'It's garbled gibberish, what shit have you bought now Dad?' Hawkins said as soon as he saw the unintelligible script.

'Shut up you little scrawny brat. You are never too young to lose your inheritance!' Lord Blessed said, annoyed at his son's little outburst.

'Can you decipher this?' He asked turning to the Professor.

'With enough time, I would imagine so, it looks like it may be related to ancient Sumer in format at a glance, but there are some clear differences. I will need time!' The Professor stated as his closely inspected the pages.

Retrieving his notes from the worn leather attaché case that he had brought with him, the Professor set to work, within minutes he had a pen and paper in hand and was taking notes and copying symbols. They all watched as he went to work. Humboldt turned the first page, took some more notes, then turned another, they were all fascinated by his level of concentration and how quickly that he had closed them all from his active thought. After five minutes Lord Blessed asked.

'Well, can you read it?'

The Professor looking up, said, 'What, oh, I will need time and I will need quiet!'

The others looked at one another, Hawkins could not help but grin, gradually they all left Humboldt alone in the kitchen to study.

****

Three days had gone by and Professor Humboldt's studies had been thorough, but he still did not have an answer to the book, something was passing him by, a clue that he had missed. He had noticed several similarities with ancient Sumerian and other Mesopotamian writings, but this was not the same, and it seemed that they had all came from this language.

Hawkins entered the kitchen; poured himself a large glass of milk, taking a big mouthful and wiping the residue from his lips. 'So, how are you doing?' He asked.

'Well, it just seems that it is not a language that makes sense, so many of the symbols are similar to the most ancient of languages known of today, but some are entirely new, and many others seem to be mirror images of symbols known from the translations of those languages we have learnt already. It Is very strange indeed.'

'What, you mean like it was written to be printed?'

As Hawkins said the last word, Humboldt, was stricken momentarily dumb.

'Of course, like it is to be printed.' The Professor said, like the penny had finally dropped.

He then opened his leather case and reached inside of the front pouch; taking out a small ink roller and ink pad, he then proceeded to roll the ink over the page. Placing a plain piece of paper upon the ink covered metal sheet, he pressed it down with a gentle force, after a couple of moments he then he removed it.

'Hmmm, very interesting.' Humboldt said as he spread his eye over the ancient text, now revealed in an entirely new light.

'Thank you, Hawkins, I think you may have solved the mystery surrounding the translation of this artefact, I think you may also have made your father very, very happy!' Humboldt said.

Hawkins left the room to find his father. As he left, he said under his breath, 'I don't think you know my father!'

Chapter 13

Behind You

Craig led Cairo away as quickly as they could, neither said a word; intent upon escaping before the man got back up or possibly the woman, Sydora came back. They dashed straight across the yard heading directly for the small wood. The low fence where Craig had entered wasn't far, swiftly climbing over it and then making way through the low underbrush. In a matter of moments that seemed to last minutes they were back with Matt at his car in the layby.

'Quick guys, get in.' Matt said.

They climbed in, 'Are you okay?' Craig asked.

'I'm fine thanks, I ache a bit, I'm a bit sore where they tied me up Craig; more shook up than anything else. But that was close, god, he was going to kill me.' She said.

'I didn't know what to do so I tried the gift; It worked!' Craig said almost amazed by the success himself, he knew now, what his Grandfather had meant when he had said,

'you must believe in the gift with all your heart, believe in it till it hurts!'

He felt he could do it again, with more confidence, before, it had only really come when no-one was about, when it had not really mattered, but at the yard, when there had been a real tangible danger, his concentration had been tested like never before. He wondered if it was Matt there and not Cairo whether he would have been successful, whether the magic would have come. Or maybe instead, he would have witnessed the murder of a close friend?

'Matt, let's get going, I don't want to be here any longer.' Cairo said.

Matt started the car as they began to drive, there was a thud on top of the car. 'What was that?' Matt asked, 'I don't know, drive fast, probably an old branch!' Cairo said, as she tended to the inch-long knife wound upon her neck, they sped away as quick as they could, through the winding roads, back to Lowestoft. It was nearly one in the morning when they arrived back at Craig's home, going in the three of them went to the kitchen and made a coffee.

'What do we do now?' Cairo asked, 'I don't want to go home, and I certainly do not want to be alone.'

'Call the police, that's what I say.' Matt said.

'The problem with that Matt, is they just will not believe you, and what if these people have links to the police. There is something going on that somehow feels very big.' Craig said.

'What, because you can move pencils with your mind? Neat trick but you are making one hell of a jump.' Matt was not convinced; he had a light-hearted personality and was naturally averse to conspiracy theories.

'Well, why else would these two be at the will and then kidnap me? He was going to kill me Matt. For fuck sake, why would it not be connected?' Cairo said.

'I think I have an idea, but for now I think we need to stick together.'

****

The Nihilist slowly came around, gathering his senses. It was a crisp morning, the light shone through the east facing windows directly into his eyes. His jaw ached terribly from the blow and it was very tender, he had been totally unprepared for the attack that had come from behind. His arm was numb, filled with the tingling sensation of pins and needles, he had obviously landed upon it when he fell, then lain on it at an awkward angle throughout the rest of the night. Getting up he walked over to the chair where Cairo had been tied up.

wringing his fingers, attempting to get the blood to flow and sensation to return to his hand. Now the blue rope was strewn about the floor; cut. The door was still ajar. The dagger which he was going to use was gone, he looked about for it, but it was nowhere to be seen.

The Nihilist checked his watch, it was a quarter to eight in the morning; he went outside, Hawkins sports car was parked at the far end of the yard, there was an acute fresh farm smell in the air. He got in the car and decided to drive to see Victoria Slattery. The Nihilist started the engine, it was a push button ignition, the engine chuckled briefly, then turned and followed up with a deep throaty roar. The Nihilist left the yard, heading back to Lowestoft, he would need to deal with the girl and whoever helped her, he suspected it was Cairo's cousin Craig, he decided he would soon pay them both a little visit.

The roads were clear, and he made good time, leaving the back roads and joining the A12 heading north toward the town; after driving for five minutes he arrived at the Kessingland bypass. Easily overtaking the rush hour traffic ahead on the short span of dual carriageway, then he slowed through the town, as thousands of people went to their daily jobs, Lowestoft was and always, it seems, will be famous for its non-functional roadway system.

Turning on the radio he listened to the local drive-time station, filling the car with upbeat pop tunes and small competitions for the local inhabitants, it made him chuckle; the sound of the local dialect he thought, it sounded friendly, trustworthy and honest. The Nihilist stopped at a pedestrian crossing, three children with a mother heading to school. As he waited, he reached into his pocket, retrieved his mobile and then he called Victoria, it rang, and he activated the loud speaker setting. The lights turned green and eventually he turned onto the relief road that slashed through the southern half of the town.

'Hello Victoria Slattery, M.P, how can I help you?'

'Hi, it's the Nihilist, I need your help.'

'Oh, okay, no problem, what an address, something like that?'

'No, I need to see you, where are you?'

'Why what is the matter, I am very busy at the moment, we are not supposed to meet, you know what Lord Blessed said!'

'We have a loose end; I need your help to clean it up!' He said finally, the mobile phone went quiet briefly, then, after a pause she replied,

'Fifteen Surrey Street, NR321LJ, type it into your sat nav, I will have the receptionist send you straight up to my office!'

The phone hung off and he continued toward the centre of town.

****

Gabby had effectively been a prisoner since the events at the seal, always watched by either Hawkins, Steve or the hideous little monster, she had cried every night for the loss of Cliff, and what had seemed like fun initially; had changed her life for the worse, forever. Then the man who called himself the Nihilist had arrived, he took a phone call and took Hawkins out somewhere, she had stayed in the living room, later the creature had left, and then it was only Steve and herself. They watched the television, she said nothing, just watched, but at all times she felt Steve was looking at her, watching her, it was creepy. Maybe if the events that now transpired were not so, then she would not think anything of it, but Gabby found herself aware of all things around her and she did not even want to be about in Steve's presence.

Gabby had finally made up her mind and she left the Manor late; telling Steve that she was going to bed, then silently slipped out of the back door. The events of the last few days had left her so terrified; her entire world had been totally shattered and her mind reeled from everything that had happened. She wanted to go to the police, but she knew they would never believe her with no body and far-fetched stories of monsters. She knew also that Hawkins father was very well connected and possibly had connections, high up in the police force!

Children's stories of monsters ran relentlessly through her mind, she felt like she was trapped. Instead, she decided that she would pack a suitcase, get her car keys and just drive, it seemed the only way out. Where to? North? To the Yorkshire dales, she had family up there, it was decided. North, maybe even further, maybe Scotland; anywhere if she could hide from the monster. Hawkins, Steve and any others that may climb out of the woodwork. Hide from the death of a friend; though inside she knew she could not hide, not from that, she knew she would never forget the sound of his screaming and she could never forget the smell.

Leaving a note to Hawkins in his bedroom as she left.

It read:

Hi Hawkins,

I am writing this as I feel I have no choice. Since the other night, and the loss of Cliff, I have decided to go, please don't look for me as I am scared. If, like me you care for yourself and your sanity you will go as well, when you left with that strange tall man this evening, I decided I would go too, I am not telling you where, only that I will never see you again.

With all my love,

Gabby

With that she was gone, into her car and then she was away, hoping against hope that Steve would not hear her as she left; would not look out of the window.

Turning up Pakefield Road she drove the long way out, going toward the Jolly Sailors tavern. The tavern had an amazing view out to sea, from there she would pick up the main road and drive across London Road South, again using the built-up housing to avoid driving accidentally into anybody she did not wish to see. Through Kirkley, past the high school and down into Oulton Broad. From there she felt she would be safe to take the A47 up to Great Yarmouth, and then follow the coastal road out of East Anglia. She just prayed that none of the others would be going that way either.

As Gabby drove, she saw familiar signs and places, places that she knew she would never see again. having not seen her family for a few days now, she desperately wanted to stop by and see them before leaving. But the thought of being caught and then being brought back stopped her making what she knew deep down could be a terrible mistake. Gabby decided she would call them when she had reached the dales, that would not be for some time.

She had always hated the A17. It was a road that seemed to continue on and on with no end. When she and Hawkins were younger, they used to joke that it was Chris Rea's road; because it was the road to Hell, she thought it was very ironic that it was the way she would now go.

****

Cairo, Craig and Matt went inside the house. As the door closed the little creature slowly slipped out from underneath the car, stalking toward the rear of the house; an amber streetlight bathed the road in an orange glow. The Gruul backed away and then took a long run up; leaping and catching the top of the garden wall, it clambered over and dropped into the garden, then slinked over to the windows to peer inside. Looking and listening but the lights were off, and the home was quiet. The Gruul could barely make out muffled voices in a room somewhere inside the house. Frustrated the creature turned and looked about, seeing the shed the Gruul stalked over toward it, with a stumbling gait. The door was still open from the night of the break in. It slipped into some of the low shelving, tucking itself out of view, it would wait for the morning to arrive. The Gruul was here to survey them, it could already see that they may become a thorn in the side, they may unravel all of the work so far completed; spoil the Gruul's chance to finally free it's imprisoned dark lord.

Since the first seal had been broken, the Gruul had been able to feel a closer presence, as the barriers of reality were loosened the closeness of such a dark and terrible force could be felt, by those who could proficiently wield magic. Currently imprisoned on a plane of existence purely consisting of rock and of earth. The Gruul though, now knew that soon contact would again be possible, already the evil master would have figured that machinations were underway that would lead to him possibly being freed, and already they would be preparing once more to take the earth, to enslave and destroy, so effectively like they had before, when, if not for the kingdom of Atlantis they would have succeeded.

The Gruul's thoughts wandered back to that time so many years ago.

It was by pure chance that the Gruul had not been captured along with the rest of the horde. An important creature in Ashtoreth's vast legions, the Gruul was tasked with reading the great omens, Gruul had read the danger and warned of the trap set to be sprung. That this battle would lead to ultimate defeat of the demonic armies, the end of Ashtoreth and his forty legions, and ultimately unending imprisonment. The great captains of the monstrous horde were unimpressed with the bleating's of a whelp soothsayer and advised the great demon prince it was now or never to attack, Ashtoreth had listened and agreed with the captains.

The Gruul was not missed when the horde marched to war with the Atlanteans, watching from afar the miserable little beast moaned and whined and as the demonic sorcerer watched the enemy trap as it was finally sprung. Easily outnumbering the Atlantean forces the demonic horde would soon have been victorious, then the vast plains that both armies fought upon opened up, thousands; both human and demon alike were swallowed by the earth, and then the water swept in from the river as its banks suddenly burst. The Gruul watched as the dust settled, watched the hopes of the master crushed. Being proven correct was of no comfort to the Gruul, the need to get back to the prince was great and that meant the Gruul would need to open the barriers between the worlds once again.

The Gruul drifted into sleep, tucked away under the table, excitement was getting the better of the ugly little creature. The Gruul forced itself to relax. Soon Gruul, soon, your master will be free, very soon!

Chapter 14

Politics, Politics, Politics

The Nihilist followed the Sat Nav's instructions, as it directed him into the centre of Lowestoft. The traffic was slow and lazy, he got the feeling that the lights would let just enough cars through each time they changed to irritate as many drivers as possible; but never enough to actually make you feel as though you were getting anywhere. The annoying voice announcing his prearranged journey finally said.

'Turn left in two hundred metres!'

Driving over two overtly large speed bumps, 'Now turn left!'

He did as the navigational voice instructed and then indicating, he abruptly swung across the road to park in a spot directly outside the building. Getting out and looking around, the Nihilist surveyed the local area around him, a very large building stood on the opposite side of the road, three stories high with a line of balconies on the top floor, the roof had been netted to prevent the numerous circling seagulls from landing on top of it. There was a sizable car park beside the building, and it was filled there was a large number of parked telecommunications vans. He decided it was probably the central telephone exchange. He turned around and walked to the two panel. glass front door of number fifteen, a receptionist was sat inside behind a desk, busy working at a computer.

He went in.

'Hello sir, can I help you.' The receptionist said.

'Yes, I have an appointment with Miss Slattery.'

'Ok, please wait a moment, what is the name please?'

'She will know who I am.'

The receptionist buzzed through on an internal line. 'A gentleman to see you Miss Slattery, he didn't give me a name.' The receptionist said.

'Thank you, please go straight through, it's the door on the first floor.'

'Thank you.' The Nihilist said, walking through the doorway the receptionist had pointed towards.

He entered her office and Victoria rose to greet him.

'Miss Slattery, a pleasure.' He said, extending his hand, she took it and they shook hands briefly, then she sat back down.

'What is the problem, I am very busy.' She said irritated.

'I will need your help, I have tried to keep you out of all of the sundry dealings, but I need your influence.'

'Why would I need to help you? I have a career to think of, standing in society; places to be, you understand.'

'I understand that Miss Slattery, but things have taken a turn. I need leverage, with somebody, and there is far more at stake than your career, I am sure that you would not be happy to incur the displeasure of Lord Blessed,' he continued after a brief pause to allow her to think, 'from what I am led to believe, you owe almost all of your political career to his machinations?'

He smirked at her, knowing that it was a telling blow; she returned his gaze with a glare, contempt shone in her eyes.

It was true that Lord Blessed had helped her career move forwards many years ago. She had been at Oxford university; volunteering to help the conservative party as an activist. However, she had ran into problems with money and drugs, as with all establishments and at all levels of society; drugs are readily available, and there was always a friend who would sell them as an answer to any problem. But they were not the answer, they were a dead-end route towards more debt, depression and paranoia. That was until Lord Blessed had taken a shine to her, they had met at a charity ball, he had been impressed with her ability as a budding politician. But he had at a later point that evening discovered her and another intern taking cocaine in the gent's toilets, he gave her an offer. Continue taking drugs and her career was over or take his help; he would pay for the rehabilitation, he would sponsor her budding career, but from time to time he'd require help in the *"other place"* as it is known in the House of Lords; or the house of commons to give it its proper title.

'Ok, Nihilist, or whatever you call yourself, what do you want? I will see what I can do for you.'

She did not like this personal threat and decided she would have a little discussion with Lord Blessed about this upstart later.

'I would like you to get an order for a raid of some description upon the home of Miss Cairo Souter, and have her family detained.'

She looked at him, he was sat there totally serious.

'You are serious aren't you, how should I be able to do that?'

'I don't know, maybe drugs or immigration; it's simple a raid, that's all, I need leverage!'

Again, she was incredulous, how did he think she could do such a thing?

'I had been informed that you may have a contact or two in law enforcement; maybe they could help?'

'If I was able to somehow influence them? And believe me, how? I am really not sure, then what will it achieve- '

'and what is in it for me?'

She had gotten over the initial shock that the Nihilist knew too much about her personal life and her rise to parliament, and had now found firmer ground, politics.

But the Nihilist was used to getting his own way in dealings, his entire life had been about leverage, threat, fear and murder. He just realised that she knew how to play the game too, obviously Lord Blessed had taught her well, he had truly spotted a rising star.

'I obviously cannot offer you money as I only keep the barest minimum to get by on, however, as you are probably very well aware, I can be very effective at influencing political rivals, I am sure I could find some dirt on anyone that you may need?'

'There is no one, so what else.'

She correctly figured this would be his next step.

'No, but there is one thing you can do for me?'

She edged toward it delicately, her mind had worked quickly when he had asked for the favour, asking herself what she wanted and it soon struck her, whatever Lord Blessed was after, it must be worth something and she would not see any of it, sure, she may be paid and thanked for her trouble, but no real gain, nothing tangible; no true power.

'I want in!'

'You what?'

It was now the time for the Nihilist to be dumbfounded and to be shocked.'

'You want in? It's just.' Victoria stopped him mid-sentence.

'Ok; get your distraction,' it was her chance to pause for effect now, 'your leverage from somewhere else Mr Nihilist.'

He hated politicians, they always seemed to spin an argument, twist your words and always gained more from negotiation than you wanted to give.

'Ok, you are in, but I need that raid as soon as possible, in the meantime, you may want to accompany me to Lord Blessed's son's home, do you know the place?'

'Yes, I know the place, Hawkins's home it's the big manor in Pakefield; next to the Tramways tavern.'

The Nihilist nodded.

****

Sydora had left Hawkins in London with his father, she had returned to Lowestoft, late the day after arriving in London; she did not like the circles that Lord Blessed held sway over, all fawning and vying for attention and favour. She felt that to be part of that shamble was to demean yourself; she also knew that Lord Blessed loved the feeling of control that he held over them all.

But before leaving she had seen Blessed; finding him in his study, drinking only the finest Brandy. They had discussed Hawkins and Gruul's involvement, and the seal they had broken together, she wondered why the demonic beast was opening seals to god knows where. Lord Blessed had said he was totally unaware of anything going on and he assured Sydora that it was of no importance to his plans, he also advised her of the gains he was to find when their venture was complete.

'Sydora have you ever heard of King Solomon's mines?'

'Of course; as has everybody, are you suggesting that you know where they may be?'

'I have from reliable sources of an infernal nature, that this book will give me the ritual to not only find it, but to open it also!' He stated in a matter-of-fact fashion.

'Just like that, if you can find the location then why do you need the ritual?' She asked, somewhat perplexed.

'It is not where that you should be asking, the location of these mines exists somewhere, but not on this planet, it is somewhere within the dimensions. So, the location can be reached from anywhere upon the Earth, but to get there requires a form of dimensional bridge, and that is why I need you Sydora, you and your acolytes.'

He continued.

'Already, Miss Slattery is assisting us in finding the correct location in or about her locale, tucked away far enough from prying eyes.'

'I feel you are confident of success, we have had to kill a girl, she is a relation of Bob Souter, his Granddaughter I believe.'

'It cannot be helped.' He said with a slight shrug of his shoulders.

'Collateral.' He added, and then took the last mouthful of the golden liquid within the glass.

She watched as he walked to an expensive glass decanter and refilled his glass with a generous double. He was a man she found repulsive, yet she was forced to work with him for the time-being; he just held too much power, and, if what he was saying was to be believed, it could only pay to be his very closest ally right now.

'What does the Left-Hand Path get out of our assistance?'

'Frankly I am amazed that you have to ask Sydora, you have heard the legends of King Solomon's treasure. By my side you will have access to them all. Eternal youth; riches beyond your wildest dreams, control of the world, it would all be mine, and yours.'

'Ok, I will arrange for some of our best acolytes to help, how many do we need, three, four?'

'Excellent, three will be ample.'

It was clear to Sydora that Lord Blessed was insane, but the offer had been a very tempting one that she could not deny. Before making up her mind she wanted to discover just what this Gruul creature was up to. She had dealt with the demonic many times before and she expected there would be far more going on than an altruistic sense of charity.

****

When Steve discovered that Gabby had gone, he immediately called Hawkins, she had not come downstairs in the morning. At first, he had figured she was just having a lay in and probably still really upset by the events that had unfolded over the last couple of days. But when she had not left her room by eleven in the morning he decided to go and see her. So, making a cup of tea he went up and entered the room.

The curtains were closed, but immediately Steve could see the bed had not been slept in. He panicked, Steve had known that Cliff's death had affected her very badly, she had slipped out at some point during the previous night.

'Hi, Steve how are you. What's going on in sunny Lowestoft?' Hawkins asked as he answered the phone.

'You are not going to like it mate, she's gone, Gabby has gone.' Steve replied.

'Gone? How, all you had to do was watch her, she knows too much; she knows what happened to Cliff.' Hawkins said; his speech increasing in speed and pitch as his nerves started to get the better of him.

'Well you will have to go and get her back, I am stuck here, till this book is deciphered, what about Gruul, can he help?'

'I haven't seen him since you went the other night either.'

'And you didn't think to get back to me.' Hawkins was at his wits end.

'Sydora is on her way back, she should be with you soon, I am coming back later with my Dad when this book business is dealt with.'

At the mention of Sydora Steve's spirits lifted, he had felt attracted to her when she had arrived the other day and he hoped she would be able to show him some of these strange powers that everyone around him seemed to possess.

'When she gets here, we will get Gabby back; we just have to find her first!'

****

Miss Slattery pulled up at the large building in Pakefield, driving in through the sombre open gates that watched the traffic go by. She drove an expensive white Mercedes, SL model, her tastes had increased along with her bank balance.

There was plenty of space at the property, she saw Hawkins car and the blue BMW, it made parking awkward, but not impossible. She went to the door, and knocked hard, the door was opened by a young man.

'Hello, you must be Miss Slattery, I am Steve, please do come in.'

'Thank you.' Victoria said as she entered, he closed the door behind her.

'Go straight on to the kitchen.' Steve said.

Gathered in the kitchen were Sydora and the Nihilist, they had been discussing the events of the last few days; Gabby's sudden departure; the Gruul's little adventures and Cliff's death at the Gruul's clawed hands.

'The police are going to start sniffing around soon, we need to have a matching story about Cliff.' The Nihilist said,

'I can help with that I think.' Miss Slattery replied.

'And what about Gabby, how will we find her?' Steve asked.

'Can you not find her with your magic?' The Nihilist asked Sydora.

'No, those I would commune with would want a big sacrifice, no, I hope that this Gruul thing has followed her, and deals with her for us?'

Victoria Slattery then added, 'If she used a car then maybe I can help with finding her too.'

Chapter 15

The Runner

Gabby had arrived at her destination early on the next morning after she had left Lowestoft. It had been a long drive, but after the first real milestone of getting off the A17, she had felt more and more relief and as the distance between Lowestoft and herself increased, that feeling had only become stronger and stronger. She would never forget what had happened, but Gabby told herself she would try to get on with her life despite that dark and evil afternoon with the Gruul.

Her destination was a small village named Darley, it was a place she had always loved to go to, due to its close proximity to the Nidderdale. When she was younger her parents would sometimes stay here with her Uncle Edward and Aunt Sally, they were now well into their seventies, but at least they would give her a bed for a few days.

Darley had not really changed at all to when she had come here last about eight years ago; there was still only the one pub, The Wellington Inn. Whatever way you looked out of the village you could not miss the beauty of the area. It was just like how she remembered it, a breath of fresh air and a relaxing escape from the scary events that had transpired in furthest East Anglia.

That first night in Darley, Gabby had said that she and her parents had argued and begged she had begged her auntie and uncle not to call them; she just asked for a couple of days and she would speak to them when she was ready. When she did go up to the spare room, she dropped her head and immediately fell into a deep slumber, the first real sleep she had gotten in days. Exhaustion had finally won through.

****

Victoria Slattery had not been idle, when she had asked to get more involved, this was not really what she had in mind.

'ANPR, very good Vicky, you don't mind if I call you Vicky, do you?' Sydora said, there was almost a purr in her voice, soft and soothing; menacing.

The ANPR or automatic number plate recognition is a series of camera's spread all across the United Kingdom, they would help the police to locate a car as it passed by. If Gabby's car had went past any number of cameras, and the chances are it had, then they would soon know, and from there they would be able to determine Gabby's approximate location and where she may be heading.

'And you can get access to this system.' The Nihilist asked.

'Yes, I have already arranged it, but I am using all of my favours up pretty quickly it would seem, and I still have to source a location for Lord Blessed before the end of the month.'

'You certainly are very well connected, Lord Blessed made a good call backing your horse; most ingenious indeed.' The Nihilist said.

Miss Slattery had two contacts in law enforcement circles one she had already spoken to; arranging a drugs raid on Cairo's parents, the other one was a local on and off love affair that she had just been tapped for an ANPR check on Gabby's car, she now just waited for the phone call.

No call came that night, one by one all of the lights gradually went off in the Manor; the house and its occupants slept. Early the next morning Victoria Slattery was awoken with a call from her friend Andy in the police force, he didn't ask questions, instead just told her he shouldn't be doing this, and it was just this once; just like the last time had been.

'There have been a number of ANPR hits going up the A1(M), two in Harrogate and the last is in a village nearby called Darley.'

'Darley, that is great, thanks Andy, I will give you a call later, maybe we can go out at the weekend if you are free.'

'Yeah sure, sounds great I will call you later.' He replied.

'Bye, for now she said.

'See ya.'

She hung up her mobile phone and went downstairs into the kitchen, she then made a cup of tea. In the kitchen she found the Nihilist, wide awake, stirring a cup.

'The kettle has just boiled, Victoria.' He said.

She was quite shocked that he was fully showered and dressed.

'Did you even sleep?' She asked.

'Yes, but I always wake early. Miss half the day and all that.'

'Well, they just got back to me, Darley, near Harrogate.'

'Come again.' He asked.

'The girl, she is near Harrogate.'

'Well I think we better get everyone up, I do love a road trip.'

They both sat at the kitchen table and drank their beverage's; the Nihilist turned the radio on, reducing the volume to avoid disturbing the others.

At nine in the morning they were all sat around the breakfast table spare Hawkins and Gruul, it was decided that the Nihilist and Victoria would stay, Steve and Sydora would go north to bring Gabby back. Steve was more than a little happy at this, he was eager to get some time alone with Sydora, she had said she would show him some magic, teach him some, this was his chance and for a woman a little older than himself, he found her very attractive, who knows. Sydora knew his mind already, she had decided she would lead him on like a little lost sheep; but give him some magical skills, it would all be down to whether he could learn how to use them.

They left in the Blue BMW heading north, the route they used was almost the same as Gabby's a few days previous. The traffic was terrible all the way; A47, A17 and then the A1(M) all blocked up and laborious. It finally culminated in a long tailback in the afternoon due to an overturned lorry on the A1(M) near Doncaster.

'What is the plan, when we get there?' Steve asked as they sat about in the traffic. It would occasionally move just a few car lengths, but then stop for another prolonged period of time.

'We get there, we locate her, we bring her back, simple.'

'This is not a fun day out in the countryside, you should have kept a better eye on her, we are tidying up your mess Steve.' Sydora admonished him, talking to him with an air of superiority, as you would scold a child.

'Steve watched the traffic slowly move, since seeing what the little Gruul could do he had desired more and more; to be able to control power like that and as the last few days had gone by his mind had lusted for power in envy and with a steadily building desperation.

He had never really liked Cliff much; Steve more got on with him because he was one of Hawkins friends, in all honesty he thought that Cliff was just stupid and a bit of an oaf. He did not like what had happened, but it had, and he would rather control power like that than be susceptible to it.

'Sydora, when we get to this Darley place, if we have the time, can you teach me some of your magic tricks. You and Gruul told me you would teach me some, it's just they seem pretty neat and all, and well, I reckon I would be more help with some kind of power like that than without.'

She looked at him, 'Do you, if I taught you, would you be ready to control the power? Would you? could you stop a monster from tearing your face off just by the force of your will? Could you?'

He looked at her a bit taken aback by the passion in her voice.

'Well probably not at first, but I saw what Gruul did to Cliff, just burned him up, I mean there are no monsters involved in that, are there?'

She smiled and then chuckled to herself, 'Ok, Steve if we get a chance, we can go through some of the basics, but we are not going to be burning anything down to start with, more like flipping playing cards with your mind!'

****

Over the two days since Gabby had arrived in Yorkshire, she had taken to walking her Auntie and Uncles three dogs Barney, Ollie and Jess over onto the nearby Nidderdale. It was calming, picturesque and just what she required, she had called her parents from a public payphone to let them know that she was alright but did not say where she was.

The second morning she was walking the dog's when a blue BMW came through the town, she was not sure but that looked a lot like Steve sat next to a woman who resembled the lady who always wore purple. Could that have been Sydora? that the tall man who called himself the Nihilist had spoken of. She ducked her head and turned away, hoping that if it was then she would not be recognised.

Once the car had gone past, Gabby quickly crossed the road. She then briskly walked down Nidd Lane, she was making for the path that followed along the river Nidd, from there she could cross to the other side of the river or turn back towards town on the path and get back to her Uncle and Aunties home. As she walked, her mind continued to throw fearful images at her. Cliff sprang back into her mind; that Gruul thing, sneering, it was all too much for her. Lowering her head, she ran the last hundred metres to the relative cover of the trees lined on either side of the lane.

As Gabby approached the river, her heart started to ease a little, though she could not stop looking back towards the lane; waiting for Hawkins, Steve and the Gruul creature to come down there at any minute. She decided to head back along the river path, all the while keeping her wits about her. On edge, it was normally a nice walk, flowers dotted all along the banks and there was plenty of shaded areas to keep the sun from burning too much. Eventually she reached the other end of the village and followed the path back toward her Auntie and Uncles.

She continued to kept her head down and hurried back; hoping that she had not been detected. She went to the spare room and closed the door, she decided that she would not emerge again for the rest of the day.

****

Sydora and Steve had booked a room at the Wellington Inn on the journey there, it was quite a small room with a double bed, but it was kept in very good condition and extremely well cared for. They had called Victoria, asking for any other additional hits on the ANPR system but there had been no more. That evening they ate in the restaurant, it was of a very good quality, Sydora had the Seabass Fillet Ratatouille, Steve settled on the Leg of Lamb. They then stayed in the bar and listened to the locals discussing the current affairs of the week, as they chatted with one another, Steve for the most part wanted to discuss magic but Sydora had forbidden him from bringing the subject up. She drank bourbon and coke, Steve drank beer, they sat at a table in front of the large, unlit open fire.

'So, do you think she is still here?' Steve asked in a quiet subdued manner.

'Vicki assured us that there had been no other pings on that ANPR system, so I think she must be, she must have friends or relatives here or very close by. We will find her.'

'What are we going to do, knock her out?' Steve asked.

'I am not the Nihilist, no, nothing so vulgar, you can leave that part to me.'

Sydora and Steve drank more and more, she had decided that she liked him, he could be an interesting distraction, he was young, fit and most importantly she was quickly discovering very loyal.

'Anyway, first thing tomorrow I will start your training, we will go out to the woods behind the Inn, we are going to move pebbles with our mind.'

Steve felt a tingle of excitement at the mention of being trained, he attempted to hide it from Sydora, but she could clearly see his anticipation scribbled across his face in the form of a very wide grin.

The rest of the evening they drank, chatted and giggled together, laughing at each other's stories and jokes, getting on very well until finally, they went to bed.

'There is only one bed.' Steve said when they arrived at their room. They both had drunk a lot of alcohol and their inhibitions had loosened.

Sydora untied the belt on her purple dress and let it fall to the floor, she looked into his eyes, with the look that said in a single moment what words could not so easily convey, and they promised far more besides.

****

Gabby had stayed in the following day, no one came to the house, her panic eased a little, maybe she had been mistaken. But to play it safe she determined that she would only take the dogs for a walk using the back route to the river, and not go through the town at all. she took the dogs for a walk the following day, getting down to the river and nothing happened. Her mind began to ease more and more, and the same happened the day after that as well.

Walking the dogs on the following evening she took the same route as she had before, hopping over the fence at the end of the garden, the dogs all easily ran underneath. As she was about to follow the edge of the field down to the river, she heard a familiar voice and her blood chilled. It was Steve.

'Hi Gabby, so this is where you have been.'

Turning around, she saw Steve stood there, beside him the woman wearing a dark purple coloured dress, Sydora just stared.

'What do you want Steve.'

Her voice came through strained and slightly higher than normal.

'You can let me go; I won't say anything about Cliff.'

'We cannot do that.' The woman said.

'No, you will be coming with us, it is up to you whether any pain is involved!'

The woman said, Gabby looked at them both, the only way to go if she was to run was towards the river, it was still about two hundred metres till she got there, and the bridge to the other side, that was probably over half a mile away.

'Ok, I will come, but let me take the dogs back.'

Gabby said, she knew there was no escape and it seemed that Hawkins new friends were not pleasant people at all, in fact they seemed to be downright dangerous; and connected!

Chapter 16

Not Quite Yoga

After returning from the yard Craig, Cairo and Matt had gotten straight to bed, sleeping in Craig's room together. Cairo felt far better with this arrangement. Craig was the last to drop off, he thought about the situation that they were all in, it all somehow tied with his Grandfather's powers. Powers that had been passed onto him, powers that to his knowledge had not been given to his father. He decided the next course of action, and there was only one real option available to his mind.

Craig had woken both Matt and Cairo early the next morning and dragged them both downstairs. The morning was warm, they had breakfast and coffee in the back garden, it was only a light breakfast, but it would suffice.

'We need to find somewhere to stay, before anybody else gets dragged into this.' Craig said.

'And we need to find out who they were, and what they are up to.' Cairo added.

'What about a chalet on the north Denes flood plain? We could all jam into one of those without too many prying eyes.' Matt said.

'Good, and that leads me to why I have got you all up so early.'

****

Craig took Cairo and Matt to the North Denes beach, there was a series of pillboxes and light wooded areas dotted all along the cliffside, till you reached the village of Corton, they would get plenty of privacy from any unwanted attention.

'Here we are.' Craig said.

They all stood in a lightly wooded area of the denes beach; in front of them was the sea and behind them the wooded and sandy cliffs swept up to the back gardens of some of the wealthier properties of the Gunton area of Lowestoft. The constant sound of the crashing North Sea waves was relaxing, and the sand was warm underfoot, they had all taken their shoes off to avoid the discomfort of walking with sandy footwear.

'Why are we here Craig?' Matt asked, 'I thought we were going to see about a chalet further up?'

'We will, later, but I think I am going to need to try to show you how to use my power.'

'How can we use your power?' Matt asked, 'I don't believe it's even real, how would we use it?' he continued.

'With training, but you must believe in it, believe first that it is possible to do anything, and then it will start to work. Look gather lots of stones from the beach, I'll see you all here in a couple of minutes.'

They all went off and gathered a number of small stones from the beach. The North Beach was a shingle beach, covered in stones washed up from the sea over thousands of years so gathering some suitable stones did not take long at all.

'Right, put all of the stones over here.' Craig said as he dropped the pebbles he had collected upon the ground; the others followed his lead.

Craig set his mind upon lifting a stone with his mind, before the other two knew what he was up to, easily lifting the stone into the air to a height of about two feet.

'Wow, Craig you've started already.' Cairo said gazing at the stone as it lifted into the air.

'Yeah Cairo, it's not quite yoga.'

Craig slowly rotated the sizable two-inch circular pebble in mid-air as the others both watched in awe.

'Look guys, it is easily possible, you need to focus, now think of a stone in that pile, think you can lift it with your mind, and it will lift, but more than anything else, you really need to believe it will lift.'

Cairo and Matt both looked at the pile of stones.

'Now concentrate.' Craig said.

Nothing happened.

'Think harder, concentrate.' He said again, still nothing happened.

Cairo, wanted to believe, wanted to focus upon the stone, her head felt like it was going to burst at the temples, in the corner of her eye she could make out the stone that Craig had lifted, she could see it was possible, she focused harder.

Matt tried and tried, he was thinking upon the stone pile, he wanted to move a stone, but always at the back of his mind he heard a voice saying you "cannot argue with gravity", "what goes up must come down", his school days were fighting him, and no matter what he did, the stone would not lift, his problem was one of belief.

Craig seeing that nothing was happening came up with an idea, as the others tried to move their respective stones, he would give them a little help. Slowly at first, he made a stone twitch, on the pile, then it drifted up lazily.

'Look it is working, it is lifting.'

Both Cairo and Matt, watched, trying to focus upon the stone, Craig had given them belief that they could do it. Like a child on a bike as a father takes his hands away slowly for the first time, Craig used the same technique.

The stone wobbled in the air, but it did not drop to the ground.

'Right Matt stop concentrating, let's see if you can both do it by yourselves?' Craig said.

Matt did as Craig asked, the stone wobbled again, but it did not drop.

'I'm doing it Craig, I'm doing it.' Cairo said gathering with excitement in her voice, 'I can do it.'

Craig smiled, 'I always knew you could.'

'Right your turn Matt, focus on the stone, keep it in the air. Ready?'

Matt focused, 'Ready.' He said.

'Take your mind off the stone Cairo.'

She did, and the stone promptly dropped from the air, back onto the pile below.

'Try again, lift it Matt, you can do it.'

'You can do it Matt.' Cairo added supportively.

Matt focused on the stones on the ground, concentrating upon them.

Nothing happened.

'It's no use Craig, I cannot do it, I think that last stone was all Cairo.' He said, a little bit forlorn.

'Let's face it, a wizard, I am not.'

They continued to mess about with the stones lifting them all that morning. But no matter what they tried, Matt could not pick it up, the stones would not move; he gave up after about half an hour. He just could not shake his belief in the physics he had been taught at school. Craig explained how you were only limited by your own belief in what you were trying to do.

****

They had not noticed the eyes that had been watching them from the dark bushes thirty yards away, the yellow eyes of the Gruul who had slipped into the car as they went to the beach. The vile beast had watched the humans as they threatened to mess up the carefully laid out plans; the plans that would open the seals and release the dark prince once again.

'Over here.' The Gruul called croaking the words out in guttural speech.

They all looked over toward the ground-level scrub where the voice had called from, trying to make out who had called out to them.

'Who's there?' Craig shouted, worried about what had been seen, and by who?

'Come out!' Cairo challenged.

'Yeah, come out whoever you are.' Matt backed up Cairo.

Slowly the Gruul slipped from the bushes with an uneven limp-like gait, they all gasped, a couple of days previous they would all have fled in terror. It was only because Craig was aware of the feasibility of such a thing existing that stayed all of their nerves. Now all that remained though was the fear of the unknown itself.

'What are you?' Called out Craig to the Gruul. 'you shouldn't be here.'

The Gruul continued to approach across the sandy glade, they could now see clearly the sallow waxy yellow eyes clearly. They all saw the wicked long claws extending from the ends of the monsters twisted hands and the ghastly black hairs that protruded from all over the infernal beast.

'I am the Gruul, you could call me a Goblin, but I am not.' The Gruul said.

'What do you want?' Craig asked, 'why have you followed us here, and if you have been sent by those others, you will be in trouble.'

'If you mean Hawkins and his lot, then yes I know them.' The Gruul croaked out. 'we can work together Craig; I can give you true power.'

'What do you mean, and how do you know my name?'

They all looked at one another, this creature knew one of their names, they all began to worry.

'Have you been following us?' Cairo asked.

Slowly they all started to back up toward the road where they had parked the car.

'We don't want any trouble,' Craig said, still slowly backing up, 'we are not interested in your powers!'

Craig had a creeping feeling that this creature was up to no good, an agreement with this thing could only lead to a bad outcome. They all retreated away, and when Cairo and Matt had reached the track that led through the copse to the car, Craig took the initiative. Steeling his mind, he focused on the stones directly in front of the approaching monster, flicking them one by one at the diminutive beast.

'Now run!' Craig shouted at the others, 'I'll call you.'

The first stone caught the creature square in the chest knocking it back, the first stone was quickly followed by a barrage of others, as they zipped one by one at the Gruul who had lifted its gruesome arms in defence from the unexpected onslaught.

Matt and Cairo were now in full sprint, following the track as it wound through the lightly wooded area toward Links Road, occasionally they would have to dodge a thin tree branch that reached over the track to whip toward their faces as they passed by, they had left their shoes.

'What about Craig.' Matt called as they ran.

'He can look after himself.' Cairo answered.

They reached the car, Matt quickly fumbling for the keys, they got in.

'Go, drive.' Cairo said.

'Where?'

'Anywhere, just drive.'

Matt started the engine, he reversed and completed a three-point turn, and then they were driving up Links road, up its very steep hill.

'I hope he is ok?' Matt said.

'Craig can take care of himself; you saw what he did with the stones.'

They turned left onto Corton Road and headed towards the town centre.

****

The stones continued to pummel into the Gruul, but the initial shock had gone, reaching its clawed hand forward, concentrating upon the molecules directly in front of the itself, hardening them mentally; forcing the individual particles to bond together, the Gruul had created a barrier from out of thin air. The stones then ricocheted away harmlessly from the beast, deflected in all directions.

'So, you do have some power.' The Gruul then reached out with its other arm, grasping towards the waves and with a heaving motion, dragged the sea toward them both.

'but I have mastered my craft over centuries, witness some true power.'

With the Gruul's exertion, an immense and freak wave of maybe four metres in height surged out from the North Sea, it came directly towards them washing over the pair, soaking Craig's clothes through. The Gruul also, though no clothes were upon that vile monster, it was still soaked through. But the Gruul had most importantly broken Craig's concentration and washed away the remaining stones.

Craig suddenly felt out of his depth; he thought to himself of what he could do, this little bastard was really good with the gift, really powerful with magic. The creature stood there dripping wet, smirking at Craig.

'I may not be that good with magic mate,' Craig said, stalling for time, 'but what I lack in skill, I make up for in guile.'

With that Craig swiftly reached both his hands down, turning his fingers as if grasping the air, then flinging them up, in an under-arm throw, launching two large shovel loads of sand at the Gruul, catching the monster in the face.

And then Craig broke into a sprint, he didn't look back, he just ran. Hoping that the sand would blind the creature long enough for him to get away, sprinting down the track, he quickly grabbed his trainers as he left.

The branches whipped him in the face as he passed through the copse of trees, but he didn't stop, he just kept running. When he reached the road, he immediately noticed that the car had already gone.

good. He thought. *I'll run to the end of the seawall and call them to pick me up there.*

Craig now risked a look back, there was nothing, just the woods that he had fled from, but then he saw it, the horrific beast stumbled out, still rubbing its eyes.

Craig quickly donned his wet trainers and started running again, heading toward the large factory and the wind turbine at Ness point further down the coast; the most easterly point of the United Kingdom.

Chapter 17

Rooftops

Craig continued to run all the way along the Sea front, the sun was up, it was late morning and the temperature was already in the mid-twenties. He was sweating profusely and out of breath from the continuous five minutes of non-stop running down the coastal sea wall. Looking behind, the creature had not followed him. Up ahead the giant wind turbine known locally as Gulliver loomed, dwarfing three or four buildings clustered around its base. He had arrived at Ness Point, the most easterly point of the United Kingdom, it was marked with a compass rose pointing to various locations around the globe and with the relative distance to them from the point where he now stood.

Under the tall turbine Craig could clearly hear the deep and low swoosh as each of the three blades swept down above the ground, Craig slowed his pace a little, he jogged onto Gasworks Road, entering into a light Industrial area, filled with businesses selling tiles, a garage and a few companies related to the green energy market.

Craig made for Whapload Road attempting to get to the town centre, Whapload Road was a wide road and either side it was filled with small local businesses. He then planned to reach the high street by walking up Spurgeon Score, there was five different scores, all harkening back to a prosperous time when Lowestoft had been a thriving fishing town, made fat off of the value of the Herring trade. He slowed yet again as he reached the steps, walking up them, when he reached the top he looked behind once more, searching for signs that the little creature had followed him. But there was none.

Entering one of the numerous second-hand shops, Craig went about purchasing some cheap clothes, he bought a pair of jeans and a white tee shirt they were both baggy but fit well enough, he purchased a cheap, small blue backpack as well, he couldn't bring himself to buy a second hand pair of shoes, instead he would put up with the squishing sensation on each step he made. The lady behind the till took five pounds for the three items, with a wave and a cheerio Craig left the store.

As Craig left the shop his mobile phone went off, it was a message sent from Cairo, it read.

Hi Craig, we are in the M&S carpark, see you there. Hope u r ok? X

Craig quickly wrote a reply as he headed south down the High Street to the car park in question.

I'm ok, will see you there. X

****

Craig made it to the town centre, walking now, occasionally looking behind. He still felt nervous, half expecting to see the creature burst out of somebodies shopping bag, but it did not happen. Finally, he reached the Lowestoft Boots department store and went inside, going in through the main doors. Craig headed for the left-hand side as knew that there was a connecting corridor within the middle of the store that he could use to get to the back of the Marks and Spencer store and their car park.

Craig made his way past the pharmacy counter. Suddenly hearing a commotion behind, he looked back; anxious, he saw a lady stretched out over the floor. She had tripped over, Craig worried, he focused concentrated upon the area, and there it was, he could sense its presence, the thing had followed him all this way, it was invisible and could not be made out with the naked eye, but he could feel it none the less.

Craig ran to the back of the department store, without looking behind he could feel the thing; chasing him, he could imagine its panting breath. Bursting through the double doors that connected this store to the next: Marks and Spencer, he saw a small covered corridor with a mesh gate on the right it was locked with an old rusty padlock, at the far end was a further set of double doors that allowed access to the neighbouring department store. Thinking quickly Craig stopped, lifted his left hand and focused his thoughts upon the old padlock on the side gate, forcing his will to unlock the decrepit mechanism, it gave with a loud crack, the double doors of Marks and Spencer began to open as a lady was having trouble getting through with two full bags of shopping, Craig quickly went through the fenced gate, there was a set of metal steps that went up on his left, he used them following them all the way to the top.

As he reached the end of the steps, a large flock of pigeons, startled by his sudden appearance flew from the roof. The steps had led Craig to a large flat rooftop, there was another set of metal steps that went to a higher rooftop on another wall. The second set of steps were above a door and a window, it looked like it was a fire escape door for some offices.

Craig then heard something clang from below, looking down he saw the feral little imp creeping up, the metal steps; visible now. The creatures clawed feet tapping the metal steps alerting Craig of its arrival, now they were alone it instead preferred to use its ghastly visage to promote fear.

Craig ran to the second set of steps, the creature seeing him run, broke into a staggering sprint, it was surprisingly quick for the misshapen thing that it truly was. Craig had decided that he would try to get higher, he reached the next level and had a clear view far out to sea, the only higher point was the Palmers department store, there was yet another flight of steps it was covered with an old Perspex and asbestos awning. Craig ran to the covered stairs and quickly went up to the very top.

Looking about there was two old air conditioning fans gently whirring away up here, they had seen much better days, the casing had broken long ago and was now laid upon the ground in pieces, it looked as though nobody had seen this rooftop in years. Three large pipes stretched across to the far side of the rooftop and a long skylight stretched along the front of the building; green algae tinged the panes of glass; they had not been cleaned in a long, long time. There was also a fire escape that went down the far side of the building. Craig stopped and he turned to face the monster.

He heard the metallic ring of the clawed feet once more, echoing up the covered stairway.

'Nowhere to go now, little man.' The Gruul croaked, 'no escape.'

'I'm not going to give up without a fight!'

'You are now going to die,' The Gruul croaked, 'such a shame.'

Craig looked at the creature, it was obviously something infernal; something from another dimension, but he had to find out what.

He remembered what his Grandfather had said about such creatures, warning the young Craig.

'you could not harm them easily on our plane of existence. No, you needed to have faith that they would be affected by a physical attack, else they could easily shake off a grievous wound like it was no more than a scratch.'

Craig guessed that this was why the church in its highly ritualised format, had reportedly defeated demons and the like; why they had successfully undertaken exorcism's.

They faced each other on the rooftop, a standoff, neither making any sharp or sudden move, the sun shone down upon them both without a single cloud in the sky.

'What is your name and what do you want?' Craig called out.

'You cannot pronounce my name, but some call me Gruul.'

'But what do you want, I could possibly help you get home.'

The Gruul looked at Craig, staring at him, trying to fathom what he was up to. At length it answered.

'No, this is my home, I have been here for longer than you could imagine,' he added, 'I will be here long after you and your bones are dust!'

'We are coming, soon my master will be back, you and your kind are in the decline!'

'Who is your master and where is he coming from?' Craig asked.

The master, Prince Ashtoreth, and his forty legions; to finish what was begun long ago!'

Craig really didn't like the sound of that; not at all.

'So, this is what you and your friends have been doing, summoning your mates is it?'

Craig knew that this conversation was soon going to come to an end and the vile little thing was going to attempt to kill him, but he needed to find out as much as he could first.

'They are fools, they want treasure; greed, one of your downfalls, but their purpose is being served.'

'You mean they do not want to free your master?' Craig continued, 'why then are they helping you.'

It then dawned on Craig as he watched the foul little beast, it started to grin; a wide grin that revealed two rows of sharp, long and uneven fangs.

'They do not know do they.' Craig had answered his own question. The truth striking him.

The Gruul raised its arms, gnarled fingers extended, Craig felt his skin start to rapidly heat up, looking down he could see his skin reddening, the creature was trying to boil or burn him, fighting the fear he focused upon cooling down, willing himself to believe he was cooling down. As he did so he could feel the alien mind fighting him; a mental duel he could not afford to lose. Concentration was his only hope.

Craig gradually lifted his arm, slowly forcing the attack back till the air in front shimmered and flickered like a heat haze. He then pushed forward with all his might, attempting to blast the wretched beast back, unexpecting of the blast the Gruul was pushed off its feet, arms flailing as it shot back.

Crashing into one of the broken air conditioning fans, the Gruul briefly teetered upon the edge, trying to regain balance. Craig then rushed forward shoulder first, to knock the beast into the mechanical system of old whirring blades. The Gruul plummeted down. Craig ran to the fire escape at the rear and headed down as fast as he could. The car park where Matt and Cairo should be was just around the corner. Where the fire escape came down to ground level. As he reached the bottom of the steps, he retrieved his phone and called Cairo, she answered.

'Hi Craig, where are you?' she said, 'are you ok?'

'Start up the car, I'm now coming to the end of the car park, I'll tell you all about it on the way home.'

As Craig reached the end of the narrow alleyway, Matt's car pulled up, Craig breathed an immense sigh of relief, he quickly got into the back.

'Hi Craig, tell us what happened?' Matt said excitedly.

'Wow, that was scary, but what a huge buzz,' Craig added, 'that thing is with those others. They are trying to open a portal; well that thing is anyway.'

'A portal, so that there may be more of those things, oh god, we've got to stop them!' Cairo said as she leaned over the seat to talk with Craig in the back.

'Agreed, but I do not know where to start.'

Matt had already gotten the car out of the town centre and on to one of the main trunk roads, it was called Battery Green Road and followed the coast until it reached the roundabout by the now empty court rooms, he turned the car left heading north.

'Did you kill it?' Matt asked.

'I don't know, I think so,' Craig extrapolated, 'put it this way, if you fell into spinning blades you would not be too healthy would you.'

'Hurhuhuhur,' Matt chuckled, 'nice one mate, down the air con unit, what a way to go.'

Craig looked at Cairo, she was still leaning back between the two seats, 'Yeah let's just hope that was enough, let's hope that is one problem down'.

****

Slowly a clawed hand reached out over the edge of the whirring and juddering machinery, then another, pulling itself up and out of the manmade hole in the centre of the building; clambering out. The monstrous thing loped over the edge and back to the safety of the rooftop. A horrific gash ran down its right-hand side, it was not so easy to kill a creature from another reality. The Gruul loped over to the edge where the fire escape was positioned, looking down from the sun-bathed rooftop. Below Craig was now getting into a car at the end of the alleyway, it then watched them speed away.

The vile little beast decided it needed to get back to the manor, it needed to get its plans back on course and could not waste any more time with these petty distractions. Thinking hard, forcing light to penetrate its body, the Gruul slowly faded into invisibility once more. The beast then began the long lope south to the Manor, it would need to rally Hawkins or some of these others that had turned up; get them to unwittingly help the Gruul free the dark Prince.

Chapter 18

The second seal

The next morning there was an animated impatience about the Gruul, it was time to move on to the next Seal. It made it known to everyone at the Manor, continually urging them all into action, during the day Sydora and Steve had both returned and they had brought Gabby with them, she looked in a bad way; resigned, upset and scared, by this time Victoria had already left on other business.

'We must hurry, the stars, the stars.' The Gruul lamented the others.

'We have others arriving soon,' Sydora said, 'three of my highest-ranking acolytes will be here this afternoon, we can go then.'

'Too late, we must go now.' Miserable that they would not leave immediately the Gruul instead stomped around like a petulant child being ignored, grumbling incomprehensible words in an alien language.

That afternoon a grey, seven-seater, Renault people carrier pulled up at the Manor, the three acolyte recruits that Sydora had talked of had arrived. Their names were Jay, Aidan and McVicar. The Gruul was in a hurry and continually urged them all into the people carrier to go to the next seal.

The sad little creature had known where to find the second seal for a long time now. Finally, things were in motion that would free the Prince; for the resumption of the war of old, as well the Gruul knew; humanity had long forgotten the past, in no small part due to the destructive capacity of humankind. The Gruul's master and the numerous hordes entrapped for thousands of years on the other hand; had thought of nothing else but.

About an hour after the three acolytes had arrived, they were ready to go, they all alighted the seven-seater; all except the Nihilist. They drove out of Lowestoft, heading north and west, the Gruul could barely hide the glee as its master would be still closer to freedom.

The journey took about forty minutes to get to Claxton, they went via Oulton Broad, then through the Haddiscoe bends and onto the old Norwich road. The hamlet of Claxton was very small, it was close to the River Yare and tucked away in the farmlands behind the town of Loddon. There was a population of two hundred and ninety-one, counted at the last census, one church; it was called St Andrews. On one side of the Hamlet were farm fields, the other side that was closer to the river was predominantly grazing marshland.

'So how will this help Lord Blessed exactly?' Sydora asked, her dealings with the Demonic were long listed, she knew there was no altruistic desire upon the Gruuls part to help; the beast would have its own agenda.

'I told you, the ritual will be stronger if the seals are broken first.' It lied, and Sydora knew it, but she wanted to see just what the demon was up to and why it was getting so animated and so frustrated.

'Ok, well keep me informed.' She said to the vile beast, Gabby looked over to the Demon, terrified of what may be about to happen. She hoped that there would be no killing this time, resignedly she sat next to Steve, hoping that their friendship would save her from any possible danger. She looked at him, he seemed calm, relaxed; she hoped it was a sign that nothing else bad would happen and she would be allowed to leave soon. He became aware of her gaze, turning to face her and sensing her thoughts, 'It's okay Gabby, I am here.'

He took out his mobile phone. 'Look, Sydora has started training me,' he continued 'I'm bloody good as well, look.' as the phone slowly levitated into the air, Gabby watched, then looked into his eyes, she could see he was enraptured by this newfound talent.

'I could show you too, if you would like? It's really not that hard once you have begun.

One of Sydora's acolytes, Aidan, looked over at Steve and Gabby as the mobile phone floated above Steve's hand, he said to McVicar who was sat opposite.

'He's better with the magic already than you.'

The three acolytes all laughed together. Sydora smiled at Steve and Gabby, Gabby did not feel comfortable in that woman's company, she sat back in the chair and said nothing more for the rest of the journey.

The Renault had taken them through the back roads of South Norfolk until they arrived at Claxton. They parked the van near the centre of the Hamlet. There was a small square green with four or five parking spaces arranged up one side, they all got out, the Gruul grudgingly wore a long coat and hat which hid its identity from casual perusal, though it did look ridiculous in the summer heat, so overdressed.

'It is this way.' The Gruul said.

They all followed the Gruul, occasionally the thing would crouch low to the ground and sniff, like a hound that was confirming the scent.

After walking for about five minutes the Gruul turned left down a very narrow side road. Barely enough space for a car to drive up or down.

'Up here.'

Again, they all followed, they had no choice, but the little devil seemed to know where it was going. After another five minutes the Gruul moved to the hedgerow upon the left and climbed through. 'We are nearly there,' The Gruul said with a definite sense of relief 'quick get through.'

It was a lot harder for all the others as they were all more than twice the Gruuls size, eventually however they had all won through the hedgerow further up, where a larger gap existed. They then caught up with the Gruul where it paced around impatiently.

****

The Nihilist had been suspicious of the Gruul since he had first laid eyes upon it. He had known about demons and the like from previous dealings with Lord Blessed, but he did not like there type and could never trust them. He decided he would not go to this seal and instead once they had gone, he would see if he could discover anything about the Gruul and its dealings.

The first thing he had decided to do was search through the room where the Gruul seemed to live, that was the lounge to the right of the front door, he opened the glass door and went inside.

The room was a mess, and it had a nauseous oversweet smell in the air, there was broken glass all over the floor from a smashed table. There was a pile of animal bones that looked like they had come from a mixture of cats, small dogs, birds and rodents. He did not want to spend any more time in here than he had to, but the place was in such a mess that he could clearly see that he would still be here for quite some time.

Whilst searching through the various bits and pieces he would occasionally find a trinket that showed an insight into the creature's thoughts, a doll with a pen-knife through its plastic chest where the heart would be. A Victorian clown doll had pride of place upon the mantelpiece, flanked on both sides by six or seven animal skulls, the clown doll had numerous chips, and its painted lacquer coat had faded with the passage of time.

Over by the bookcases, which were on the wall beside the door, there was not quite as much rubbish; it was like the creature would throw stuff down or drop whatever it had in its hands. But the bookshelf was not in the same state of chaos and disorder. The bookshelf was filled with all manner of different books, whether the Gruul read them or not the Nihilist was not sure, they ranged all the way from books of nursery rhymes, and history books to the occult and religion.

He continued looking through the flotsam and jetsam littered about, it struck him that this was the second time he had searched through someone else's life in recent weeks, only this one was clearly far older than the last. He went behind the couch in the corner of the room, moving the chair forward a little, he found there the Gruul's bed. Blankets and clothing had been laid like a nest in there, he could not see inside but it did not smell good, the Nihilist slipped out his mobile phone, turned on the torch app and the video camera, and then he gingerly crouched down and reached his arm through the demon shaped aperture in the blankets and old clothing.

****

The Gruul had taken them to a cornfield there was quite a steep gradient, sloping down towards the hamlet close by. All the fields had recently been harvested, the dirt had dried; sun-baked and was sturdy underfoot, signs of the recent harvest were strewn all over the field, dried leaves and the occasional damaged cob, they were all stood in the top corner of the field, tractor tyre tracks imprinted the earth where they had turned in the past.

The wind whipped and whistled here, and this corner was almost alive with the sounds of the wind, like it was warning those that had gathered here to go That they were unwanted, across the field a small murder of crows pecked at the leftovers from the harvest not fifty yards away.

'Get rid of them,' the Gruul said to the acolyte Jay, 'they are not welcome.'

Jay ran towards them, waving his arms and scaring the birds away, they flew further down the field and landed, resuming their purge of the waste that littered the dusty field.

Jay returned moments later, the Gruul looked over at the crows, unhappy that they had not left the field in totality he decided they were not enough of a threat and continued.

The corner of the field was overshadowed by a single gnarled oak tree, twisted branches reached out from the hedgerow, moving animatedly within the grip of the whispering wind.

'Now focus upon me.' The Gruul demanded, 'all of you.' It croaked looking at each of them in turn. they all gathered around the Gruul, close to the thing; concentrating upon the diminutive little monster. All except Gabby that is; she was surrounded by the acolytes, McVicar and Aidan, who could easily grab her if she made a break for it. She didn't dare move and instead just stood there.

Gradually the winds seemed to lessen, the whistling died decibel by decibel, and the cool feeling of the rushing air slackened somewhat.

'It is working,' The Gruul croaked, 'do not lose concentration.' The little creature urged the others to focus their thoughts. The tree above lessened in its movement as the winds had gradually died off.

'Now, it is time, you; bring her forward.' Pointing at Aidan, he did as he was told, grabbing Gabby by the arm, he was strong.

'Don't fight darling it'll be quicker that way.' She tried to resist his grip but Sydora took hold of her from the other side, Steve said nothing, just watching with an impassive look upon his face.

'Help me Steve, please, help me.' Gabby cried, but Steve stood there, half paralysed from fear and half exhilarated by the chance to control such power as he was now witnessing. Struggle as Gabby did, she could not break the grip of Aidan and he dragged her to the centre of the gathering that had formed in an informal semi-circle around the ancient tree.

'Do it, hurry.' The Gruul urged, as Aidan held her tight, he now had hold of both her arms, she looked over her shoulder to see Sydora walking calmly forward a small oriental dagger in her hand. Gabby could smell the acolyte's breath, it was stale from cigarette smoke, this was going to be her last memory; she gave up and just closed her eyes. She felt very close movement and tensed ready for the death cut.

But instead she felt the acolytes grip soften. Then he slumped to the ground, Gabby opened her eyes, looking down at her feet; the acolyte laid, holding his neck in a futile attempt to stop the dark red blood that pumped freely and with wild abandon from his jugular, the blood, eager to escape his body, and Aidan's eyes slowly glazed. The dry earth started to rumble slightly, and Gabby quickly retreated toward Steve. Then Aidan's body was gradually consumed by the very earth, as the dry soil all about the body cracked and split open; till it had fully disappeared from view. Then the winds gradually picked up once again.

Gabby ran over to Steve, briefly hugging him, then remembering that he had done nothing, she pushed him away. 'You bastard, you are a fucking bastard Steve, I will not forget that!'

The dead body had disappeared into the ground, like it had slowly been sucked down, and now there was just fresh turned dirt and the stirring of the wind once more. The Gruul however was watching something else, after the second seal had been broken, the insidious little beast had been ready for the crows to attack once more. But they had not, instead they had all flown to the trees dotted about in the hedgerows, all that is apart from two, they had immediately taken flight; south.

'No time,' the Gruul said, 'we must get to the last seal straight away. There is no time!'

****

The Nihilist swung the camera phone about inside the little demonic nest; attempting to video all corners within, hoping to find a clue to this Gruul's motives. After a few moments of blind video capture, he slipped his arm back out, then left the room in a hurry. The Nihilist had been careful not to move anything too much, he was not sure what demons classed as tidy and what was messy.

In the kitchen he made himself a drink, watching the jumpy footage that he had taken; inside the nest he saw that the thing had been eating somebodies' cat, the poor creature had obviously experienced a horrid death and now there was only messy, bloodied bones from the tail to its waist.

'Well I guess at least he eats what he hunts!'

He thought to himself, the Nihilist did not have any compunction about killing he had committed the act several times in his life, however, he thought to kill with no reason other than self-gratification was absolutely vile and the worst thing anyone or anything could do.

The only other thing inside the nest of clothing and blankets was a small staff, maybe three feet long. It was very ornate and looked to maybe be made from some yellow metal, maybe gold, bronze or brass, the top of the staff looked like it had some kind of embellishment, maybe a winged scarab but he had not gotten good enough footage to clearly make it out, the other end was capped with a sharp spike. He decided he would not go back in there, just yet.

Chapter 19

Bonds Weaken, Arms Reach Through

The noise echoed through the dark and wretched tunnels; a sound of tumbling rock and sliding debris that rumbled toward the two guards who had watched relentlessly at their master's decree. When the low rumbling din rolled over them, they readied their sharp weapons thinking somehow it may be an attack, they waited both motionless; listening and waiting, fearing to breathe, then after a long pause, one looked over to the other and said,

'What could that mean?' its voice high and sneering.

The other stayed still, peering silently into the darkness ahead, it wore an eye patch, it had lost its eye in battle an age ago.

'It might be worth a look, go get a section and check it out, since the master declared the seals were being opened, it could have something to do with that.'

The creature turned and ran toward the central cavern, excited that it may be bringing the news of upcoming slaughter to the Dark Prince. Delusions of grandeur filled the demonic things head, as it hastily passed through the dusty tunnels. It failed to notice that the wooden torches that burned in the sconces along the hewn tunnel gently flickered unlike before, a breeze was coming from somewhere, another sign of the barriers between that this and the earth's reality were coming close to each other; closer toward concurrence.

****

In the very centre of the main and largest cavern; upon a risen plateau stood the stone palace that had been erected to house the prince Ashtoreth. It was a twisted craft of unworldly artifice, a curtain wall with jagged crenellation's surrounded the donjon, stretching around with its high towers set at regular intervals. Twisted minarets crowned the top of the donjon, all built with some unnamed black stone. There was a great black barbican that squatted like an unspeaking guardian directly in front of the terrible keep.

The guard arrived but his thunder had already been stolen. A great crowd had gathered, looking up at the walls of the Dark Lords stronghold. High above, upon the walls the banners of Ashtoreth's great legions were gently moving in some draught from another plane of existence. The large gathering there knew exactly what this meant. Skimshall, as that was the name of this particular creature slowed to a walking pace and asked one of those whether the Prince was aware of what was going on?

'Has anyone advised the Prince Ashtoreth yet?'

Two turned; one spoke.

'We await the decree, he will be here soon,' The thing continued 'we are ready, we will be free.'

The vile horde had no set form or build, all shapes and sizes; each and every demon was different. Some were large others small, the skin colours ranged from dark green, to sallow pale leather. There was others with scales, and multiple limbs, more limbs than us humans, some were biped and others quadruped, they all waited as one for their master. They were armed with vicious weapons, sharpened cruel spears, wicked swords and axes; they were ready and eager for war, a return to the old ways.

The gathering waited for about an hour before the Dark Lord Ashtoreth finally made his appearance. In that time the body of the acolyte Aidan, who had been sacrificed at the second seal had materialised, it had been dragged from one of the outlying tunnels where the body had been discovered, to the Prince's palace. His body had then been torn to pieces and eaten, as anything that came to this pocket vision of the abyss would usually be.

Striding up the rough chiselled steps the Dark lord reached the top of the black stone barbican, he looked down over the vast horde, gathered below. The immense cavern was filled from hewn wall to hewn wall with his loyal subjects. A great cheer rose up as he appeared for them all to see, their master, whom they all despised yet were all fanatically loyal to; it was through fear he secured their loyalty.

'What a great host I see before me.' He began, 'The second seal has been broken. Already I can now affect the other world from afar, it is not long my friends, not long now at all.'

The mass cheered, many slamming weapons onto the face of their shields, a great din echoed throughout the immense chamber.

'Soon the High Priest that had foreseen our imprisonment will have sundered the third seal, and we will be free.'

The clamour was deafening within the vast central cavern, Ashtoreth lifted his arm, beckoning them all to cease, gradually the noise trailed off, and the echoes fled down the exit tunnels.

'I will send a thousand warriors to search for the portal. We will be back soon, vengeance, and victory shall finally be ours.'

The mighty legion below cheered and battered their shields once more, Ashtoreth withdrew from the top of the barbican.

'I want my best magi sent to the palace Donjon.' He demanded as he walked down the stairwell, a multitude of hangers on were there; eager to please their master, hungry to win favour and advancement.

****

The central hall of Ashtoreth's great dark palace was a large octagonal space about two hundred metres across, it had been made entirely from solid blocks of stone, the workmanship was of the very highest quality, anything less would only bring a swift and ugly demise to the artisan guilty of such shoddy work. There was a great fire that burned at one side of the hall, several braziers were positioned at regular intervals about the walls. High stone arches lifted the ceiling a great height into the shadows above, interspersed evenly upon the eight outer walls were four exits, each exit was thwarted with a double set of metal doors, heavy, very strong and almost impervious.

Four ghastly creatures had been summoned, they were all bedecked in ragged clothes and wore no armour. They were demonic sorcerers of repute within the legions of Ashtoreth. Three were all kneeling in front of the demon prince, heads touching the stone floor, the fourth, a slug-like thing bowed its head low. The Demon prince sat upon his great throne, imperious and stately. Beside him his dragon-like mount slept, curled away behind the throne, its massive bulk heaved with every breath that it took. Across Ashtoreth's lap was a great staff at least ten feet long, it was made of a dark wood and had been carved with intricate workmanship to look like a serpent; no detail had been spared.

'I have summoned you here to attempt to contact the Gruul upon the other side,' He said to them all, 'you have access to my laboratory and libraries should you find the need.'

'How master, we have tried before.' Asked one of the gathered magi-demons, not daring to lift its head from the submissive position upon the cold black floor as it spoke.

'Two of the seals are now sundered, we must contact Gruul, then we can bridge the gap once the final seal has been cast aside.'

'Of course, master, what message do we send, if we are successful?'

'We must give Gruul strength, with contact we can help ensure the attempt to bridge the gap from here to there is successful.'

'Should we begin now?' the same grovelling creature asked, it appeared to speak for all of them.

'Yes, begin straight away.'

They all slowly rose and then backed away cautiously; showing the utmost of respect at all times.

****

The Great library within Ashtoreth's palace, was a long oval hall, it ran alongside the Great hall and had two levels. There was a solid set of stone steps at one end that permitted access to the balconies upon the topmost level. Each and every space of the walls had been filled with books and texts. The collected knowledge of a demon prince and his armies' conquests.

There was a multitude of long rectangular tables set out in neat rows down the centre of the ground floor. Some had been moved and a large altar set in the very centre of the created open space.

Within, the demon-magi had begun their attempts at contact with the Gruul, concentrating upon bridging the gap; unsuccessfully it could be said. They were now conducting blood sacrifices, invoking thaumaturgy to increase the power of the summons, but so far none there could break the barrier and reach to the other side; to contact Gruul in Earth's reality.

'It is useless, there is no chance, we need the third seal removed before any contact can be made.' Said one, its claws drenched in the blood of an unfortunate demonic wretch that had been on the wrong side of a ruling from the Dark prince. Its ribcage had been opened while the thing still lived, its ribs now opened like the spread wings of a bird; its ribs had been unfolded, allowing the organs to be extracted at the insidious needs of the dark sorcerers gathered there.

'We must continue, the boundaries will weaken, and we will be ready as soon as the alignment occurs, we must contact the Gruul.'

'Continue searching the tomes for a ritual that will help.'

After a number of hours, the slug-like magi who had been looking for books on the higher level of the library found a book that may have what they were looking for. It was titled 'Horribilis aspectus. Et afficit non modo' sliding on its singular slimy foot till it had returned to the grisly scene in the centre of the hall.

'This one will help.' The thing said, holding the book out, another took the book, read the title and nodded,

'Good, good, this may be the one.'

The demon that had taken the book was the most senior of all of the four that had been gathered, it had two arms that ended in vicious, sharp crab-like pincers, its body was covered in horns and its hide was a shade of dark burgundy.

'You have done well Slac. Read it, find anything that may be of use.'

'Yes master.' The slug-like Slac answered.

It retreated to one of the tables further back, to begin reading the tome, hoping to find a ritual that would empower their magical endeavours; to reach out of the pocket dimension they had been imprisoned within for so very long.

It was as Slac studied this particular book that the breakthrough came, a ritual that may be the answer, it was located near the end of the tome and would require a lot of blood, a new type of magic circle would need to be drawn upon the floor, candles created with the blood of the living and the attempt would need a minimum of six casters to be successful. Immediately Slac called over the master sorcerer.

'This one; read it master, it may be just what we have been after, now some of the seals have been broken, the dimensions may be close enough to make contact.'

The master sorcerer took the tome with one of its crab-like clawed arms, and read the open page, after a few moments it said.

'We will try this, prepare the hall, you; pointing at another of the sorcerers, go and bring two more slaves, we will need their blood, and you,' pointing to another, 'summon more casters, we need all those we can get and quickly, all of you. Slac, help me begin preparing the area.'

There is no such thing as a 'day' in a pocket dimension and time does not exist as it does in our reality, but the sorcerers had gathered all that they could; toiled to prepare everything that needed to be prepared and then, finally gathered with extra magi from the highest circles of mastery to cast this ritual of reaching.

The library was filled with the sounds of the dark misshapen living, miserable things invoking the darkest of magics; summoning the worlds to allow their conscious to reach across meta-physical boundaries and defying the laws of physics to allow communication with one of theirs so very far away. Blood was spattered all across the floor, yet they all stood their impassively continuing the magics, at the head of the circle stood the master sorcerer, its crab-like claws risen over head, a demons heart within its pincered grip, dried dark blood covered its arms to the elbows and its face was coated in the ichor and gore of the sacrificed, all about the sorcerers continued to murmur in an alien language; in a monotonous tone.

Then it stopped.

'Gruul here me now. It is I Shimozel!' The master sorcerer said.

Chapter 20

Black Winged Warning

It is proven that crows are one of the most; if not the most intelligent bird on the earth today, they can recognise and remember a human face, and warn other crows of any potential threat that may be posed. They can problem solve and are one of the few breeds of bird that are known to be able to use tools. It is thought that we gave birds a lot less credit for their intelligence than they were always entitled to.

These two particular corvids were loyal to Bob, they had been his most loyal friends for years. They were even there when Bob had died. Each day the two birds would land upon the statue in his back garden and wait for him to feed them both, every day they were there; without fail. A mating pair, he had nicknamed them Russell and Cheryl, they knew him, and he had used the gift to give them a purpose. A purpose which they served even after his passing.

They were tasked with helping Bob in monitoring the three seals, the task that Bob had undertaken selflessly for so many years. They would report to him, what had happened close to them. Usually nothing to worry about but, now at the very time Bob had died, the seals had come under attack. Two had now been sundered, only the third seal stood locking the Earth's mortal enemy away; imprisoned in another reality.

The two birds had flown fast and far, they had watched as tasked by Bob, now they needed to get to the master's successor before it was too late, flying on glossy black feathered wings, searching for the quoted heir. The events at the second seal proved beyond any doubt that the forces of evil were once more in ascendency, long had their vigil been, but now at least, it would prove that it had not been in vain.

The two birds knew Craig's face, but they had not been introduced in a formal context. Craig had fed them many times when Bob had not been about, but he knew nothing of their vigil, they had landed upon the statue as they always did, and they waited, Bob's wife, Elisabeth had come out and fed them, one swooped down and ate, and then the other, but neither flew off as would be usual.

****

Matt dropped off Craig at the end of Reeve Street, they had arranged to meet up at Matt's later, they hoped that these antagonists had not discovered where he lived. Craig just wanted to get some things and let Grandma Liz know that he was going away for a bit. Craig walked down the road till he arrived at the front door. Grandma Liz was in the front room watching a daytime television quiz show.

'Hello dear.' She said as he entered the house.

'Hi Grandma,' he said, 'I'm going away with Cairo and Matt for a couple of days, I was just getting a few things.'

'What about your work, you will never get a deposit for a house if you keep taking time off.' She said, worrying.

'Don't worry about that, I have taken a holiday.' He lied.

Craig had already realised that when he finally walked back through the doors at the call centre, he would have some explaining to do, or quite possibly, he may just get asked to turn around to leave.

He went through the living room; up the steep stairs and then entered his room. It hadn't been tidied since the break-in, but his Grandmother never went in their anyway.

Throwing a few changes of clothes, some pairs of socks and some clean underwear into the bag that he'd purchased from the charity shop, he then proceeded into the bathroom and grabbed his toothbrush. Then he went back downstairs to the kitchen; took a bright green apple and bit into it. The apple was juicy and had a good crunch as he took the bite, he looked out of the window in to the back garden. He saw the two crows perched upon the statue in the garden.

'I guess I will see you guy's later.' He said more to himself than to the birds.

However as he spoke it appeared as if they were looking directly at him, he wondered whether they had been fed; deciding they had not Craig opened the cupboard beneath the sink and grasped some of the dog biscuits that they used to feed the pair and threw them a dozen brown treats out of the back door.

'There you go guys.' He said and closed the door behind, then he walked through, taking another bite of the apple.

'Right Nan, I'm off, I'll be back in a few days.' He said.

'Ok dear have a nice time.' She replied; he knew that she was more interested in the quiz show than what he had actually just said. Craig left, closing the front door, he immediately headed off towards Matts home.

****

Matt arrived at his ground floor flat with Cairo, it was late afternoon and the sun still shone clear and bright. Matts flat was just on the outskirts of town, he kept it very tidy, it was decorated in the latest style. There was lots of prints of different woodland scenes, they were hung with taste; frames and curtains all matched in a dark grey.

They contrasted well with the walls, which had been painted a lighter shade of grey. He had two bedrooms, a kitchen and a living room in the premises, the property had been decorated in the same style throughout. He had four black leather seats in the living room, they all faced towards a large fifty inch plus size flat-screen television.

They went inside, Matt headed directly for the kitchen, Cairo sat down in the living room.

'Do you want a cuppa?' Matt called through.

'Yes please.' She answered back.

Soon the comfortable sounds of a kettle boiling floated through into the living room, quickly followed by the smell of fresh coffee as the brews were being made. She decided to continue with Craig's training back on the beach, looking about Matt's living room she saw a small, waist high, grey bookshelf in one corner. There was a mobile phone charger on top of it, a small lamp and a photo of Matt with his mother and father taken when he had been at university. Above it was his degree, framed in grey to match the paintings hung elsewhere within the property. She began to concentrate upon the charger lead, hoping that it would move; it didn't budge.

'I cannot do this.' She thought to herself, but she knew she had to try once more.

Doubt began to sink in to her subconscious.

'What had Craig said. Believe it, believe with all you have.'

She took a moment to resettle her mind, then she raised her left arm, closed her eyes and reached out with her mind, forcing herself into believing, a belief with everything she had that the lead would lift into the air, Cairo did not open her eyes she just kept her mind on the cable, kept willing it higher.

Matt came through, 'Hey Cairo, what are you doing over there?' Matt asked as he entered the living room with two steaming mugs of coffee in his hands.

Fearing to lose her concentration, she opened her eyes slowly still trying to keep her mind focused upon the cable. Instantly she could see that the cable was floating erect pointing to the ceiling; she was relieved it had worked when Craig was not there. She turned her head to face Matt and the cable dropped from the air as soon as she stopped thinking about it.

'You did it, Cairo, wow, you are good at that gift stuff.'

'Look I want to be able to help Craig if there are any more of them. I'll bet those others who got me in that yard can do this stuff as well.'

'It looks like you have already got the hang of it.'

'We will see.'

Matt put the two cups on the table, as he did, Cairo focused her attention on him, thinking that she would lift him from the ground.

Nothing happened, 'Well I've got a way to go as yet.'

'I hope Craig isn't too long, I think we need to stick together; work out our next move.' Cairo said.

'Yeah, I think you are right.' Matt replied as he took a sip of coffee, Cairo followed suit, taking a sip as well, she put her mobile phone upon the table, and concentrated upon it, she wanted to make it ring, focusing with all her might, and then.

'ring, ring, ring, ring'

'Are you going to answer that?' Matt asked, wondering why she had not swiped the phone from the table which would have been normal for Cairo.

'It's ok Matt, I was trying to make it ring with my mind.' She said, Matt could see she looked a bit shocked, amazed that she could do it.

'Wow, this is crazy Cai,' He was visibly excited, Matt had a natural positive attitude to everything, light-hearted and good to be around.

'At this rate you will be better than Craig by the end of the week.'

They continued to drink their coffee as Cairo's phone rang again.

****

Craig had made his way across town, on his way he had went to a shop and bought some snacks, inside the shop, some children waited ahead of him to pay the cashier for their sweets,

It must be about 4.00, to 4.30.

Craig thought to himself. Patiently waiting he was watching the cars go past, then he noticed outside perched upon a wall on the far side of the road; a crow, odd, but he almost thought it was looking toward the shop, toward him.

Nah, just a coincidence.

He decided. The children left the shop and Craig stepped up to the cashier, he paid and exited the shop, as he left the crow still stood there on the wall.

'Go home Russell, or Cheryl, whichever one you are.'

Craig almost joked, he then set off toward Matts flat, turning left.

About twenty-five minutes later and Craig had arrived at Matts home, he had kept looking behind and at least twice more he had spotted a crow upon a roof, or one suspiciously flying in his general direction, he had begun to worry a little.

Could it have been that these birds had been keeping an eye upon Grandpa all this time?

Craig walked up the small tarmac driveway toward the front porch of the flat and knocked upon the door, no answer. So, Craig rang Cairo's mobile phone instead.

'Hi, Craig, what's up, are you ok?'

'Yeah, when is Matt going to fix his doorbell?' he inquired, 'I'm outside.'

He hung up and soon Matt was at the door and opened it. 'Hi mate, how are ya, any trouble?'

'I'll tell ya when we get inside.'

Craig followed Matt inside, they joined Cairo in the living room.

'Hi Cairo.' Craig said as he sat down.

'Hi Craig.' She replied.

'I'll put the kettle on,' Matt said, 'I feel like another.' He added.

'I'm ok, thanks.' Cairo said turning down a second brew.

Craig began telling his assumptions to Cairo, he spoke loud enough that Matt would hear in the kitchen.

'I think those bad dudes may have been watching Grandpa Bob with a pair of crows for years?'

Cairo looked at him for a moment.

'Are you, possibly being a little bit paranoid Craig?'

'Well no, I don't think so, listen, all the while I have lived with Grandma and Grandpa, there have been these crows, and Grandpa would feed them, well they were in the garden earlier today and I think,' he stopped briefly, 'I think that they have been following me today; Just now in fact.'

Cairo nodded, accepting his point, 'There must be hundreds of crows about town Craig.'

'Yeah, but I think they have followed me here, well one of them anyway.'

'Well call it a coincidence Craig,' Matt called from the kitchen over the sound of the boiling kettle, 'but there is two in the back garden right now!'

Craig and Cairo got straight up and rushed into the kitchen, joining Matt, he was looking out of the window, they followed his lead and looked, there they were, two crows, both looking into the kitchen window, blackened silky feathers and beady black eyes.

'What should we do Craig?' Matt asked.

'I'm not sure, I guess there is only one way to find out.'

With that Craig went to the back door, Matt followed behind, then unlocked the door. Cautiously Craig advanced towards the two birds as they were perched on branches in a pear tree, in the garden. The grass was parched and patchy due to the recent summer heatwave.

As Craig got close one of the two birds, flapped its wings and then let out a raucous cry.

'Mwawk, mwawk, mwawk.'

Craig focused upon the bird, feeling for words within the black feathered bird's mind; the bird just stayed perched there, beading Craig with its brilliant, shining opal eyes.

The thoughts and images started to materialise within Craig's mind, he could see the love that his Grandfather had given this regal creature. He could see the hatching of young crows, and a life, long lived upon the wing. He then also saw his Grandpa explaining to these creatures that Craig could be trusted when he had gone, and he saw the birds perched there watching solemnly at the funeral. It brought a lump to his throat and he could feel the tears ready to fall from his eyes again.

'What is it that you are here for?' He asked, and he waited.

Then the images of what had happened earlier came to his mind; flooding in, he saw the events that took place in the Norfolk countryside, he got the perception that they wanted him to follow them before it was too late.

Then   the   images   faded.

Chapter 21

The Mason's Deal

An Aston Martin had arrived at the plush black metal gates, it was late, the night had fell, blanketing the opulent countryside residence into total pitch blackness. It was so far into the countryside that no streetlights had been encountered for about twenty minutes, only the bright pale halogen beams from the 'Rapide S' made navigation possible, indicating; Hawkins turned down the long snaking driveway toward the large mansion. The building was beautiful in every aspect of the word, built in a 'u' shaped layout, there was an east and west wing; the décor was Corinthian throughout the entire exterior.

Pulling up at the wide marble steps outside a large set of ornate front doors, Lord Blessed and Dr Humboldt got out, they made their way up towards the main entrance, as they arrived at the doors, Hawkins drove the high end luxury sports car to the garage space at the side of the mansion.

One of the double doors opened and Lord Blessed along with Dr Humboldt were greeted by a young man of about twenty-five, he was impeccably dressed in a full dinner suit. His name was Stuart Miles and he had been the butler here for two years now.

'Hello Miles,' Lord Blessed said, 'how are you keeping?'

'Very good sir, thank you for asking, may I take your coat?' He replied.

The foyer was very elegant, it had been painted white and every surface almost glowed from the reflected light, the floor was a checkerboard of large black and white tiles, with a dark red carpet positioned centrally throughout.

'Are they all here?'

'They have all been waiting in the East wing sir,' Miles continued, 'I'll take you straight through.

'Thank you, oh, and can you make Dr Humboldt here comfortable, see to it that he is well taken care of, and anything he needs is obtained for him immediately.'

'Certainly sir, this way please.'

Hawkins came through the front door as Miles led them all into the property from the foyer.

Throughout the property as they walked it was clearly apparent that the building had always been kept in exemplary order, the marble tiles were clean, and the walls looked as if they had only been painted a few days previous. They followed the hallway for a couple of minutes. There were expensive antique paintings hung along the wall, they passed three low circular white tables as they followed the corridor towards the eastern side of the building. Upon these tables were white busts in the roman style. Numerous doors opened onto this central corridor. Made of a dark brown sturdy wood, they were all closed. On the right, about halfway down a solid wide stairwell gave access to the first floor above. It was made from the same type of wood as all of the interior doors within the property.

They all stopped at a door that Miles quietly opened.

'Here we are Dr Humboldt, this study should be very agreeable, if there is anything else you need please just ring the bell.'

'Thank you, eh, Miles.'

Dr Humboldt went inside; Miles closed the door behind him. Miles then ushered Hawkins and Lord Blessed toward a great pair of white-washed doors at the far end of the corridor.

Opening the doors, Miles announced the guests.

'Gentleman, Lord Blessed and Hawkins Blessed.'

The pair walked into the long east wing room, like all the other rooms within the building on the ground floor, it had white-washed walls, portraits hung upon the walls and the floor was black and white checked marble tiles. On the centre of the far wall was an open fireplace, it was unlit, the ceiling was high, and an expensive looking chandelier bathed a long oval teak table in yellow light, the table was surrounded by ten or eleven gentlemen, all dressed in expensive suits.

'Lord Blessed, a pleasure to see you again.' Said the familiar voice of David Smith.

He was sat at the table, Lord Blessed and Hawkins moved over to the only two empty chairs available at the table, in the centre of which was a silver tray it had two bottles of wine; one white, and one bottle of red. There was also a decanter filled with a brown liquid, one of the men stood and poured two glasses of the brown liquid into some brandy glasses and took them to the new attendees.

'Thank you, well, what have we missed, speak please.' Lord Blessed asked.

'We have an agreement within the fraternity, but will you agree to it?' announced one of the gentlemen sat at the end of the table.

'Come on; out with it, we will see where we go from there.'

'The brotherhood has agreed that we will help you if you agree to a fifty-fifty share of the wealth gained.' Lord Blessed interrupted him as he choked on the swig of brandy he had just taken.

The mason continued 'We can facilitate the wealth gained through a number of channels and from there we can assure that no questions of where or when it came from shall arise.'

'Fifty-fifty, are you nothing but thieves and beggars?' Lord Blessed could clearly feel his blood boiling, the whole venture had cost him considerably already and as far as he could see, these gathered here were going to make immeasurable wealth just for a little bit of money-laundering. A bit of murmuring in the background as Lord Blessed, Hawkins, Sydora and her acolytes conducted an intense and potentially deadly ritual, did not equate to a fifty-fifty share.

'We know you need us Lord Blessed, you would have gone directly to the right-hand path if that was not so,' he continued, 'I am guessing there are sects within the path that you or your people do not trust, and so you have come to us. We want fifty percent.'

Lord Blessed leaned back in his chair, he looked at David Smith.

'And you agree to this David?' He asked.

'They wanted seventy-five!' he said resignedly.

Leaning forward again and putting both his elbows upon the table, Lord Blessed picked up a pen and fiddled with it as he thought of the cost of the deal, at length he said.

'Twenty-five, and I will always funnel through your set up, there are others involved and they require their slice of the pie as well.'

The chief negotiator of the masons now had to think, about the table, gathered were some of the top ranked masons of the United Kingdom, and they were looking at him, some with faces which displayed acceptance, others could clearly be seen showing a more negative attitude towards this figure being presented.

'I will move a little, thirty-five; we will take control of all the financial movement and-,' he paused looking at the gathering, 'and I want full disclosure as to any other projects of this nature with a five percent cut!'

'The wealth we are talking about here is beyond your wildest imaginations; all of you, you cannot understand the gains that are to be had here.'

Lord Blessed looked at them all, slowly pausing at each individual face about the table in turn.

'David, you know you are fucking me over here.' He swore in his public-school accent, it sounded out of place, like the words did not fit his vocabulary.

At length Lord Blessed answered their demand.

'I think it is a bad deal, but in the spirit of cooperation I will agree. Thirty-five percent, all financials in your hands and five percent of any additional ventures of this nature.'

'And finally, there is one last thing we require also,' the head mason announced, 'the final end of the Nihilist.'

'Agreed.' Lord Blessed said.

Lord Blessed then stood up and left the room.

The gathered masons all clapped the conclusion of the meeting, Hawkins, who had been quiet all this time was not really interested, he knew everyone was going to get rich, including himself and so really couldn't see what all the fuss was about. But it did appear to Hawkins that the masons were more than a little happy with the deal they had just achieved.

****

Later that night Lord Blessed sat within a large trophy room at the rear of the property, the room had windows looking out over the grounds on three sides, the view in the summer daytime from here would have been very nice, now, at night all that could be made out was the silhouette of the treeline in the distance.

Inside there were stuffed trophies of a previous owner, grisly badges of pride from a barbaric past, a stuffed lioness stood in the centre of the room upon a brown bear-skin rug, which was stood on the tiled marble floor. There was several busts of various animal heads upon the one wall, in the centre over one glass door that opened out into the rear grounds was a plaque which clearly displayed the mason's symbol of the square and compass displayed together.

Lord Blessed sipped his brandy looking out, he had given away a lot of wealth today, he was not happy about that, the power that came would still be his, sure but he had in the previous half an hour given away possibly billions of dollars' worth of gold and jewels, at least the wisdom of King Solomon would still be his.

The door opened behind Lord Blessed, someone entered behind.

'So finally, you bear the courage to explain to me David.' Lord Blessed said without turning.

'I have searched about the premises for you I assure you, I am sorry for what happened there, nothing I could do.' David said.

'Do you know how much that has cost me?' he asked, 'millions. BILLIONS.' Lord Blessed's voice raised in anger.

'Come on Alfred, you stand to make far more than that, I don't know how much you have given away to others, but you knew they were never going to move easily.'

'Well it is done now, I have been robbed, Vicky has been arranging a place for the final ritual, she has told me that she has the perfect place in mind, she will be contacting them shortly.'

'This is excellent news, it will all be over soon, and we can all count our money, and you will be the richest man upon the planet, and Lord Blessed, you will be the most powerful man on earth!'

Lord Blessed rose from the chair and turned to face David.

'Yes, you are correct, I will be, that does not mean I have to like it and I have not got to this place in my life by throwing money down the back of furniture or lining the pockets needlessly of august organisations like yours.'

'You have a way with words Alfred that must be said but come look at what you have won here today. They will now fall in line, you have bought the freemasons, not one of them will risk losing this lucrative deal.'

'They had better!' Was all that Lord Blessed said?

Lord Blessed did not mention the Nihilist.

****

Later that night Hawkins had walked outside and wandered over to the large converted barn annex that was now a large garage. Inside was a number of nice cars, including his father's Aston Martin. He did not like what had happened over the last week, his life had been relaxed, laid back, but since Gruul had taken him to the place in the woods everything had been turned upside down.

The question that kept going through his head was; is it all worth it? Already Cliff had died just so his father and he could be rich, sure he had not known that Gruul was going to kill him, or that Cliff would push the envelope and attack Gruul; but, since then his view of Gruul had changed. Now Hawkins saw that the thing was actually just a vile little monster, a monster that, to Hawkins own horror, he had nurtured. All those dead cats and birds; he did not like to think about it, but he was in too deep now.

He could only trust his father; he knew what he was doing. Then, when all of this was over, he could sit back and enjoy life again, get back to the way things were, the way they used to be; though in reality, Hawkins was aware that his life would never be the same ever again. He would not be able to lie to himself and deny that any of this had ever happened.

'Son, what is on your mind.' Came the familiar voice of his father from behind.

Hawkins turned.

'Hi Dad, I was just thinking.'

'What were you thinking?'

'Is all of this worth it, I mean we already have all the money we can get. What do we gain?'

'I understand Hawkins, my son, but do not worry, we all have fears, that is natural when stood on the precipice about to dive into the dark hole of greatness. When this is over, we will have anything we could ever want.'

'But Cliff, will there be any others? I don't want anyone else to die.'

'We already discussed Cliff in London; he should not have attacked Gruul. But that is all over now, I'm sure there will be no other, unfortunate casualties,' he then added 'it's nearly over now son!'

Chapter 22

The Book Reads Thus

It had started raining the following day and it wouldn't let up, it was raining hard at that. A north easterly had brought a chilly storm in from northern Europe, the clouds were dark and low, there was a threat that the storm would bring with it thunder and lightning.

Dr Humboldt stood in the orangery watching the storm, he had been studying the grimoire now for what felt like weeks, to him it had been an absolute delight at first, but now he felt an eerie kind of despair. This grimoire was not nice bedtime reading, after the breakthrough, various parts of this dark tome had made themselves known to poor Dr Humboldt's virgin mind. The language in question was a precursor to Greek and shared many characteristics with it. Now he was nearly ready to give his presentation to Lord Blessed, and, leave these mad people that lurked wherever he looked, to their own devices.

He was unsure whether Lord Blessed would be prepared to undertake some of the darker aspects of this ritual that were transcribed in this book, but he planned to be long gone before the answer to that question were to arise. Dr Humboldt would very rarely drink before he began this undertaking, now however he had found solace in bourbon, at this moment he sipped at a double.

The book explained many rituals of different and dark nature, explaining things ranging from the creation of love potions and amulets that brought luck, to communing with the dead and conjuring beings from other planes of existence; other realities.

Once he had deciphered the major points of the language, he had advised Lord Blessed of the different spells and rituals within. Lord Alfred Blessed had insisted that he focus upon a particular ritual, it was a way of opening a portal to a pocket dimension that Lord Blessed referred to as King Solomon's mines, the ritual did not call the destination that, however. Taking another sip, he wondered what may go wrong; was it possible he could be unleashing something on the earth that was not supposed to be here, he did not want to think about it.

He had seen these people here, they were pleasant and friendly enough, but he knew there was a lot at stake, and that he would not just be allowed to leave. Like that girl in Lowestoft, they had hunted her down and brought her back. There was no escape for her, and she had contacts far away from all these people, no he was trapped here, he would need to see this thing through and then just get away when they were busy with the ritual in question. Dr Humboldt just preyed they knew how to deal with anything if it all went wrong?

Finishing his Bourbon, Dr Humboldt headed back to the study. He opened the solid stained wooden door and entered. The room was small and square, no more than five metres by five metres, with a high ceiling, three of the walls were filled with books upon shelving which rose from the floor to the very top of each wall. A large window greedily took up the fourth remaining wall, the heavy curtains were drawn.

The floor was marble tiled in the same manner as the rest of the ground floor. There was a white table with two chairs which dominated the floor space, the only thing upon it was Dr Humboldt's notes that he had been making upon the grimoire and the language within, the magical tome itself and large a selection of pens and crayons. He closed the page he had been working on. He locked the door on the way out and went upstairs to the bedroom he had been using; then he went to bed.

Laying there he could not get to sleep, the thoughts running through his mind; a sacrifice, it just repeated in his mind, every time he neared sleep, it appeared again; a sacrifice and he would be awake again. Then the thunder and lightning began. The storm had threatened to materialise all day but had not dared approach during the daylight hours. Now that night had fell the storm had no such fear. It was a violent storm; ferocious. Dr Humboldt could hear clearly the rain, as it lashed at the one window in his room in a frenzy, trying to get in. Like the rain even feared the lightning, and the deafening thunder that boomed brief moments after each bright, electrical flash.

The storm almost shook the building it was so close, it must have rolled straight over the town of Beccles on its way south. Hawkins knew they left tomorrow, Dr Humboldt would give his presentation then they could get this over and done with. He could then forget about books and rituals and such. Forget about Gruul, get away, maybe the Caribbean, or maybe go live with his sister in Italy? Just get away from all of this, he did not need it and certainly did not want it, he was rich enough already.

David felt guilty that he had not fought harder for a better deal for Lord Blessed, he had already ascertained that the help from Lord Blessed with his career would cease, David was on his own now, a flash lit the room, it was followed by a series of quick flickers and then the roll of the thunder ensued, almost immediately afterwards. He wondered if Lord Blessed would outwardly stymie his career or could it be something far worse, something final? At least it would not be at the Nihilist's hands who was doing the finalising. David eventually drifted into a disturbed restless sleep, interrupted by the angry weather outside.

****

The next morning was bright, the rain had ceased, the clouds had broken up. The storm had drawn out all of the natural smells, outside the property everywhere on the estate had a strong clean smell; of fresh grass and tree sap. Hawkins had awoken early, driven to the local shops and bought some odds and ends. He waved at a gamekeeper who was working by the gate as he arrived back, the gamekeeper waved back in response. Driving up the long twisting approach to the mansion, he spotted the Doctor standing outside, he pulled up next to him and exited the Aston Martin.

'Morning Doc.'

'Hello Hawkins, up early?'

'Yeah, I wanted to get one of those breakfast drinks.'

'Oh, I'm finished by the way, we can be on our way later on today, I've got most of it down, it's not good though, it's really dark.'

Hawkins nodded, he didn't really want to hear any more about this last ritual, he just wanted it over with and then he could make up his mind from there. But, then again, he figured when it was over at least he would be far richer.

'Good, I take it you are coming with us?' Hawkins asked.

'Well no, I have been employed to decipher the book. I planned to get my fee and go back home.'

'Oh, my Dad will be disappointed, you know he likes to look after useful people, and I would imagine he views you as very useful indeed.'

'Well, I don't want to-, I mean I hadn't,' Dr Humboldt stumbled on the words to say, he did not like confrontation, and he felt that he was a bit cornered at the moment, 'I guess we will have to see what happens next.'

They went inside, Miles had been stood by the door, waiting for Dr Humboldt, he opened the door as they climbed the white Corinthian, marble steps toward the main double doors.

'Have you eaten?' Hawkins asked.

'No, I was now going to get breakfast.'

'Ok, I will see you later.' Hawkins headed for the gym in the western wing of the building.

Passing through he spotted a number of different people there, most he recognised as masons who had gathered at the meeting two nights ago, they were friendly enough, but they all seemed to have an air of superiority to them; arrogance he thought. He decided that he did not like it. And so, he did not like them either.

He worked his back and arms in the gym that morning, determined to get some gains, channelling all of the negativity from the last two weeks into raw aggression, it worked. He would always do this if he had a problem, sure it wouldn't get an answer to anything, but the muscle gains could be amazing.

Later Hawkins had showered, cleaned up and went to the same room where the deal had been made, three nights previous. Gathered inside was his father, Dr Humboldt, who currently stood and two of the mason's, David Smith was one, the other person who had been leading the negotiations at the meeting the other night. Hawkins hurriedly sat down, as his father glowered at him, lifting a pen from the paper that he had been writing with.

'I'm sorry Dr Humboldt, please carry on.' Lord Blessed said in his deep voice, clearly irritated by the interruption.

'Err, thank you, sorry, right where was I,' Dr Humboldt thought for a second, regaining his composure, 'yes, the ritual must be undertaken below ground, there are to be a minimum of twelve practitioners, assisting the ritual and a main spellcaster who is known as the foci.'

Lord Blessed continued to write, at the mention of twelve practitioners he looked at the head mason who nodded, he went back to writing.

'There will be a sacrifice to all of the great elements, fire, water, earth, air and a flesh counterpart, of which the dagger used must be drenched in the blood of the moon the night previous.'

'The blood of the moon, this is to happen in two days-time?' The mason said.

'You did not tell me it was to happen in two days.'

'It is time, it waits for none of us,' Lord Blessed said, 'If the book had only been deciphered earlier, you would have had more prior knowledge.'

'Can I continue?' Dr Humboldt asked.

'Yes, yes, go on.' Lord Blessed said, irritably.

'Ok, the blade must be drenched in the blood of the moon, which I guess relates to the blood moon eclipse happening in two days. The sacrifice must be a soul free from lust and pleasure for gold; without dreams of riches.' Dr Humboldt looked at those gathered he was not comfortable with these powerful serious men, none of whom seemed to flinch when the mention of sacrifice entered the conversation, he was worried; he was also trapped, and he knew it.

'The circle must not be broken by flesh other than the sacrifice once the ritual has begun, to do so could have unforeseen consequences; possibly even calamitous.'

Again, none of them budged or moved, they just watched him listening, Lord Blessed had been taking notes at all times.

'A trance-like state must be attained by all those that conduct the ritual, until completion, until the portal is opened, that leads to a reality that consists solely of the gold and riches; within will be found the wealth of all those who have conducted this ritual before, but more than that, the very essence of this dimension is solid gold; it is minable.'

They all started to smile, at this description, the thought that the gains were unending brightened all sat who there. Hawkins could not help but grin either. Riches beyond any scale of thought; wealth unimaginable.

They all clapped.

'Thank you, Dr Humboldt, you have proven why you are top of your field, I thank you for the very hard work you have done here, on behalf of all of us.'

'That's no problem at all Lord Blessed, So, those are the main points, whenever you are ready Lord Blessed. I will take my cheque and leave you all to it.' Dr Humboldt said.

'Not so fast my dear fellow, we need to ensure that it works before we pay you. How will I afford your exceptional fee if there is no riches?'

Dr Humboldt spotted the trap too late.

'But I have done what you have asked, I have deciphered the book, I have translated it for you.'

'And I thank you for that, but as we agreed in London, I would give you the proof that magic exists, and that means, you will be there when the ritual completes. I will give you your handsome ten figure cheque at that very moment,' He paused for effect, a skill he had mastered, 'and not a second beforehand!'

Chapter 23

The Third Seal

There are few things in life so terrible as the fear of letting somebody else down when they need you most. That was the feeling that Craig felt at that time, stood there just looking into those black orb eyes, they blinked sporadically, but there was an intelligence that Craig felt too.

He knew that this was what his Grandfather had done all his life, a sacrifice of all his efforts for a truly altruistic ideal; to protect without any thought of reward, some seals that may never in his lifetime come into any danger. But at the very end of his life they had, a coincidence? Craig was not sure, but whatever; he would take the weight upon his shoulders now, all those lessons made sense, all those enigmatic discussions in the hypothetical. It was for this moment and onwards.

'We will follow you.' He said to the bird, he then turned and went indoors, where Cairo and Matt still stood in the kitchen, watching.

'What happened?' Matt asked as Craig came in.

'They are on our side; they want us to follow them; to stop those people doing; I feel something really bad,' the other two both looked at Craig, he answered their thoughts, 'I think these two have been helping Grandpa all those years, whatever they want us to do, it's important; and probably, very dangerous.'

'Following crows now, and I thought my life could not get any stranger? Where are we going.' Matt asked.

'I don't know, its somewhere rural, but unfortunately crows don't have maps to point things out, but we can follow them, they will fly there.'

'I'll get the car.' And with that Matt had already grasped his keys that hung upon a key-rack by the back door.

They all went outside to Matt's car and got in it, sure enough, the two crows flew overhead in a westerly direction.

'There they go, they are heading toward Oulton Broad.' Cairo said, pointing as the two black birds lazily flew up ahead, Matt started the engine and pulled away.

They made their way through the slow traffic on Normanston Drive, moving whenever the line of traffic moved, stopping whenever the line of traffic stopped. Each time they stopped, the two crows would circle and then land in a tree, on an aerial or chimney pot, but always they were in sight. Finally, they arrived at the roundabout near the train crossing, and as by the law of murphy the gate lights began to flash.

'This is so typical Craig.' Cairo said.

'I know, you could not make it up, whenever you are in a hurry, a bloody train, when are they going to sort out this bleeding road system.' It was a phrase that every driver in Lowestoft had used many times.

'Can we go through the Haddiscoe route?' Matt asked, thinking about pulling a U-turn and driving a different route out of town.

'I think the birds have decided which way we are going, so we are stuck here, I'm afraid.' Craig said resignedly.

After a couple of minutes, the two-box train came sliding in past the crossing from Norwich, it stopped at the adjacent station and then people began to file out, past Matt's stationary car. The gates lifted, and they were making way again. The crows launched high into the air and continued to lead the otherwise blind trio towards the site of the third seal.

****

The Gruul had urged them all to hurry to the last seal as soon as possible, when a demon says as soon as possible, they really mean now or there will be serious repercussions, they do not trouble themselves with laws, remorse or empathy, they are selfish, self-serving things and could kill on a whim at any time.

As demanded by the demon they all made their way back to the Renault parked by the village green, Jay and McVicar were upbeat, did they even know that the third acolyte, Aidan was an insider, a spy? Gabby was not sure, Sydora and the rest of them, especially that vile little monster were fine with yet another death. Gabby did not know where that man stood in the sway of things but, evidently, he wasn't on Sydora's side, or so she claimed on the way back to the Renault. It did not change the fact, she was in terrible danger, and they had decided not to kill her there and then, for a reason.

They got in and started off, Gabby was again flanked on either side by Steve and this woman, Sydora. They made their way through the back roads, towards the last seal, the Gruul was sat in the front, next to Jay who was driving. Occasionally the Gruul would give Jay directions; 'Left here.' Or 'Straight across.' When they reached a roundabout.

They made steady progress heading through Loddon and then toward Bungay, both were small towns in the Norfolk and north Suffolk countryside.

When the Renault finally reached Bungay, they turned onto the back roads, toward the smaller farming villages in the area south and west of the town. They had been driving some time at a hastened pace. The road they followed meandered about, this way then that, fields and farms either side and all around until they reached Flixton. There is an old tavern known as 'The Buck', it had a small aeroplane museum nestled behind it, from the road you can clearly see old aircraft within the field, a Hawker Hunter, a Buccaneer and Lightning are amongst the collection there. They turned off to the left, about two miles further up the road at a village named Wortwell.

'Where are we going?' Gabby asked.

The Gruul looked behind,

'We are nearly there, not long now.' It croaked in its horrid cracked voice.

Gabby sank back into the chair.

Was her fate the same as that other guy? Maybe he would have been able to save her? Is there another spy?

All these questions ran through her mind, she could only pray for a miracle. She saw a sign fly past, it said Homersfield, Gabby had never heard of it, if she escaped, she quickly realised she wouldn't even know what way to run.

'There were no landmarks that she spotted that would easily give her any clue as to how to get back to Bungay, nothing that she would be able to use as a heading, just fields and small wooded copses filled with dark green trees, until they turned into the village, it was just a straight road with cottages on either side of the road.

****

When Matt had finally gotten out of Lowestoft, he put the pedal down, but was soon to discover that the phrase as the crow flies is decidedly accurate, because although Matt's car was far faster than the crows could ever fly, they would never follow the road. They instead crossed directly over the fields, and that meant also that Matt had been led via the back roads, avoiding the quicker Beccles and Bungay route entirely.

'This is crazy, Craig, can you tell them to follow the road or something?' Matt asked, frustrated, he already knew the answer.

'I don't think they would understand Matt; we will just have to follow as best we can, at least they are stopping to let us catch up.'

The car burst out of the back roads, onto the A145, the crows circled briefly overhead then flew over the fields upon the other side.

'Fuck sake, really?' Matt said, clearly frustrated by the meandering route that they took.

'Look over there.' Cairo said, pointing up the road about a hundred metres, a small backroad left the main Beccles to Halesworth route upon the other side. Matt sped down it. It was called Kings Lane according to the sign upon the other side of the road. Another sign a little further on indicating that they were heading toward Redisham. The crows had driven them forward till they emerged out of the farmlands and backroads on the Bungay to Halesworth road; the A144. But again, they didn't stay on it, just cut straight across, disappearing into the back roads once more enroute toward Rumburgh and always onward toward the St Elmham Hamlets.

Clouds started to gather in the sky, as if from out of nowhere, threatening a heavy storm but for now the rain held off. Eventually they pulled up, the two crows swooped toward a larger river, the Waveney, they had been following a small beck that was a tributary to this larger river at a small brook where it joined the faster running body of water. The crows perched upon a tree that overlooked the river, the crows then started to get mad, swooping around in angry diving sweeps, like they were attacking.

'Craig what is going on, what are they doing.' Cairo asked as she strained her eyes to see.

'I think we are too late; look over there.'

Craig pointed, on the far side of the river a group of individuals hurried away across the fields toward a village in the distance on the far side of the river.

They had arrived too late.

****

The Renault stopped in Wortwell; it was close to the main road from Beccles to Diss the A143. The Gruul had taken a roundabout route to disorient any onlookers, to camouflage their destination. They had arrived, just a quick walk down to the river and then the final seal could be sundered.

'Get out quickly, follow me.' The Gruul whispered in its hoarse cracked voice; it had already alighted the vehicle, the others exited the as well and they followed the beast as it quickly loped down a narrow track.

'We must hurry, they are coming.' Was all the Gruul would urge.'

Soon they were crossing fields, making towards the river Waveney, the ground was hard due to the summer weather that had been unusually hot this year, baking the ground. The few storms that had blown through had successfully done little more than run off the desiccated, cracked soil.

Arriving at the river the group quickly arranged themselves upon the bank, hastened by the Gruuls demands. They all concentrated upon the water, focusing their attention upon an unseen seal. The Gruul insisted that it was down there within the depths, the creature was in high spirits because there was not a crow in sight.

Forcing their minds to open the seal was far harder here as there was nothing that could be seen. They all waited for Gabby to be thrown to her fate in the depths. But nothing happened, the ritual was not working.

'Harder, concentrate harder.' Demanded the Gruul, they did as the thing demanded, but evidently for some, this seal was just not going to open. The Gruul looked at each in turn, finally focusing upon one of the acolytes, McVicar who stood beside Gabby.

'Keep trying.' The Gruul repeated, this time as the gathering focused the beast turned and leapt, grasping onto McVicar's body, then with a quick repeated stabbing motion, thrust its dagger-like claws into the acolyte, he died quickly, McVicar uttered a scream that quickly turned into a gurgle as his lungs began to fill with blood. The acolyte had been totally unprepared for the quick and savage attack. Choking upon his own blood as he fell into the swirling river, the Gruul jumped clear. McVicar's corpse was soon enveloped by the waters.

Now as the blood mixed with the waters, a swirling pattern formed in the water that had not been there before, the blood made the whirlpool pattern readily visible to the naked eye. From the depths a sucking sound was briefly heard from below, like a plug had been removed from the bathtub, then the sound went away, carried upon the wind. A circling wind that brought forth storm clouds, conjured from some unseen place out of time and out of synch with our own reality.

Across the river two black specks had arrived upon the horizon, flying upon black wings, the crows were here again, the Gruul figured they were calling allies.

'You stay here, stop them, we are leaving, to complete the ritual.' The Gruul ordered the last acolyte, guessing correctly that this Craig would soon be here, Jay would stop them, or hold them long enough for the Gruul, Sydora, Steve and Gabby to escape.

****

Running over the fields, Craig, Cairo and Matt could clearly see the two birds diving at something ahead, attacking, claw first whoever was there. Craig wondered whether it would be that Gruul beast again? It could not be, he had seen it fall into the air conditioning machinery upon the rooftops, or maybe there was more than one of them? Craig hoped not. They ran across a farmer's field, that was too dry for anything to grow; it waited eagerly for the rains. The crows were obscured by two large twisted oak trees that squatted over the tributary onto the river Waveney.

The crows dived relentlessly and repeatedly at the acolyte as he stood on the far bank, they attacked, scratching at his face and pecking at his eyes. When one swooped down the other prepared for another diving attack, preventing him from concentrating; removing from him any opportunity of creating any magical attack and breaking any concentration that he may try to attain.

Craig burst onto the far bank and saw the stranger stood there throwing his arms up to fend off the incessant and repeated diving crow attacks. Craig then saw the bloody whirlpool within the waters. He knew then also, that this man was one of them, but who was he? Cairo and Matt quickly joined Craig upon the bank, the acolyte seeing the others arrive fled, harried by the crows as he retreated from the riverside.

'Aren't you going to blast him, stop him or something?' Matt asked. Craig began to centre his concentration upon the retreating man, but with the crow's relentless assault, Craig did not want to risk harming them.

'No, the crows will see him off, I am just worried about what has just happened,' he continued, 'I think this all may have been for nothing and I have failed Grandpa!'

Chapter 24

The Legions Gather

The third seal had opened; a deafening clang echoed throughout the underground rocky kingdom prison of Ashtoreth. None there could escape the thunderous clamour; the sound of millions of tons of earth and rock collapsing, falling on each and every side of the steep-sided pit. The pocket dimension had almost been opened back to the earth, and the Dark Princes armies were ready to march forth once more. With so many baying, violent and evil denizens, animosities had already re-emerged within the demonic hordes, eager to harm and slay, they were already flexing their deformed muscles and grinding their hideously sharp teeth.

The moment Aidan's body had been discovered the entire kingdom of Ashtoreth mobilised. The din from the blacksmiths quarter as they sharpened old and crafted new weapons for the armies. Scouts had been sent out; into the outlying tunnels. They had been tasked with finding the portal and not to return until they had found it, upon threat of a slow and painful death. When it was finally reopened, they would be ready to march to freedom. This was the time of Ashtoreth's ascendency, this time he would not fail, this time he would take the Earth for himself.

The third seals opening was announced by a sudden uprush of water which oozed through the rocks toward the west, flowing through the myriad tunnels, washing away anything that wasn't firmly secured, flotsam and jetsam was washed close to Ashtoreth's pocket kingdom and the central caverns. When the waters subsided the bedraggled but very dead body was left within sight of some of Ashtoreth's subordinates.

The scouts climbed over rocks and clambered upon rubble. They searched on high stony plateaus and delved down into low sheer gorges, but it was all initially fruitless. Where there was no way through, they blasted through, where there was no way up, they erected scaffolding. The search would not be a failure, on this occasion they would force through, their epic quest would be a success; and they would be ready.

It was a diminutive creature only known as Yakk that made the crucial breakthrough. Yakk stood under three feet tall, a dirty yellow complexion; Yakk wore nothing other than a ripped, torn and heavily stained smock, it stunk of sweat, urine, faeces and last night's meal. Armed with a small rusty sword. The beast wore a slightly too large metal, conical helm and carried a dented, battered shield. Yakk was almost comical in appearance, but like all of the other denizens that resided here, would not give any quarter in battle, finding glee in pure destruction, purely for destructions sake and was cursed with an evil avarice like all the other demonic creatures that were trapped here. Yakk had been repeatedly bullied by all of those that were of a larger stature. That was the way in this devilish city, that was the order of things, But, like all the others here, Yakk was fanatically loyal to the Dark Prince Ashtoreth.

At the decree to scour this underworld prison for the long-hidden portal, that led to the plane of existence that they had all been ejected from. Yakk had been picked, as had many others search for the portal. All of Ashtoreth's demonic legions both high and low, had at the very least, been trained the rudimental basics of defence, there were some things in the outlying tunnels that were not subservient to the Evil ruler Ashtoreth; things that were here before the demons had been imprisoned. Yakk wanted to find favour with the Dark Prince, whichever demon or creature located the portal would find favour, that would mean power; and the portal meant lots of power.

The tunnel search went on and on, fruitless in endeavour, Yakk was on the verge of giving up. The journey the little demon had made had been far and wide, long had the beast ranged alone through Darkened passages, with only itself for company. It was ill fortune that turned into propitious reward for Yakk. The demon had almost succumbed to an unfortunate rockslide whilst clambering up to a higher previously un-investigated ledge, but it had proved fruitful, the landslide gave Yakk access to the ledge, and it had unveiled a small hidden passage, previously unexplored by others; save the all too common spiders that were everywhere.

Much later, after finding and following the narrow, natural fissure, Yakk arrived at a crack barely large enough for the diminutive creature itself to squeeze through. Most others would never have made it. Heavy-heartedly, Yakk placed the battered shield upon the ground then slowly began to squeeze through; the tight, claustrophobic crack went twenty metres or so. Yakk had contorted its back and the pain was excruciating, but finally the little thing won through and the passage widened upon the other side. Yakk dusted its clothes down and then continued on this ancient and lonely, natural route. The passage was occasionally lit by strange fungus that glowed with soft purple and white colours.

It continued to draw the little demon on for what seemed like many miles, till it finally spat Yakk into a very large cavern. Within the centre stood a great altar and on either side were two immense circular mirrors that faced each other, towering over the altar in between, a film of dust covered everything within the large cavern. Yakk ran over toward the mirrors and altar and began to brush the dust off.

'I've found it, I have found it. Yakk said to itself disbelief in its voice.

'It is the portal; it is the portal!' Yakk exclaimed, his disbelief was followed by a high-pitched squeal. Hopping up and down with glee, a sadistic, selfish glee, revelling in the delight that not only would the rewards be beyond measure, but the carnage could continue once more.

Yakk turned around, first he checked about that there were no other tracks, then the creature decided to hasten back to the tunnels and the Dark Prince. Great reward awaited at the feet of Ashtoreth, maybe a captainship of one of the legions, Yakk hoped and Yakk dreamed.

****

Yakk made it back to Ashtoreth's great and terrible, black walled palace, when the little monster stood at the gates, the two guards initially would not let Yakk through.

'I want to see the master.' Yakk asked the guards.

'He doesn't want to see you, get along, off with you.'

'It is important, I need to see him now.'

'The only way you will see him is on a plate for his dinner.' The second guard stood there, laughed. It was a horrible and malicious laughter, at the firsts jibe.

'Yeah, fuck off whelp.'

They were not going to let Yakk pass, but the little demon did not want to let on why the urge to see the master was there, else they may take the knowledge to Ashtoreth themselves, and gain the favour.

'I must see him; it is more important than either of you.'

They both looked at the small demon stood in front of them, Yakk knew that it was pushing its luck. The two stood in front were both at least twice Yakk's size, there was no going back now.

'Look you little shit, if you don't fuck off, I'm going to poke holes in you till you are empty of blood, then I'll stretch your skin over my shield.'

The other slowly reached down to its sword which was still within its sheaf.

Yakk backed up a little.

'Fine,' Yakk said, 'Ashtoreth, Ashtoreth, Ashtoreth.' The little fiend screamed in its high-pitched voice.

The two guards, advanced toward Yakk.

'Why you little shit, I'm gonna spear ya in the guts.' Said the first guard.

As they advanced, Yakk retreated; still screaming the Dark Lords name at the top of its voice.

The first demon guard jabbed with its spear, which Yakk parried away with the small shield, the other stalked sideways, preparing to attack on Yakk's blind side, it would be brief, Yakk was doomed and Yakk knew it.

****

The ensuing blast swept Yakk clean off its iron shod, booted feet, the stalking sword-armed demon's body was wracked with a blast of dry, sandy air that stripped flesh from bones, penetrating between chain armour rings, and critically damaging skin, eyes and anything else exposed, the first; armed with a spear and shield cowered back; this attack could only have come from the Dark Lords mount.

Above the two that still stood by the towering black barbican gate was the dragon that Ashtoreth would ride to victory; massive scaled claws held firm to the top of the jagged crenelated walls. Its craned neck was ready to send down another blast, if this great and terrible beast was hungry then it would happily hunt, kill and then eat any demon it encountered, the noise had drawn it to investigate. The dragon didn't want to kill the guard, but things can happen when you work on an empty stomach.

'I have found the portal.' Yakk shouted to the dragon-like creature quickly; fearing that the fiery hot sand blast may be aimed at Yakk next. The gigantic beast opened its terrifying maw and exhaled once more, this time the demon guard armed with a spear felt the super-heated sandy blast. Yakk watched as the guard was visibly stripped back to the bone with the abrasive nature of the dragon's lethal breath weapon. The sheer ferocity of the blast was intolerable and Yakk cowered back still further, curling up, waiting for the dragon to finish off poor Yakk next. Instead he felt the ground shake as the enormous creature dropped down beside the little demon. Yakk was picked up by the dragon's mouth, then taken by flight as the giant winged monster launched into the air with a multitude of powerful wingbeats. Thrust forth at the tip of the monsters long scaly nose, Yakk had a clear view of the city below, as they rose higher and higher Yakk could clearly make out all of the other demon-folk busying themselves; readying themselves for when they would emerge forth from this demon-bound prison. Up ahead Yakk could clearly make out the great and terrible palace. Yakk would either feed this magnificent yet terrible beast or meet the Dark Prince and possibly survive; Yakk prayed for the latter.

****

Yakk sat in the centre of the great octagonal hall of the palace, the little demon felt terribly small, impossibly small. The dragon had descended from the large hollow in the palace roof above, dropped Yakk at the foot of Ashtoreth's throne and then stomped over to the large area behind the throne where it always slept.

All things in here were too large for this pitiful little creature, the throne was far too big, the pillars that held the high ceiling up were thicker than the largest trees alive upon the earth today and the engravings of wanton destruction and carnal repugnance that covered all surfaces were of a size that would take the breath away of anybody who were to behold them.

Yakk had never been here before, the lesser whelps had no access to the Dark Prince, so Yakk waited solemnly until finally a large set of double doors opened behind, Yakk dared not to look, it was the Dark Prince Ashtoreth, the waiting was over and now Yakk hoped that the location of the portal would bring favour, it may bring a swift death as well, but there was only one way to find out. Ashtoreth strode to the throne and then sat down. Even when seated the dark prince towered over the diminutive Yakk upon the floor. Yakk looked up; Ashtoreth sat with his serpent staff in hand, laid across his lap.

'So, you have found the portal, whelp.' He said

'I have master.'

'Where is it, you will tell me.' He demanded of Yakk, his voice carried across the chamber, reaching all corners, then returning in echo.

'It lies in the western caverns, far out, but it is hidden beyond a narrow fissure, your excellency.'

'And what do you want for this knowledge, think hard as too much and you will feed the dragon, too little and I will eat you myself.'

Yakk knew that to demand too much would be seen as a threat to Ashtoreth's power but to ask for not enough would be taken as an insult to the Dark Prince's power, such as it is that all demon-kind play evil games with one another.

'I want power like all other demons your excellency, but I would like to command the first legion to leave this rocky prison.'

'Interesting whelp, you want power and the glory of heralding my return to the earth.' His voice carried easily throughout the chamber.

'I have served faithfully your excellency; it is a fitting reward for finding the portal.'

Ashtoreth looked down on the hapless Yakk, if Ashtoreth was to give this great honour, he easily had the magical power to mutate this small demon's form into a killing machine or whatever he determined appropriate, according to whim.

'You will take a mining party to this fissure, you will then lead them to the portal when you return, I will then make up my mind. Remember whelp, my dragon is always hungry.'

'Thank you, your excellency, I will not let you down.'

Yakk said bowing as it retreated, this was a test, whomever returned to give word that the passage was finally clear would reap all of the rewards, Yakk realised that the mining team would all be a lot bigger but if Yakk could just avoid being eaten?

Chapter 25

Too Late

The crows ceased their assault upon the hapless acolyte as he neared the far side of the field; he was in full retreat, they both veered off and up; high into the air, then agilely banking to the right, Craig, Cairo and Matt watched as the birds rapidly disappeared off into the east.

'We must find out where they are going.' Cairo said.

'Can you speak to the crows again, maybe we can get the crows to follow them.' Matt asked.

'I can try but I do not know how to summon them here?'

Craig attempted to summon the birds back to this location; tried to contact them with his mind.

'Help me guys, just concentrate on calling them here.'

They all focused as Craig had asked, trying to reach out to the now distant specks which would soon disappear from view completely. The three friends; though they had been too late to stop the seal being sundered, all had not been lost. They reached out to the flying specks, calling them and slowly the two birds banked right once more, it appeared that they had begun to respond, lazily the two large black birds swept around in a wide arc; they were returning.

The two crows landed in one of the trees by the riverside, their beady black eyes looking down, the larger of the two called.

'Mwawwkk, mwawk, mwawk.'

Almost like the bird asked for orders. Craig quickly pierced the bird's mind with his own, beseeching the bird to follow the acolyte and his friends and then return to Matt's home, and tell them where they have gone to. The bird cocked its head, tilting slightly toward Matt, like it listened to an unheard voice. comprehension dawned within those black beady orbs, then as one; both of the crows leapt into the air, flying off. Back in pursuit of the retreating acolyte who was now departing the field and about to cross into the next.

'Did they understand?' Cairo asked.

'Yes, I think so, they seem to recognise what I am thinking, almost like they are reading my mind at the same time that I read theirs,' Craig looked at Cairo and Matt.

'It's really weird, but it almost feels like they have been doing this sort of thing for years?'

'Well, I hate to break your tender bonding moments Craig, but we better get going, do we know where to go from here?' Matt asked.

'Yes, we'll head back to yours, the crows will return there when they know where those others have gone and from there, we can make our next move.'

They all hastily ran back to Matt's car, he reversed in the road and started back the way they had come, through the back roads. None of them were familiar with the back roads of the area but it felt that the return journey was twice as long.

****

The Renault had started away as soon as the last acolyte had returned, he had several scratches over his face and arms from the dive attacks of the two crows. Running up to the seven-seater the door was quickly flung open from the inside.

'Get in.' Sydora said.

He did as was asked, the door closed, they reversed and then they were speeding away back out of Wortwell the same way they had come in.

'Where are we going to now?' Steve asked.

'We must prepare for the ritual.' The Gruul said in its croaking voice.

'Yes, Victoria was finding an ideal location for the ritual, so we better go and see her!' Sydora said.

'Can I go then?' Gabby asked apprehensively.

'Oh no, no, you have a special purpose,' Sydora replied, 'you are more important than ever, but don't worry, you will be fine.'

The car turned right onto the A143 quickly picking up speed as it headed in the direction of Lowestoft. The traffic moved along in procession as it quickly caught up to a tailback created by a slow-moving tractor. There was a heat-haze up on the road ahead, and the Renault went along irresistibly with the flow, like a stick in the fast running river. Eventually entering Lowestoft from the Somerleyton road. They were quite unaware of the two crows that swooped from tree to tree, close by; watching them from above, shadowing and following them.

By the time they arrived back into Lowestoft, the bulk of the rush hour traffic had left off for the day. Joining the artery roads, making for home; slowing the journey still further, but continually they went east. Finally getting into Lowestoft from Oulton village. The traffic was particularly slow today, there had been a car crash in Oulton Broad and it had slowed the traffic to a snail pace. It took over an hour to fight through and to get to Victoria's office, but by the time they had made the town centre, the bulk of the traffic had gone the other way. The Renault pulled up outside and they all went in to her office apart from the Gruul who remained hidden in the car outside.

'Hello there, Miss Slattery is now closing up for the night, can I take a message?' The receptionist asked as they all entered into the reception area.

'No please tell her that Sydora is here and wishes to see her immediately,' Sydora continued after a brief pause, 'it will not wait.'

'Well, I'm sure-, just then the receptionist was interrupted by the door towards Victoria's office; it opened, and she walked through, stopped as she immediately recognised all of those gathered that stood in the reception, Victoria said to the receptionist.

'It's ok Cheryl, you can go, I will lock up.'

With that the receptionist started collecting her things from the desk quietly.

'Please come this way.' Victoria ushered them all through to her office, they all piled in, the two men stood whilst the two spare chairs were taken by Gabby and Sydora, the office was small and with the five of them in together, it was very cramped. Victoria sat at a large comfortable chair behind the wide wooden desk in the centre of the room. There was a picture of the Queen and Theresa May upon the far wall, a large window stretched the entire length of the north facing wall and there was bookshelves filled with various texts about psychology, socialism economics and the like. These shelves crowded the other two walls and flanked the door.

'Hello everyone, it's good to see you all again, I hope you have all been as busy as I have?' Victoria said as she sat down in her chair.

'I think that rummaging around the summer countryside would be viewed as a lot of fun for some, but it's not really my cup of tea.' Sydora spoke for all of them.

'I have arranged a location that fits all of Lord Blessed's specific requirements, it is south of Halesworth.'

The crows landed upon a lamppost close by, one looked to the other and it flew off, the first stayed and watched for maybe five minutes or more, then that one too sprang into the air and flew south.

****

The crow had landed on the roof, she then glided down onto the small grassy lawn in the back garden at the rear of Matt's flat, walking with that awkward gait that all crows seem to have when on the ground The large black bird made its way about on the lawn, every now and then cocking her head to one side, then she would start poking about with her beak, after worms, spiders or other titbits hidden in the undergrowth. Continually stopping to looking toward the property she was patient, checking the door, to see whether the new master would come out; hopefully with a tasty reward for the endeavours that her and her partner had undertaken. She flew up to the old wooden fence and perched on there, after enjoying a couple of unfortunate insects she had picked up and eaten, she would now wait.

The wait was not too long, birds and animals are blessed with a body clock that seems to be surprisingly accurate, but when she saw Craig's face walk past the kitchen window, she immediately began her cawing call.

'Mwawk, mwawk, mwawk.' With each call she tilted her head low then lifted it to the air, on the third caw the back door opened and out came Craig.

'Hello.' Craig waved.

The bird stirred a little but did not fly off, Craig concentrated and fixed his mind upon the bird, attempting to get a mental image, relaxing himself in stages, allowing the images to come, and they did. He saw the Renault driving into the town centre, then the images as they got out, the clarity that he could see in these images was quite alarming, he could also see the very building they went into.

Craig knew the road in the town centre well, everyone did, it was a busy thoroughfare which led into the high street. He then conveyed a message to the crow perched upon the fence.

'Thank you, that will be all for now.'

The bird just stood there, it cocked his head, then a single word just came repeatedly to his mind.

'Treat, treat, treat!'

'Oh, I see, I will see what I can get.'

Craig went inside and started looking through the cupboards, all he could find was a biscuit tin, of which he took a couple, went back outside and crumbled them about the lawn. The crow flew down and began to peck at the morsels on the ground.

As Craig came back in Cairo approached.

'Where did they go, did you get any answers?' She asked.

'They went to a building right in the centre of town, I think we need to go there.'

Matt entered the kitchen, he turned on the oven.

'Well first we are eating, I'm starving and so must you two be, no excuses.'

Cairo and Craig both looked at Matt, they knew they did not have a lift if he did not eat, they were also both very hungry.

'Okay, you win this one Matt, what are we eating?'

'Yeah seems as you put it so eloquently mate, we will go out later on this evening.'

That evening they all helped Matt cook a delicious casserole, Matt was a good cook, he enjoyed cooking and was always watching the celebrity cooking programs on television, his book collection was in no small part a shrine to the cooks Delia Smith, Jamie Oliver and Gordon Ramsay. They ate and forgot the outside world for a while.

****

The trio left Matt's about an hour after dinner, it was now gone seven O'clock, it was still light, they decided they would keep an eye on the building and make their move from there. The crows could help as well with this, Matt stopped the car outside. The street was empty; other than a single car parked outside, there was a light on in the upstairs office.

'This is the place; I think someone is still here.' Craig said.

'You know that is the Conservative party for Waveney headquarters, don't you?' Matt said.

'Come on, let's see what they know, I think they will be surprised to see us waltz up.'

They got out of Matt's car and went to the door, Craig concentrated briefly upon the lock, the mechanism clicked, he then pushed the door quietly open. They all crept in.

'Quietly, guys.' Craig whispered.

They moved over to the door on the far side of the reception and listened, somewhere inside they could hear a woman talking, though they were unable to make out clearly what was being said, it seemed as though she was talking on a phone.

'Let's go.' Craig whispered once more, his voice barely audible, they sneaked through the door, as it closed it made a slight creaking noise, they stopped in their tracks, Craig thought he could hear his own breathing so loudly that everyone would be able to hear it. Nothing happened, aside from the faint discussion now audible from a room up the stairs, they crept towards the telephone conversation in the room ahead.

At the door, Craig stopped again, it seemed that there was only one person in the room, he prepared momentarily waiting for her conversation to end, then once she hung up, he then barged the door with a solid left shoulder, it flew open wide, catching Victoria Slattery totally unprepared, she spun around sheer fright within her eyes, she was trapped.

'What do you want, go away or I'll call the police!' She said, the words lacked force due to the shock of being startled.

'Sleep!' Craig said with a strange, almost hypnotic lilt in his voice.

Immediately, Victoria slumped to the ground.

'What have you done Craig; she is our MP?' Cairo said.

'It's alright she is asleep, I think we will need to question her, to find out what is going on!'

'Where though?' Matt asked.

Craig pointed to the other side of the road to a big square building, it was the local telephone exchange, built with three stories it was a bland ugly building. Craig had worked on the second floor for a national survey company in his first job after leaving school, when the company had moved to another town, he had then found work at the Hoseasons call centre.

****

In the early hours the rain began to fall, highlighted by the flashes of occasional lightning which would always be accompanied moments later by a blast of rolling thunder. At length Victoria started to come back to consciousness. Taking stock of her surroundings she saw Craig, Cairo and Matt, all facing her, there was dim orange street lighting creeping through from some long windows, half covered with damaged and dishevelled blinds. The room was very long, maybe sixty metres, there was a large number of partitions, each with a wooden computer desk set out in groups. It was a call centre Victoria realised, though there were no computers in any of the stalls; she figured she was just across the road from her office on Surrey Street.

'What do you want?' Victoria asked.

Craig stood up and walked closer.

'We want to know what you and your friends are up to.'

'What do you think you will get by kidnapping me; torturing me? I won't talk.'

'That's not as far as your pals wanted to go on me, they were happy to settle on killing me.' Cairo said, as she leant back on one of the desks with her arms crossed.

'No, we will not be so violent, I am just going to read your memory and then wipe this whole incident from it. Thanks to your friends I have started to realise just how powerful this gift can be!'

'You will not get away with this.' Victoria said.

'But you won't remember, so maybe we will. Hold her.'

Cairo and Matt grabbed hold of Victoria, she struggled but thankfully was not nearly strong enough to fight the two of them off, Craig just stared at her.

'Tell me where you are going next… Tell me.'

He stared directly into her big blue eyes, she fought the intrusion, it felt uncomfortable, a mild thumping feeling, almost like her brain had grown within and was straining in the cramped conditions within her skull.

'Forget us, forget how you got here…… And now, Sleep'

With that she slumped, she struggled against Matt and Cairo and sagged in their grip.

'Got it?' Cairo asked.

'We've got it!' Craig answered.

Chapter 26

The Discovery

The Nihilist had been busy, he felt that he had been left increasingly out in the dark, he was just sat about waiting at the manor. He knew this Gruul creature was up to something and he had decided he would try to find out more. They had been due to come back but were now long overdue; grudgingly he re-entered the Gruul's lair.

Inside it was exactly as he had left it, a mess, a smelly mess, he walked over to the bookshelves, looking through the various titles, most he could not read, they all seemed to be written in many different languages, none of which he could understand. Slipping one out at random from the shelf; he opened it, the words were illegible, littered all about the flowing alien script were pen and ink sketches of various flowers and herbs, alongside these sketches were lots of little imp-like creatures, some with insect-like wings, others wearing chain armour, carrying shields and weapons. The Nihilist could not name any of the plants inside, flicking through the pages further, he decided there was nothing here he could learn.

He continued along the shelf further, every time a car went past outside, he would look up to the bay window that faced the short drive, but no Renault pulled up into the driveway.

The next book he slipped from its nestled spot within the packed shelf was older, again written in a different language though still incomprehensible, he was not sure, but he thought it maybe Hebrew. Flicking through the pages, the Nihilist immediately realised that the book contained some kind of encyclopaedic descriptive of creatures, monsters and the like.

It was beautifully illustrated, whether it was some long dead author's attempts at naming imaginary monsters in the night he was not sure, before he had met the Gruul he would have said so immediately, but now, that was not so sure. Another car went by, he looked up, it was not the others return; the Nihilist continued. He went back to flicking through and scanning this interesting bestiary.

He then wondered whether, the Gruul's race was maybe listed in this tome. Looking through, he was amazed at the lifelike pictures of things that just should not be in existence, things that walked on two legs, four, winged beasts, and spider-like creatures, but all were in this book, which was in the possession of this specific creature, this Gruul, the Nihilist wondered whether all these things really existed; somehow in the back of his mind now, he knew they did, somewhere, somewhen.

The next few pages he went through were liberally sprinkled with a myriad mix of strange monsters, some beautiful and amazing, others grotesque and despicable. Toward the rear of the book he found a page with a picture that looked similar to the Gruul, there was five other creatures upon the two facing pages, they were all different from one another, the centre creature looked like it was some hideous cross between a slug or snail and a malformed human, beside it was a dark red skinned creature, whose two arms ended in plated crab-like claws, covered all over its body with a great number of horny protrusions. At the far end of the illustrations that could easily have been the Gruul.

It was smaller than the rest, it had the same goblinoid look with the same bowlegs as the Gruul did and was covered in the same course thick black hairs. Then the Nihilist realised they all held a staff similar in appearance to the one he had spotted in the creature's nest, he looked over to it, nothing had changed around the chair and no eyes peered at him from within.

Checking the window again, he went back to looking at the staff in the illustration, then checking the video he had made earlier, they were the same, this was probably the Gruul pictured in a book about demons, the Nihilist wondered why the little creature would be referenced in such an old book. At length he continued, flicking further through the last few pages of this old tome, the last couple of pages were interesting, they seemed to detail a large human-like creature wearing a crown, it sat upon a dragon-like beast with a staff carved into the likeness of a serpent. Thoughtfully he slipped the book back into its niche.

The Nihilist continued further along the titles upon the bookshelf, slipping another out, again he could not read it, but this one had no illustrations, after flicking through to the end he put it back. He looked at a couple of other tomes sliding them out, but with much the same results, so he put them back.

The Nihilist stood back taking in the whole of the book shelf once again, it was then that he noticed a space where a book was missing upon the shelf. He looked about the room for this elusive book, maybe this one would have the key to unlock this beastly and enigmatic creature?

Scanning the entirety of the room again, this time he got results, on the chair in the niche made by the bay window was two books, a very old thick text, leather bound with the title in gold leaf and a large modern ordnance survey map book in softback of the United Kingdom. They looked like they had recently been read.

Glancing out of the window, a car pulled up at the junction outside, the Nihilist quickly took the two books and sat down near the door, it was practically the only part of the floor that did not have broken toys, dirty clothes or some other unsavoury items strewn about, or the door would have jammed.

Flicking through the map book first he discovered lots of scribbles and notes within. He thumbed through the pages until he reached East Anglia, there was notes written in an alien dialect filled with illegible symbols and glyph's, but what intrigued the Nihilist most was the triangle drawn between three points, one went to a wood close by; it was called Mutford wood, the second point was very near a small village named Claxton and the third terminated at a point between two villages called Wortwell and Mendham.

The other maps within the book had been scribbled all over, strange notes in the devilish dialect, he had never seen before. He lifted the other leather-bound tome and then quickly looked out of the window again, no sign of the returning group yet so slipping back by the door the Nihilist studied the pages. It was beautifully illustrated like the others but this one was full colour, and it had been preserved beautifully. The book was written in the Latin alphabet, in a medieval

French he surmised. His ability to read French was terrible, and something that looked as though it had been written about two to three hundred years ago would be simply impossible, he opted to look at the pictures for any clues as to what the text was about and why it was evidently related to these seals that Gruul had had everyone running around the East Anglian countryside for.

After twenty minutes of looking through the tome, he came to a section that piqued his interest, there was a map of what looked like England long ago, when it was still a connected part of Europe, when the Doggerland existed. The Doggerland extended from what is now Holland to England before the sea enveloped it over eight thousand years ago.

The map had some notes that Gruul had probably written going by the alien characters which aped some of the eerie writings here and in the other books he had looked at, but also a triangle which could quite easily have been this area.

The Nihilist's mobile phone started to quietly vibrate inside his pocket, he retrieved it from his pocket; it was Lord Blessed, he answered.

'Hi, Lord Blessed. To what do I owe this pleasure?'

'I need you to come to Heveningham Hall,' Lord Blessed said, 'they are expecting you later, please check that our rooms are ready for when I arrive.'

'Sure, but Lord Blessed there is something I really think I should let you know about the little goblin thing-'

'It can wait, this is more important, I'll see you there in a few days.'

The phone went dead.

****

The Renault people carrier turned into the short drive, the Nihilist in the blue BMW was long gone by now, the occupants all piled out heading in via the front door. Inside and Steve immediately headed for the kitchen, to fill the kettle and make drinks for everybody. Gabby looked for ways of escape but wherever she went it seemed that there was somebody close by; easily within arms-reach of her, Sydora and the acolyte Jay took Gabby into the living room. The Gruul hastened into its room to the right of the front door, closing the door quickly behind.

The sound of the kettle gently warming water came through into the living room, increasing in intensity as it gradually boiled.

'When are we going to this Heveningham hall place?' Jay asked. He was tall and powerfully built, intelligent, with blonde hair and brown eyes, he had come from a family that had been tied to the right-hand path for a long time; many generations before him, when a car crash took both of his parents, he fled to the left-hand path, the loss had touched him; left him empty deep inside. Now he was devoid of compassion for others as there was nothing he could have done. He blamed the universe, and so he had slowly studied the darker arts of magic, dabbling at first. But the lure of unrestricted power eventually took hold of his soul, now he had a powerful ally in the dark powers of magic.

'We go as soon as we get another call from Lord Blessed.'

Lord Blessed had called as they were on their way back to the Manor, he had advised them to wait in Lowestoft till he called them with instructions; they were then to go to this Heveningham hall. Currently he had sent the Nihilist to inspect it and prepare rooms for them all.

'When will that be, I hate waiting.'

Steve came through, carrying an oval tray filled with coffees and teas, a sugar pot and a milk bottle.

'Help yourself to milk and sugar.'

They all took a cup, apart from Gabby, she just sat there, looking at Steve. She noticed the way that he only had eyes for Sydora, the infatuation was clearly visible, it made her feel a little sick. Sitting back into the comfortable seats around the large tasteful living room, they relaxed. Steve turned on the television, the weather lady was announcing the weather, tonight a freak storm was showing, it looked like it would last for the next few days at the very least. She said it would very likely be torrential and prolonged.

'Oh, that is just great, did Blessed say whether this ritual was going to be undertaken inside or out?'

'He didn't say, I just hope it is inside, that does not look good.'

'Could it have anything to do with Gruul and these seals we have been opening?' Steve asked.

'Don't be stupid, that would have nothing to do with it, get back to flicking cards with your mind.' Jay said sarcastically.

He was not a fan of giving people access to magic without the proper checks, some people would likely be a danger to themselves or to any others around them.

'He's ok Jay, leave him alone,' Sydora said, 'Steve, the seals we have opened will just help the incantation, we have unlocked ley lines, they will empower the magic during the casting of the ritual, that is all. They are nothing to do with the weather.' She eased Steve's apprehension and his ego, but not her own.

****

The Gruul closed the door behind as it entered its lair, snuffling around, instantly it picked up the scent of the tall one's after-shave, he had entered whilst they had been away. The beast stumbled quickly to its nest behind the sofa and climbed in, feeling for its staff, there it was. The little monster then clambered back out, extricating the staff with it, lovingly, it rubbed the cold metal haft, then looking around for evidence of what this Nihilist had been doing in here and just what if anything, he may have discovered.

The Gruul sniffed and snuffled about the room climbing over the piles of rubbish that were littered about, he found where the Nihilist had sat, but then continued, he had been to the book shelves. There was not much sign of disturbance about the room, but the book shelf had been disturbed, the thin covering of dust all about the large unit had been disturbed around three or four different books. The Gruul quickly sniffed close at them, they had the Nihilists scent all over them. The books themselves would not give away too much information, after all there was very few people on this planet that could actually read them. The Gruul then remembered what he had been reading, turning quickly, the two books were upon the settee as before, scrambling over to them the Gruul sniffed at them voraciously taking in all the tiny air particles; greedily checking them for signs of the Nihilists presence. He had looked at them!

Chapter 27

Dimensional Alignment

That night the storm clouds gathered, coalescing upon the East Anglian countryside; a dark sponge soaking the night-time stars one at a time. The clouds were heavy and very dark, as they expanded and rolled over the land, looking for something, covering the earth, relentlessly.

The storm brought rain that would not abate, a relentless rain that lashed at windows and whipped with the wind, it was countrywide, and it was unexpected, coming from nowhere; but there was a heat in the air as well, stifling, humid and close; a closeness that was palpable, that closeness made sleep almost impossible. If and when you finally had found some sleep, a blast of thunder would shock you back to wakeful consciousness.

The thunder and lightning attacked the earth, like nature had finally had enough, jabbing the ground with electrical attacks, the sound of a far off fire engines sirens, hurrying towards an emergency could be heard in the distance; to put out a fire could be heard far away, but the sky had no pity, the assault from the clouds continued regardless.

Not all things hid away from this terrible freak storm; there are other creatures on the earth that are not native here, trapped in ages long past, but defied leaving by our laws of physics. Some of those things revel in the closeness of the other dimensions, and those same things had emerged tonight.

Revelling in the agitation caused by the friction of these different realities as they interacted violently with one another, they knew that gaps in existence could soon appear; to creatures not of this dimension they could feel the dimensional shift like we could feel a change of wind direction upon our faces. The few of these beasts that could control magic and an even smaller minority which of those that were highly skilled enough would attempt to contact their home planes of existence, praying that this portal that the arcane storm heralded would soon open, would lead to their respective reality.

****

There was another that watched the storm excitedly, in an overly warm room in the suburbs of Pakefield, it had dragged out its dirty rags and retrieved its ancient ornate metallic staff. The Gruul now sat in a hastily cleared space upon the floor of its room, eyes closed as it whined at an eerily high pitch. The noise was disturbing to all those in the house, but none would dare enter the room. The flashes of lightning would briefly illuminate the messy room with this lonely, entranced figure sat within the centre.

The Gruul's call was not for humanity however, or for any creature native to the earth either for that matter, this was a call to prepare for the re-emergence of an ancient planar superpower, the arrival of Ashtoreth. Slowly things were creeping from their crevices about the world, hearing this call, on top of this unearthly storm, the call became irresistible.

'Hear me, Gruul... Hear me!'

It broke Gruul's concentration, a voice that it had not heard in so very, very long, came into its mind, as clear as if spoken within this same four walled room.

'Hear me Gruul, Hear me!'

Again, there it was, a calling from across the planar boundaries. The Gruul stopped whining, then started to listen, slowly more words formed within its twisted mind.

'Gruul, it is I Shimozel, can you hear me?'

The Gruul slowly answered.

'Yes Shimozel, I hear you.'

'The seals are being broken; communication is possible between us finally.'

'I have found, and sundered the seals, Shimozel.'

'We have found the portal on this side, even now we clear the way to march forth once more!'

'This is excellent, it is only a matter of days till the final ritual begins, the duped are anointing the blade; we will not fail!'

'Do the duped suspect?' the eerie voice crept into the Gruul's head with ease now, questions and answers defying time and space, floating through the dimensions.

'They suspect nothing, I allowed the duped to discover the deceitful book of riches, they think they will be rich beyond their wildest imaginings.'

'Once again, greed becomes one of our greatest weapons,

'There is one other problem this side.' The Gruul said aloud.

'What-tell all, is it in your power to deal with

'I am currently taking steps. The grandsire of the seal guardian is strong in power and has quickly developed his skill with the gift.'

'What is your plan?'

'The power of the planar storm has awoken many forgotten things.'

'Is there any that may be used to nullify this…. Problem?'

'I think so, I am currently calling out to the things that have awoken, we will see what answers the summons?'

This is Marvellous Gruul, you have done well, the Master will be very pleased, we will see you, soon, very soon!'

The thoughts trailed off, like they had been blown away by the raging, angry storm outside.

The Gruul produced a vicious and devious smile, it had been hiding for centuries, now it appeared because demon-kind would finally be unstoppable, the world at large was totally unaware of their impending return, and that meant they would also be totally unprepared. The vile centuries long plan of a diminutive demon had come to this nexus point, to this moment, the only possible thorn in the Gruuls plans was a man named Craig.

With the storm though came other possible allies; trapped on this plane of existence could maybe be induced to stop the guardian's grandson. The Gruul began the onerous haunting whine again.

****

Sydora had not been able to sleep, after love-making, Steve had quickly fallen asleep. She now stood naked at the blinds, looking out at the lashing rain as it whipped at the windows and created rippling patterns on the street below. The streetlights bathed the road in orange light.

Occasionally a blast of brilliant white light would momentarily illuminate the scene from a speeding car or flickering electrical flashes from the storm above would briefly strobe the street. Sydora felt the closeness of the worlds, but she did not know why, her skill with magic; with long years of study and practise had attuned her senses and she had become sensitive to the planar movement as a result, but this felt heavy, like a weight on her shoulders as if someone else's hand pushed down forcefully upon her back.

Then the Whining began, at first, she thought it was the wind affecting an aerial or a loose cable, but as she listened more attentively, she realised this was not so, it came from downstairs. She retrieved her purple silk shift from the floor and slipped it on, then quietly she stalked out of the bedroom door. Sydora had dealt with demon-kind many times through ritual, though never in the flesh.

Her many dealings using blood magic had taught her to give them a healthy respect when it came to treachery. Any deal they wanted to sign, usually came with a very heavy price, some would say dealing with demons cost you your soul; often they were correct.

She crept down the stairs and the whining sound got louder, Sydora was correct; it was coming from the glass door that was the Gruul's lair, she slipped up beside it and listened. For long moments the eerie howling, whining sound emanated from within, was it calling to others, or in pain? She was not sure, she just listened to the awful sound that was coming from within, then it abruptly stopped.

She was about to creep back up to bed when she heard Gruul begin to speak in its cracked and croaking voice. She could only hear what Gruul said but the monster was talking to something or someone, but the language was not one she had ever heard before, she quickly realised that Gruul was in conversation with others of its kind. A quick succession of flashes lit the hallway briefly, then plunged it into a deeper darkness than before, the thunder rolled in deafeningly loud and close. More of the garbled speech came from within. Then the one-sided conversation ended. The Gruul started to whine once more, she listened for a while longer but Gruul did not resume the conversation, at length she crept back upstairs and slipped back into bed beside Steve.

****

Inside a wood just to the south of Lowestoft; nestled between the A12 Ipswich road and the B1127 a creature about the same size as a large badger lifted its ears to the air, through the torrents of rain that repeatedly battered the trees within, it could clearly make out the high-pitched sound. The rain ran down in rivulets from its smooth flanks, well developed muscles were taut over its entire body, the beast had two tusks that protruded out from its lower jaw, the creatures mouth opened vertically with no lips, multiple rows of jagged, sharp and wicked teeth that were clearly visible. The length of its spine was protected with a series of shield-like carapace plates.

It was an abomination from another place, trapped here, now it had awakened and would soon feed on whatever it could get its infernal jaws around.

It sniffed the air attempting to discern where and whence this call in the only language it would understand came from. Slowly it walked to the edge of the wood, padding through the sodden wet ground as it was batted relentlessly by the strong gusts of wind and the pounding watery deluge.

'All hear my Call, I am the Gruul and my message is clear. Hunt down the Grandson, he bears the mark of combat with me, know my thoughts and know my mind, hunt him down and extinct his line!'

An image appeared within the beast's terrible demonic mind, an image of Craig, the creature's whole being became fixated with this image, an intense desire to rend and tear, to gore and bite. The monster slowly left the wood, walking onto the field that separated the woods from the main A12.

Something else heard the summons also, within Lowestoft, an old church nestles upon the Pakefield cliffs, built in the Norman manner of churches. Within this solemn place, another creature standing in the shape of man left the graveyard, it had been here so long waiting for a summons to the world, this creature had a mind far superior to that of the badger-like thing, however. This possessed a malice that was matched with intelligence. It was tall well-built and wore a dirty dark green trench coat, that looked not out of place in the 1930's, though now it was stained with mud and dirt, underneath he wore a black polo neck jumper, black jeans and a pair of worn army boots. It came out of the graveyard and turned left, following the coastal path out of town, south.

It had once been human and was once called Dietrich but through the use of a forbidden ritual undertaken at the time of death, he had cheated the grave, now Dietrich stalked at night and thirsted for the warm taste of blood, feeding on the occasional drunk individual that would pass by and the late night dog walker, he did not kill, the creature had lived here since the Napoleonic wars had ended, undisturbed, now this summons was irresistible, he could not help but heed the Gruul's call, such was the power that the Gruul commanded.

****

In another part of town, a solitary person stirred. The storm that raged outside, it had brought her back to consciousness. Her thoughts raced through her mind, where was she, how had she got here, she then remembered, Craig's group had burst in and taken her to this place, the call centre above the telephone exchange upon the other side of the street from her office.

Victoria got herself up off the carpet-tiled floor, dusted herself off and then started looking for a way out of the building. After a couple of minutes she had found a double doorway that led to a solid set of concrete stairs which went up and down, there was a window that was being battered continually by the rain storm, she went down the stairs and came to a long hallway, a flash of lightning briefly lit the area, plunging it back into a gloom, the only light shed was from a green fire escape sign. There was a number of doors from this hall, but the one that announced that it was a fire exit was the one she went toward, getting to it she was able to activate the locking release system from the inside, she walked into a small foyer, and with the same system upon the front door she was soon out onto the rain-drenched Lowestoft street.

The rain was twice as bad when she stood in it as when she had watched it lash upon the large window inside the building. Stood upon the front steps she was instantly drenched. Gathering her sense's, she ran through the driving rain back to her office, the light was still on inside. Victoria was too occupied to look up to the ominous billowing clouds, dark greys and deep purple notes to them, as she dashed through the terrible weather. Tinged by the light pollution from below, it was a haunting freakish scene. But she was quickly out of the rain and ran up to her office; she collected her phone, turned off the light and left. On her way through the reception she grabbed a rain coat that hung upon a rack behind the desk and left. Locking the door on the way out, then quickly making the short distance to her car parked outside.

Victoria started the engine and pulled away, as she did, she called Lord Blessed on loud speaker.

'Hello who is this do you know what time it is?' he said.

'Lord Blessed it is Vicki, we have another problem.'

Chapter 28

The Car Accident

The storm could be felt all over East Anglia, it did not move; it had just settled there, slowly rotating over a vast area of England and north western Europe. Craig, Matt and Cairo had all headed back to Matt's, now their impromptu base of operations, before the storm had come in. They were all unaware that it could have anything to do the Gruul, and its accomplices.

They needed to plan a way to stop this scheme that the Gruul had set in motion from happening. They did not like the idea of having to go out in the monster storm, but they did not like the idea of hanging back either.

'This storm does not look like it is going to clear off any time soon; and besides, Cairo doesn't want to get her hair wet!' Matt joked.

'Don't blame me Matt, you're the one who is spending the most time pampering yourself after a shower.' Cairo retorted.

'I don't think it is going to wait for us, if google maps is correct this Heveningham Hall is tucked away in the middle of nowhere and besides I don't think Gruul will be hanging about either.' Craig said.

'Can we stay at this place?' Matt asked,

'I don't think so, that Victoria woman has contacts there, they are staying as guests, I do not think this hall takes paying guests, they have booked for tomorrow and the following day. My guess would be for us to travel down there, book into a cheap hotel in Halesworth, then just keep an eye on the place.'

'I will make some calls.' Matt said, pulling out his mobile phone.

'Though I would like to go now as well Craig, I just do not think there is anything to be gained by going straight away. Let Matt get us some rooms close by, we can go tomorrow; early,' she continued, 'they will not be going anywhere.'

Reluctantly Craig agreed, that night they all tried to get as much sleep as the storm would allow, but the constant howling of the wind and a persistent knocking sound of a nearby sign, battering upon a wall, prevented any but the heaviest sleeper from slumber.

****

The storm raged through the night, and when the dark went, the storm stayed, if it looked ominous and foreboding in the dark, with the coming of daylight it was truly terrifying, the clouds were thick, and had been tinged with a ghastly purple aura. The rain fell heavy still and the drains in countless places were backed up, many roads were flooded and the rain-water ran freely down the streets and avenues.

Matt had booked two rooms in a hotel in central Halesworth, it was called the Angel, it stood at one end of the quaint, pedestrianised town centre. It had been a central focal point of the town since the sixteenth century, inside it had a vibrant atmosphere. Being one of the two primary places to go in Halesworth on a night out without leaving the town.

They all piled into Matt's Black Ford, stopping off at Cairo's to pick up some clothes and then heading south, out of Lowestoft, towards Halesworth on the A12 London Road. They had packed light, determining that they wouldn't need too much, taking only enough clothes for a couple of days, and left very early, hoping to avoid all unnecessary traffic.

The purple tinged clouds rippled and billowed unnaturally, at all times tipping millions of gallons of rainwater down upon the earth; the lightning had not given up either and the roads were choked to overflowing from the continuous irresistible deluge.

'Shit, this isn't going to stop is it.' Cairo said as they followed a lorry towards the Kessingland bypass.

'No, I'm thinking that it may never stop, it's just going to get worse.' Matt said.

'I am beginning to get a bad feeling about this, look at the colour of those clouds, I've never seen clouds that colour before.'

They all looked at the lively agitated sky. Craig turned on the radio, hoping to get the local weather report, but all that came through was static, he changed the channel, static again, flicking through all of the pre-set channels; there was nothing but crackling white noise.

'That's not good; either we have a naff aerial, or this storm is affecting the radio?' Craig said.

'I suspect I know which.' Matt said.

The lorry went around the roundabout and headed onto the bypass, Matt followed behind road, then accelerated as he aimed the car at the inside lane of the dual carriageway. Matt hurtled down the two-lane road, no other cars were on it, they quickly chewed up the length of the road. Matt overtook the lorry long before reaching the roundabout at the far end. Leaving the bypass and the lorry behind. The lorry had given them plenty of space to increase their pace and Matt was quite happy to do so. All the while Matt's wiper blades were fighting unsuccessfully to keep the windscreen free from rain.

'Here we go, we've got loads of clear road.' Matt said.

They sped along for another five minutes coming close to Benacre, when Cairo shouted watch that dog. The rain did not obscure Matt's view to the point that he could not see the dog. Matt swerved to miss the sprinting creature as it came across the road, steering successfully to avoid it, but the creature changed its angle of advance and increased its pace.

'It's charging at us.' Cairo said.

'Oh god look at it, it's no dog!' Matt said as he attempted to evade unsuccessfully the now all too obvious monstrous quadruped.

Thump!

The black Ford Fiesta caught the charging beast as Matt attempted to avoid it. But doing in so the car lost all grip; Matt was helpless as the vehicle aqua planed off the road, plunging down the ditch on the other side of the verge.

The car rolled over and over, as it slid down into the narrow irrigation ditch. they were all butted around, saved from instant fatal injury only by the seatbelts that they were all thankfully wearing. Earth became grey sky and grey sky became earth again, as the car rolled violently to a stop. The windscreen cracked and shattered, falling in covering all of the occupants in glass. The car had finally wedged itself between the fence on the other side and the bottom of the water filled irrigation ditch, the roof had partially collapsed in upon itself.

****

Cairo recovered from the accident first, the way the car had left the road she had been kept out of the water, she could see that Matt was partly submerged, luckily his head was above water, his seat had evidently broke from the floor during the crash, and had kept him safe from drowning, he was not conscious and not responding however. she was not sure exactly what had just happened, her mind was confused, she turned to look to the back seats of the car.

'Craig are you ok, Matt, Matt can you hear me?' She called panic-stricken.

Matt did not respond, but she could hear the sound of Craig stirring behind.

'Craig, I think Matt is hurt pretty bad are you okay?'

'What happened?' Was all Craig could find to say.

'We crashed, something ran at the car, Matt swerved to avoid it, a dog or something.' Cairo said.

'Aarrggh.' Matt said as he slowly came to.

'Matt are you alright.' Cairo asked.

'Over the- argh moon Cairo. No, I think I have hurt my leg, it hurts really bad.' Matt said through clenched teeth, clearly in a lot of pain.

'I think I can get out ok, I will call an ambulance.' Craig said this as he opened the passenger's side door that now would open vertically if at all, it still opened and wasn't jammed; he clambered out.

'I can get out too.' Cairo said, she managed to squeeze through the shattered front windscreen, Craig help me get Matt., Craig hopped down onto the bonnet and helped grab hold of one his arms.

'Matt, undo your seat belt, we can get you out.' Cairo said.

Matt depressed the release button and the seat belt slackened.

'Right be careful guys.' Matt said.

They pulled him out slowly, with much wincing and accidental bumps, they had gotten him free as well.

'I'll call an ambulance, Craig you go ahead, I'll call you, I am going to stay with Matt.'

'Are you sure, I mean, aren't we stronger together?'

'Craig if what you said about this Gruul thing is true, then we cannot risk them being successful, you need to go now!'

With that Craig called a taxi as Cairo called an ambulance, none of them noticed the mauled creature limping away from the front of the car, from where the impact had dragged it too into the ditch, and where now it was slowly retreating, attempting to get out, so that it may heal and then attempt once again to kill this human, so single minded was the image placed inside its head by the Gruul, the possibly fatal injury that it had sustained in the crash would not stop it from this forcibly imposed purpose.

They all waited for about ten minutes; the taxi pulled up first.

'I'll see you two later, Cairo look after him.'

'I will Craig, I'll get to you as soon as I can.'

Craig got in.

'Alright mate, looks nasty, what happened?' the taxi driver asked. Craig lied that he lived nearby, had heard the accident and came to help, advising that an ambulance was on its way, as they made off, the tell-tale blue flashing emergency lights were coming from Lowestoft, it was the police, an ambulance would not be far behind.

'Where to anyway mate.' The taxi driver asked in a broad Suffolk accent.

'Err, Halesworth, the Angel inn, please.' Craig said as he looked out of the rear windscreen.

****

None had noticed the lone figure that watched from two hundred metres down the road, stood in a dirty dark green trench coat, polo neck jumper and army boots. But he had watched the whole episode, he let the taxi drive away and waited as the monstrous badger-like creature limped closer. The creature got close and he lifted it easily out of the ditch, he then carried it quickly across the road, and through a gap in the hedge upon the other side of the highway. He laid the creature on the ground and looked at its wounds, they were grievous but not fatal, the creature's shoulder had been heavily dislocated, and the front right foreleg was broken, with a nasty tear to the leathery skin that ran the length of the beast's flank. He decided he would need to take time to heal this creature. His powers could mend and twist flesh, mutate it, such were his abilities with magic. He gathered up the creature and headed for the woods upon the far side of the field, unseen as the torrential rainstorm concealed Dietrich's retreat with the injured creature.

The blue lights, flickered on the roadside, a police car and an ambulance had arrived, the two creatures had made it to the safety of the dark wood that was shrouded in the murky deluge unnoticed.

Cairo and Matt were quickly taken into the ambulance, it was confirmed that Matt had probably broken his leg, the police asked some basic questions, took a breath test, then let them go together to the James Paget hospital, north of Lowestoft.

Cairo and Matt hoped that Craig would be ok alone.

'As soon as we get to the hospital, you can go Cairo, he may need you, I'll be okay.'

'First we will make sure you are ok, then I will go and help him.'

They went through Lowestoft without too much trouble, making south and going via the Oulton broad bridge, it was still early, and the morning rush hour traffic had still to materialise.

****

Sat far away in the manor house in Pakefield the squat, evil creature smiled its evil grin, The Gruul had witnessed all of the unfolding events with glee, its malicious mischief knew no bounds.

'Get back to the safety of the woods, I have use for both of you still.'

The telepathic message stretched through time and space, unlike radio transmission, this message was unhindered by the planar storm that raged all around.

'So, the son of the guardian was on his way to stop the Gruul's plans.' The Gruul thought to itself.

'I will be ready. I must plan for him a lovely surprise!' The Gruul looked forward to dealing with Craig once and for all. This human had already bested it once before, now the Gruul would be better

prepared, this time Craig's demise would be assured, this time it would be painful and this time it would be very slow.

Chapter 29

Heveningham and the Angel

The Nihilist had arrived during the evening as the storm was beginning to take hold, he drove the blue BMW along a narrow, fenced road that ran through the centre of the picturesque Heveningham grounds, well-kept fields and woodland stretched in every direction. There was a large lake with abundant reed-bushes crowding its banks on the Nihilist's left and an ornate folly stone bridge crossed the lake in its very centre. The sun was out, it had been bright but now it duelled the rain clouds for space in the sky, the clouds were winning, blotting out the suns attempts to warm the earth with thick voluminous clouds. The grass was scorched, it eagerly awaited the rain that was beginning to fall; gaining in intensity until it fell with wanton abandon. A little further down the road the large stately manor came into view on the far side of the lake.

The building had been built in the eighteenth century, it had been partially rebuilt after a fire in 1949, originally designed by capability brown, it was now a very important part of the local life, with a prestigious car event, several annual firework displays, live bands and festivals throughout the year.

The Nihilist had driven the full length of the lake when he came to a long metal bar gate, he indicated and turned up the drive, making for the main building, as he went by he saw a curious half subterranean structure to his right, it had a front door and a roof but it could clearly be seen to continue into the hill it was built upon.

The Nihilist went past and approached the vast stately home, it stood upon a long hill that dominated this part of the grounds, looking down imperiously upon the lake and all the grounds that surrounded. The rain, which had increased in tempo as he had arrived ran down the stone and pebble drive, forming large puddles on the edge of the track, the purple tinged clouds made the immense mansion look like an imposing fortress, defending privilege and wealth in all its imperial forms. He slowed the car, following a sign directing him to drive to the side of the property, he followed it towards a semi-circular set of buildings to the left of the main structure. There was five or six vehicles parked here already. There was a large British racing green Range Rover covered with dirt along the sides, it looked as though it had been working in the fields as the rain had started and had made a mad dash for the buildings and the dry as the rain had intensified.

The Nihilist got out, he pulled an umbrella and his large bag out with him, he then quickly opened the umbrella to take shelter from the rain which was falling heavier and heavier by the second. Checking out the Range Rover he could see that there was an overweight gentleman with long sideburns and a grey shaggy beard who wore a flat cap inside; writing a text on a smartphone whilst he sat in the driver's seat avoiding the rain. The Nihilist walked over, as he approached; the driver peered up.

'Hallow there, can I help?' The rural gentleman said as he wound the window down.

The Nihilist could hear the rain drumming heavily upon the roof of the large four-wheel drive car now.

'Yes, hello, my friends and I are staying here, a Mr Blessed and Miss Slattery have organised it, I am here to ensure it is up to their demanding standards.'

'I'll call Mr Hunt, I'm sure he will send you in the right direction.'

The groundsman in the green Range Rover then closed the driver's window, leaving the Nihilist stood in the rain and made a call on his smartphone.

****

The taxi dropped Craig at the rear of the Angel, the building was in good order, not sanitised as some may say, but well kept. He had not escaped the clouds and the storm, it seemed that whenever he had looked up at the sky on the way down the clouds had been angrily moving, intimidating and threatening; all the time throwing down rain with the occasional accompaniment of a lightning strike, there was no sign that it would relent at any point in the near future.

The tavern had a small car park at the rear, it backed onto the restaurant part of the tavern known as Cleone's, it was a popular local restaurant within the town, often very busy. In the summer the beer garden was always full, tonight if the rain continued it would be empty, however. The only people who would dare go outside would be those who braved their addiction to have a cigarette, before quickly getting back in.

Craig paid the driver, thanked him and quickly dashed through the back doors, he was soaked and had no spare clothes as they were all in the back of Matt's car. He wandered through to the reception. Inside, the tavern was sliced into three separate sections. The Restaurant was situated at the back. Along the left-hand side was the bar area, which was in itself divided into two smaller sections; a main bar area and a quiet snug with a rear window, and the hotel area filled the right-hand side of the tavern with a reception at the front. A small set of steps went up to the rooms that were all on the first floor. In the very centre of the building, there was an area which may once have been open roofed, it was like a crossroads to all of the different parts of the tavern.

Craig wandered through the tavern, all about people were having breakfast, the morning service was brisk. The talk on everyone's table was of the storm, and the lack of sleep that people had had; due to its heavy downpour and the harsh but abundant lightning and thunder. Craig went continued through the tavern till he arrived at the cubby-hole that was the hotel reception.

'Good morning, how can I help you?' The young lady at the reception asked.

The reception was filled with small local posters for places to go and things to do, it was disordered but quite quaint and very Suffolk. The young lady was very pretty, her hair was blonde and tied up, it was dreadlocked, her cheekbones were high, and her makeup made them look angular, she wore a navy-blue shirt with the angel taverns insignia upon the left breast, it was very flattering to her physique as it hugged in all the right parts.

'Hi, I've booked two rooms for a few nights, it's under the name Souter, I was hoping with all this rain to book in early.' Craig said.

'Oh, you look drenched, unfortunately your room won't be ready until later in the afternoon.' She said.

'I thought you may say that, I really am not too bothered by the state of the room, I just got caught totally unaware by the weather and I do not have a change, I was hoping to get some clothes in town, so really I was hoping that you may be able to make an exception this once.'

Craig stared at her, forcing her mind to except his suggestion as the common-sense thing to do, he had not attempted the gift on a person before, it felt terribly strange, like he could hear echoes of her thoughts.

There was a brief pause.

'Well I think you could do with getting out of those things,' she said, 'you are room seven up the stairs on the left, I will have one of the team bring up a dry pair of trousers and an angel inn shirt for you.'

'Thanks.' Craig said as she passed him the key to the room.

He turned and went up the stairs in the covered courtyard area, within the centre of the tavern.

He walked about in the room, it was spacious and tastefully decorated in browns and teal, the bathroom was clean and there was a double bed that looked welcoming. The walls were bright and held a clean appeal. A few minutes after he had entered a gentle knock on the door came, he went and opened it. The young lady from the reception was there with a small pile of folded clothes, and an umbrella.

'Here you are, to get you by till you get some of your own,' she smiled, 'that's my umbrella though I want it back when you get back, today.' She smiled.

'Thanks.' Craig said as he returned the warm smile.

He closed the door behind her, quickly went into the bathroom and put on the clothes that the dreadlocked receptionist had brought, he looked himself up and down in the mirror, the clothes were a little tight around the side, but they fit well enough and that was the main thing. Craig then went down into the pub and ordered a full English breakfast, it arrived about five to ten minutes later. He hadn't realised how hungry he was until he smelled the hot food on the plate in front of him. He could feel himself salivating and quickly got stuck in, eating with gusto; as he ate, he thought through his next steps, the Gruul would even now be moving toward Heveningham Hall. He would have to act swiftly.

****

The Nihilist walked toward the large doors of the main building, the rain now drumming down heavily upon the umbrella, the wind would repeatedly attempt to whip it from his grasp almost every time he took his attention from it. When he neared the large front doors, they opened, a well-dressed woman came out, she wore a waterproof wax jacket and walking boots, she was in her sixties, her hair was thinning and she had small features upon her face, her eyes were narrow and hawk-like, and they were deep brown in colour.

'Good day, I am guessing you are Lord Blessed's runner.' Her accent came directly from a sixties' finishing school, arrogant with a note of condescension running through, like the Nihilist was below her. He ignored the condescending remark.

'Hello, yes Lord Blessed and the rest will be here later, I am to ensure that all of the requirements have been met, please take me to the rooms.' He replied professionally.

She did as requested, ushering him inside, they followed a long corridor that went to the right, on the way she announced facts about various works of art, the Nihilist did not listen, he merely followed, uninterested; taking in all doors and stairwells, preparing a mental map that he may need if things were not to go to plan, it was not that he did not like art, more that his job had nothing to do with it and so he had no inclination to hear about the fortunes and history of this beautifully restored property that this lady was obviously very proud of.

She arrived at the far end of the building and announced the history of the four rooms that Lord Blessed's entourage would be staying in, defining the lineage of prominent others who had stayed here in the past.

'Lovely.' He said, cutting her off in mid-flow.

She gave him a look that could curdle milk, the hawkish eyes focused on him.

'Now can you take me to this out-building that has been arranged please?' He said, ignoring the contemptuous looks, that were thrown his way.

****

Craig had finished his breakfast. Looking outside, the storm raged as it had started; torrential. He decided that the umbrella was his best chance and headed into the pedestrianised thoroughfare, he had noticed a gun store immediately before the town centre and figured that waterproof clothing would be in abundance there. Craig stepped outside, the rain immediately bombarded him with an uncountable watery barrage, a heavy deluge which disempowered the individual, evoking an opinion to wait the storm out before any activity should be enacted upon.

Grudgingly Craig opened the umbrella, it was black and white with the Angels insignia on it. He stepped outside. The noise of the rain hitting the upper-side of the umbrella was very loud, a constant drumming with no timing or consistency, just the dull repeated pounding upon the canvas directly above his head.

Craig wandered down the street, it was deserted. Most of the shops had opened, but the customers were avoiding this dreadful weather, only those who had no choice would be out in this today. After what seemed like the longest five-minute walk of Craig's life he had arrived at the far end of the thoroughfare, there was a roundabout with three exits other than this road that he had approached from, across the other side of the roundabout he could see the shop in question, he hurried over.

There was no traffic, so he quickly made the other side of the roundabout, it was only about one hundred metres to the front doors. Inside he could clearly see rack upon rack and row upon row of shotguns and air rifles, pump actions and breech-loaders. They were all here in abundance. In the rear of the shop he could just make out clothing racks filled with jackets and camouflage clothing. But the shop was closed!

Chapter 30

The Drenched Blade

The Nihilist followed the lady in the wax jacket to the outhouse in question, it was built into the ground, it had a front door and a roof that disappeared into the ground, it was very much in keeping with the time that it had been built. it was nicknamed the icehouse by the staff at Heveningham Hall as it allegedly was once used to store the ice for the nobility many years ago.

The lady produced a powerful hand torch, that she switched on to show the Nihilist about inside. There was a small circular room and a small flight of stone steps which led down. The stone stairs joined a corridor; they walked on, guided only by the cold white light from the powerful torch in the woman's hand, they were finally there, she opened a wooden door that allowed entrance to what was a very large open rectangular area, dirty and dusty flagstones covered the floor.

There was a damp smell within, like that of dirty clothes left for too long, foetid. There was six pillars that ran in two rows of three down either side of the centre of the subterranean chamber. It was clear that the room had not been used for an awfully long time, the only adornment to the room now was some tattered and broken furniture that had been pushed to the far side of the room and a table of basic design that looked like it was from the last century, the table was stained from years of damp penetration.

'This is perfect, may I take the key now, I have things to prepare.' The Nihilist more stated, rather than asked.

She frowned, then passed him the key.

'I only have this one torch.' She said.

'That is okay, I have candles.'

She passed him the key, he then watched as the light from the torch retreated as she left the underground structure. He produced a candle and lit the wick, it flickered in a slight breeze that came through the large open space, causing the shadows on the walls to dance and move in the dim light.

The Nihilist knew he must act fast, and so before he did anything else he quickly went to the tattered furniture at the far side of the room, opened his large bag that he had brought with him, and took out a long three and a half foot soft bag, he then gently undid the bag slipped the long contents into the broken bits and pieces of chairs and tables. He then had a last look around before leaving the icehouse and making his way back through the driving rain toward the main building and the rooms at the east end of the building.

****

Lord Blessed's entourage arrived at midday on the following afternoon; after the Nihilist, the same day that Craig had arrived at the Angel Inn. A small convoy consisting of Lord Blessed's Aston and two black Audi Q7 SUV's, they turned onto the Heveningham Hall estate and parked in the semi-circular area beside the Nihilist's BMW, they all got out. Within moments the lady in the wax jacket had reappeared from the building to greet the guests, she had an umbrella in a dark green canvas, she walked briskly over to the cars as they arrived, eager to get them inside and away from the heavy grey rainy deluge as fast as possible.

'Good afternoon, Lord Blessed, we've been expecting you.' The lady said as she quickly darted out her hand to shake his.

He did not reciprocate, as he got out of the sports car, he just quickly opened an umbrella, Hawkins who stepped out upon the other side had no such way of keeping dry, he was very quickly drenched, all he could do was pull his jacket close and hurry toward the door.

'Hello, where is my friend, you can collect our things later and send them to our rooms.'

Hawkins ran to catch up with his father, the other men from the Masons were all getting out of the SUV's. They all had black umbrella's and moved as a large group toward the main entrance behind Lord Blessed. The lady with the green umbrella and a wax jacket led the way. She knew that this peer was very influential, her attitude to him was a stark contrast to the treatment she had shown towards the Nihilist yesterday.

Once inside the immense property they closed their umbrella's and hung their drenched coats in a large cloak area. They then all followed the matronly woman as she led them down the right-hand corridor. Again, she explained the works and objects of art, the history and geography; in a trained educational and informative manner, till they finally arrived in an open plan seating area, surrounded by doors. On a very comfortable and expensive looking sofa, lounged the Nihilist; he slouched back with his feet on a low table, and a very large glass of Brandy in his hand. The open bottle stood proudly on the low glass table easily within the Nihilist's reach.

'Lord Blessed, greetings.' The Nihilist said, raising the glass in salute.

'Sort yourself out, Nihilist, we have far more important things to do, than just lounging about and drinking.' Lord Blessed said in his deep booming voice.

The Nihilist stood, he was changed now, he wore a pair of blue jeans and a white tee shirt, he kept the large brandy glass in hand, however.

'Everything is in order Lord Blessed, I have been waiting that is all I could do, the others are not here yet.'

'They are not here? Most strange, I have spoken to Victoria, she will be here, she ran into some trouble that is all.'

'Was it the Grandson of the guardian?' The Nihilist asked.

'Yes, I think so, now listen, tonight we must prepare the area, for the ritual. What does it look like?'

'It is good, very good; you will like it Lord Blessed, lots of space, underground, away from the building, Vicky has done you a great service, everything you asked for.'

'I knew she would, when Sydora gets here I want you to go with Her, David and Mr Humboldt and prepare the underground chamber, I will consecrate the blade tonight, we can then start when the time is right.'

'Oh, one more thing Lord Blessed, it's about Gruul.'

'It can wait Nihilist; we have more important things to deal with than the imp.'

The Nihilist figured he would bring it up again later, before the monstrous wizard arrived.

****

At the Manor House in Lowestoft the storm had been unrelenting; throwing everything it could at the grey brick property. Sydora, Steve and Jay had all been waiting for Victoria to return, but still they heard nothing from her. The Gruul had been busy within its lair, occasionally they would hear murmurings and babblings from within, but they saw no sign of the beast making any appearance. Gabby was beginning to think that maybe she would get out of this alive, she just needed to hold her nerve.

Much later Vicky's car pulled up onto the drive, she stepped out of the car and dashed to the door, the rain quickly soaking into her clothing, she wrapped the door repeatedly; hurriedly and the door was opened to let her in.

'Hi Steve, sorry I'm late, that Craig and his friends got hold of me.'

'Are you okay, did they hurt you?' Steve asked as they walked through into the living room.'

'No, but I need to get some dry clothes, Gabby have you got any I could squeeze into?'

Gabby looked up, she nodded, hoping that if she was helpful then they would leave her be.

'My clothes are in the backroom to the right of the stairs.'

'Right I am going to get changed, we can then be on our way.'

The door opened behind them once more, the Gruul stalked out of its room, brooding.

'Hurry we are late; time is against us.' It croaked.

The Gruul stood wearing a braided belt and harness, various animal bones and skulls hung from it, a long dagger hung within a scabbard on its side, the imp also held onto a staff about three foot in length, it was made from a golden metal material, spiked at one end and embellished with an intricate beetle upon the other.

Half an hour later and they were all on their way to Heveningham hall. The rain fell free and heavily from the ominous, strange and unnatural coloured clouds. They passed the site of Craig, Matt and Cairo's car crash, unaware of who's car it was; most gave it no heed, the Gruul however knew well what had happened, a vile grimace crossed the creatures fanged features. The Renault people carrier sped through the clogged roads, the traffic was bad, all vehicles driving at low speeds due to the terrible weather, no one on the roads was in the mood for going fast. The continual rainfall was easily overloading the windscreen wipers of all of the slow-moving vehicles.

Eventually they had turned off of the A12 and passed Halesworth, the clogged traffic had reduced once the Renault had left Halesworth, the roads now had flooded in multiple locations, then finally they turned onto the Huntingfield road which would take them to Heveningham hall. All told; a journey that would normally take around forty minutes had taken over an hour and twenty, such was the state of the roads and the affect that it had had on the ebb and flow of the rush hour road use.

They turned onto the estate and made their way to the parking area, clearly visible were the black Audi's, the Blue BMW and Lord Blessed's Aston Martin. They were greeted by the Matron of the house, she smiled at Victoria. The matron had met Victoria many times before and the matron in her wax jacket was happy that out of this group of strangers who had arrived here, there was at least one of them that she was familiar with.

'Miss Slattery, a pleasure to have you stay again, please come this way, we have set aside the entire west wing for you and your entourage, we have also set aside horses from the stables, though with this weather I would imagine that can wait.'

'Thank you, Maggie, hopefully the weather will let off and maybe there will be a chance to go for a ride about the estate, tomorrow.'

The Matron; Maggie led them all into the building where they joined Lord Blessed, and the rest, The Gruul had quietly slipped out of the Renault and had made its own way to one of the stables that surrounded the parked cars. The Gruul decided it would wait out here.

****

That night the group discussed the plan for the ritual, it was decided that Lord Blessed would lead the ritual, the others would be in support. The atmosphere was one of eager anticipation and excitement, they drank expensive Brandy and French champagne that had been sent with compliments from the family cellar, Gabby sat and drank, she could not ease into the atmosphere, it just seemed that she knew they had something in store for her, but everybody was being so nice, she wanted to believe that they had other; nicer plans for her.

As the discussion continued Lord Blessed took Hawkins, Sydora and the Nihilist and went out to the corridor, closing the door behind them.

'I require your assistance outside.'

'Really Dad, it's pissing down out there.' Hawkins whined.

'What do you wish us to do?' The Nihilist asked.

'Nothing much, I want a little protection whilst I prepare the blade this evening, and with this storm I will need to use magic to complete it. Sydora I want you to prepare the circle in the icehouse.'

'What about Gruul, he would do it for you.' Hawkins said.

'I would not advise that Lord Blessed, he is up to something, and I don't trust the little shit.' The Nihilist warned.

'Gruul is okay, harmless even. I have dealt with its ilk many times before, Gruul can wait.'

Later that evening Lord Blessed, his son, Sydora and the Nihilist all went outside, they decided to leave Dr Humboldt. The storm raged above, throwing all it had at the earth; attempting to wash away everything below. They walked to the Ice House, Lord Blessed stood in the centre on the hill behind the entrance, Sydora went inside the building. Hawkins and the Nihilist flanked Lord Blessed as he placed the ornate sacrificial dagger reverently upon the ground, directly in front as the three men stood on the rainy, muddy hillock and then stepped back a couple of paces. The portly Lord then raised his arms out and up to the sky, he emptied his mind of thoughts about where he was, what was going on, what was at stake. Calmed his mind, then slowly believed the clouds would part, that the moon would break through.

The angry clouds raged, moving with an unnatural life of their own, the call of Lord Blessed affected them; the heavy purplish cloud cover above began to split, but the formations reacted negatively to his call. As clouds parted so more would rush to cover the stars immediately, spreading across the clear sky above. Then gradually as more and more clouds came to plug the gap being forced through the heavy shroud, a vortex began to form, slowly rotating in an anti-clockwise direction, this in turn pulled more clouds over to the local area where they were folding back upon themselves above, and finally punching through to the calm clear, night sky beyond. They stood outside in the rain for what seemed like hours, as the cyclone had gradually formed.

The three below the clouds gradually felt the rain ease where they stood till it had ceased completely. The clouds swirled angrily, occasional jolts and electrical follies darted through the clouds erratically; emanating from the rotating maelstrom. Directly above the blade, the starry night sky shone through; bathing the dagger in white moonlight.

'Now we wait for the moon to do the rest!' Lord Blessed said.

They turned and left in the direction of the hall, they made it to the stables and parked vehicles.

'You three go on inside, I need something from my car, I'll be there in a minute.'

The Nihilist and Hawkins did as he requested.

They did not see the Gruul creep out from hiding underneath the muddy Range Rover.

****

Craig stood in the rain outside the shop, deliberating his next step, eventually he justified breaking in because if he did not it may hinder his attempt to stop this monster and its accomplices. Relaxing and thinking about the lock, he turned the handle and it opened easily. Craig figured there would be an alarm so he figured he would need to be quick, dashing to the rear of the shop he grasped a large backpack, a small tent, a pair of walking boots in size nine, a combat jacket and some combat trousers. Then he headed straight back out of the shop, focusing on the lock, he heard it click once again. Craig turned right making his way to a park just around the corner on Saxons way. There he hid in the children's play area. Correctly figuring no one would take their children out in weather like this. Craig changed in the children's play castle awkwardly slipping on the combat clothing, he waited here for a long time; a police car sped by with its blue lights flashing but nothing else happened. Eventually after he was sure that there was no other police activity he made off, following the direction given to Heveningham hall on his mobile phone's map app.

He was determined to stop them, at all costs!

Chapter 31

The Ritual

Craig made his way to Heveningham hall, the hard driving rain was terrible, lashing at him relentlessly attempting to stop him in his tracks. It had taken more than two hours to arrive at the large stately mansion grounds by foot.

He set up his stolen tent in a hedgerow in the woods that faced toward the Hall from the other side of the lake; he figured from there he was close enough to keep an eye on what was going on without easily being spotted. Close enough to react when they started this final ritual. Craig had spotted the Blue BMW, the Renault and Victoria's car. he did not realise that the Aston and the two Audi SUV's were involved with the Gruul's accomplices as well.

The tent was low domed with a single front zip, it was grey green in colour, and blended in well with the ground cover in the woodland, Craig sat down and watched from inside the tent. The trees protected the tent from the worst of the rain fall, the aromas of the forest were released into the atmosphere by the rains that freely fell. The warmth in the air and the deluges humidity atomised the local area to such an extent, that the moisture was visible in patches of mist that seemed to creep through the trees almost everywhere.

The storm swirled above in a lunatic formation of shades in grey and purple, the whole scene was terrifying, forbidding and ominous. The purple tinge had an unwholesome affect upon the observer. Craig watched for what seemed like an age, nothing happened accept the rain continuing to fall and the sky would occasionally be rent with a downward cascading blast of lightning. It would light the hall in a menacing fashion.

He then noticed the black metal fence which bordered the road on this side of the lake, perched there in the rain stood hundreds of crows, Craig wondered, he calmed his mind and then called out to two crows in particular, but there was no response

****

Eventually the light began to fail, and the evening gave way to night. Craig realised that he would need to get closer, some lights had turned on in various rooms in the hall but there was no way of knowing which rooms Craig's quarry were in, if any.

Craig opened the Umbrella he had been given in the Angel Hotel and advanced across the field, it was very muddy, he was thankful he had taken the walking boots when he had had the chance.

He approached the metal rail fence, the crows called to one another, most flew; two stayed and as he closed with them, he realised he had done have at least two allies.

'Well guys, glad you both showed up, I think it all ends here, do me a favour, just keep an eye out for me.' He asked the crows, as he climbed through the fence.

Craig neared the manor, his attention was drawn to the clouds on the right of the hall, they had begun to agitate, gradually stirring and rotating anti-clockwise. He watched as a slow and gradual sense of fear crept up within, this had to have something to do with the monster and its accomplices. Craig followed the fence around toward the revolving clouds, fearing what he may see, unable however, to draw himself away.

After five minutes of walking toward the alien shifting winds and clouds, he began to feel the power of the storm, as he had made it closer to the central eye, the fury of the winds and the rain intensified; it felt like every loose pebble or stick was being deliberately thrown in his direction.

'I hope they haven't got the power to do this to me, or I'm fucked.' Craig thought to himself.

With stinging eyes Craig looked on, he could make out the small Icehouse building stood on the hillock beside the palatial stately home, partially submerged into the hill that it was built into. To Craig it appeared to be directly below the eye of the raging storm.

'It has to be more than a coincidence.' He thought.

Craig continued to watch, he wasn't sure, but he thought he could just about make out three or four people walking away from the outbuilding, toward the main hall. Craig would investigate further, he made a long curving route through the field close to a man-made lake and then crossed the road, finally arriving at the low building. He stealthily crept toward the door, trying the handle he soon discovered it was locked. He concentrated on the lock.

'I think I should think about becoming a burglar if I get out of this.' Craig thought to himself in jest.

The lock clicked, he turned the handle and cautiously entered the Icehouse.

Craig made his way down the pitch-black stairs and followed the corridor till he reached the large open space below the earth, he had been forced to use his mobile phone to light the way ahead. The large rectangular room below was sparse of places to hide, within he could see the broken and dilapidated chairs and tables at one end, the floor had been marked with what looked like powdered chalk, unlit candles stood at all of the main terminating cardinal chalk points; in what seemed like a circle with a five pointed star within the middle, there was several strange symbols marked out in chalk within the circle as well, other than this it was bare. Craig crept over deciding to hide within the broken furniture, he determined that he would then wait. Settling into the debris, Craig noticed a long, narrow wooden object out of place, upon closer inspection he recognised it for what it was, picking it up gently, fearing to make any real noise in the darkness he took his phone light to the object to inspect it. Someone had stowed a sword down here, Craig concentrated upon the blade.

****

Lord Blessed led the group out to the Icehouse through the rain, they could all clearly see the fast-rotating clouds above, leaves, sticks and loose debris tossed and danced about in the circular winds, unable to compete with the strength of the cyclonic winds. They all walked past the stable area, the cars parked were repeatedly buffeted by the strong winds and driving rain.

They reached the Icehouse and opened the door, then went inside, Hawkins looked up just before entering, directly into the clear sky above, surrounded by the rotating clouds, little rain fell here, he waited for the Nihilist to retrieve the dagger from behind the Icehouse where it had been left earlier.

'Got it.' He said.

Hawkins let him through, then closed and locked the door behind. He turned as the Nihilist ignited a powerful torch, bathing the small circular room in a brilliant white light.

'Ready, let's go.' The Nihilist said, after an affirmation from Hawkins.

They followed behind the rest of the entourage down the dank stairs which led into the ground.

Lord Blessed's group filed into the large rectangular room below, Sydora walked quietly from candle to candle, lighting each in turn with a tube-like fire-lighter. They gave off little light in comparison to the battery powered torches that various members of the party held, after each candle had finally been lit Lord Blessed stepped forward, he took off his jacket and passed it to David Smith who stood close by on his left.

'Douse your torches everyone, your eyes will become accustomed to the light, it is time.'

They all walked about the circle as they had discussed the night before, each had an allotted place; each had been given the words they would need to recite, and all stood there had memorised their part.

The Gruul was sniffing the air about, dressed in the outlandish outfit and carrying the yellow metallic staff, the creature slowly walked about, in no hurry to take a place at the circle upon the ground.

'Gruul, take your position, hurry up.'

The creature stepped round after taking a last large sniff of the air, then loped over to the place where it had been allotted to stand, the Nihilist noticed in the dim light the creature had arranged upon its belt a blade in a place that made it very easy to draw, such was the way his mind worked. The Nihilist looked over to the rubble in the corner, he would be ready if that thing had anything unexpected planned.

Gabby was stood next to Steve, she looked around at the eerie scene before them, they had assured her that she only needed to do what they said and she would be fine, but then she had seen this group kill without remorse, the creature that slowly stalked about; that she had thought was cute; now however she knew that its heart was black, a callous ugly vile thing, both inside and out.

'Let us begin.' Lord Blessed said.

He took a deep breath, paused a moment and then gradually released it with a slight wheeze as he forced himself to relax.

'Lord. Bring us an opening to other worlds.' Lord Blessed began.

The others all intoned behind him in unison 'let us see other worlds.' They repeated it together, all with their eyes closed, deep in concentration.

'Lord. Give us an opening to another dimension.'

The others continued behind.

'Let us see other worlds.'

'Lord. It is time that we open a path to the realm of Solomon.'

'Let us see other worlds.'

Craig looked around, it was eerie and dark, they were all deep in concentration, looking at each in turn, he felt that what they now undertook should not be allowed, as if it was forbidden, but he did not know how to stop it. Then he realised that the Gruul was not speaking in the same language, the creature croaked but it was something unintelligible, like it chanted in an ugly demonic language.

'Lord, with this dagger we offer the flesh that will bond the path to the two worlds.' Lord Blessed produced a long ornate dagger and held it aloft.

'Let us see other worlds.' They all continued the chant apart, from the Gruul who continued to gurgle out unfathomable words from an unknown script.

'Lord, we offer you flesh as a sacrifice to the realm of Solomon.'

'Let us see other worlds.'

Craig gradually felt the ambient room temperature drop, it was a chilling thought, at first barely perceptible, but before too long the room was clearly and discernibly colder, as if they stood within a refrigerator and had suddenly turned the thermostat down.

As the ritual progressed a strange phenomenon began to transpire, within the circle a vertical white light began to appear, occasionally brilliant white sparks would flash from within. As the spectacle progressed, the white light elongated vertically both up and down, only it did not cease to grow once it contacted the flagstones below or the ceiling above. Instead it seemed to materialise in spite of them. It was a dimensional rift, a tear in the fabric of reality that would bind two different dimensions together, a pathway from one to the other.

'Lord, we beseech you to help us bridge the realities, we offer you this sacrifice.' Lord Blessed's voice was high and strained now, echoing off the walls, his face illuminated clearly from the bright white light immediately before him.

'Bring forward the sacrifice it is time.' He stated.

Gabby looked to either side, suddenly fearing that this was the moment, she prepared to run, though she knew they had locked the door to the outside world.

The Nihilist opened his eyes with a start, he felt the heavy grasp on both arms, as he was thrust forward toward the bright light, he struggled attempting to free the grip on either side but it was too strong, for some reason he felt he had no strength within his body at all, he then realised he had been played all along.

Looking about, he saw the masons, they did not like him and Sydora; she and the left-hand path despised him, then he looked at Lord Blessed. It was then he realised why his strength had suddenly gone. Blessed pointed with one arm outstretched clearly in his direction, he had taken the Nihilists vigour, his magic was all about and all-powerful. How easily had it been to do this, then Lord Blessed began to advance toward the Nihilist, like a fly within the web.

Craig's mind raced, he knew he should act, before it was too late, but he was frozen with fear, indecision. Part of him wanted to help the Nihilist, but the other side of his mind thought that it was poetic justice that he should succumb to the very people he had been helping. He watched as the nihilist was thrust into the circle, the bright light obscuring all colour from his face and clothes, till all that could be seen was his outline, immediately before the flickering rip in reality, this rip that attempted to stabilise itself, within this world, to gain a beachhead in our reality.

The Nihilist struggled, but it was futile. He could barely even lift his arms, the two masons on either side easily kept hold of him, and now all he could do was wait, as he did, he relaxed; prepared, mouthing to himself a soundless farewell to the world; and he readied himself, the only question was throat or heart? He could not believe that at the end of his own life he would honestly have that question run through his head, that that would be the last thing on his mind before he died.

'Hold him; Nihilist, I want you to know, it is nothing personal, you will understand.' Lord Blessed spoke from just behind the Nihilist but blinded by the unstable rift he could not see anything.

'Fuck you Alfred.' Was all he could find to say.

'Oh, come on, with a title like that why should you care?' Lord Blessed replied, grinning.

He then stepped closer, the Nihilist could hear his wheezing, heaving chest, excitement dripped through Lord Blessed's very being and was audible in his speech.

He lifted the dagger to the Nihilist's throat.

Chapter 32

Better Never Than Late

Craig watched, he knew then, that there would not be another chance. He had frozen within the moment and realised if he did not act now it would be too late. The overweight Lord Blessed had approached behind the Nihilist, Craig watched as the knife was raised to his throat, Craig forced his mind into action, demanding his body to act upon his thoughts and, grudgingly; like a teenager being forced out of bed, he moved into action.

'Lord, to you I give this sacrifice.' The dagger was placed against the Nihilist's throat; then Craig arose, standing with his arm stretching out and focused on pushing the Nihilist with all his might, forcing him away from the dagger and Lord Blessed behind him.

The Nihilist was knocked from his feet onto the floor several yards away, almost instantly. Lord Blessed looked about and spotted Craig stood at the corner of the room.

'Who is that, what are you doing here.' Lord Blessed demanded.

They all looked about and saw the lone figure, arm outstretched in the corner. Within the chamber they all stared toward Craig; surprised.

'It is the son of the guardian.' Sydora said.

'Get him.' Lord Blessed said.

Within the circle of chalk, the brilliant white crack began to flicker and fail, struggling to keep purchase within our reality, only the Gruul still paid heed, the creature was not interested in human affairs, it had never been interested in our affairs; instead the creature continued to open the portal, taking action whilst all the others were distracted by the unwelcome intruder. The Gruul began to mutter in the croaking broken voice again.

'Lord, I that have served you willingly, now offer you flesh, flesh to make the bridge from one reality to another complete.'

With the diminutive creature's magical incantation complete it took out the dagger from its sheaf upon its belt and strode forward, unafraid of what it would do, eager to serve its master unwaveringly, willing to die in order for its dark lord to return.

Craig faced toward them all, preparing a mental defence.

'Stop, it's not too late, you have all been tricked, by that little monster.' He said, they stopped in there advance toward Craig.

'What are you talking about?' Lord Blessed asked, slowly edging toward Craig who was trapped in the corner of the room.

'That creature, it is trying to open a portal to wherever it's master resides; its planning to free him.' Craig said.

The brilliant white rip in the fabric of time was pulsing with an irregular timing, it was becoming more and more irritated, almost as if it had grown impatient with being called into being, but know wished to leave as quickly as possible, like it wanted to retreat to whatever part of reality it had existed in before in peace undisturbed.

Dr Humboldt who had stood at his allotted place within the circle was terrified, he had just witnessed what he thought would never ever happen, he had witnessed Lord Blessed about to kill a man in cold blood. He had also witnessed the formulation of a rip in reality that led to another world, he believed now. He believed in magic like he believed that without air, he would suffocate and die.

He wished he had never believed now, but that would never be so, now this young man had appeared in the corner of the room and possibly saved the Nihilists life, but he could not concentrate upon what was being said, what was happening, his mind was in freefall, tears ran unseen by the others down his face.

Gabby slowly backed away from the circle, when the Nihilist had been thrust forward, she breathed a sigh of relief, but it quickly dawned upon her that they may have other needs for her to be there, then when Craig had stood up in the corner of the rectangular room and everyone gathered there had looked his way, she took that moment to back up toward the exit, only slowly, but to give herself a chance of escape, she needed to have a clear run at the door first.

Sydora, turned to face Craig squarely, she prepared to snuff out his existence with a word, to squeeze his heart till it would burst within his chest.

The Gruul; whilst all others faced toward Craig, had drawn the dagger from its belt, the dagger that had also sat bathed in moonlight the night before, and now the Gruul moved toward the back one of the mason's, stood staring at Craig, furthermost back from the rest.

The mason was totally unprepared for the dagger that pierced his heart, as the Gruul plunged it deep from behind, at all times gabbling in its croaky broken voice a jumbled unintelligible language. The mason died quickly, falling to the ground, his blood quickly darkening the dirty flagstones upon the floor. With that the mason gurgled and he slumped to the ground. He clutched at his chest uselessly as his lifeblood fled from his body. Another mason had seen what had happened and turned to the Gruul, but his attention was split, with the blood that ran and the portal that now had steadied in its undulating, irregular pulse.

The white light slowly increased in size, growing, opening.

The Gruul with its metallic staff in hand had quickly began to etch foul symbols within the fallen mason's blood, even as he still laid there, choking upon his own blood that now had gotten into his lungs from the fatal wound that he had taken from behind. The symbol was a balance to the portal, directing it across the realities, connecting it to another place in time, another dimension. And now, as the white light had started to increase in size, it also began to change colours; from brilliant white it gradually faded and dulled. The rift now almost seemed to fall away, like clouds rippling down into a pit, only this pit was not in the ground and had no up or down, it fell into itself.

The clouds disappearing within themselves as the portal had finally opened.

Craig looked at the number of people he faced, he knew now that he was dead, that these men and women would soon kill him, he waited for the attack that would come any second, Craig had prepared a mental defence, hoping to stop any magical killing attempt, he figured that he would be able to foil any casting directed at him for a short while, he just needed for the portal to collapse and it would be over, whether he lived after or not.

'You are in a pickle now aren't you, its Craig, isn't it?' Lord Blessed said.

'We have come too far now to worry about your petty righteous fears young man, so we will be opening the portal, and you shall be dead before the gold starts rolling out.'

Some chuckled behind Lord Blessed, but then the Gruul struck the mason from behind, the mason's gurgling distracted all of those gathered there momentarily, they could all see as the man died upon the floor and the Gruul had started scrawling in the blood. But it was the portal that had captured everyone's attention, it had steadied and was now opening, it now seemed to be falling in upon itself as reality split open bridging two worlds, joining a rocky barren place the earth; a place that could be seen far away upon the other side.

Craig saw the exhilaration appearing upon Lord Blessed's face, a look of success, of victory. Craig acted, with a thought of intense violence, he mentally thrust forth, blasting all in front of him with a physical thrust of positive energy, launching the broken furniture was sent towards the Lord and all his allies, they were pushed forcibly back, they had been unprepared for Craig's onslaught and, though it was never going to be fatal to any of them, it had given Craig some time.

The Nihilist had already been knocked to the floor, he had witnessed all that had transpired, he awaited the final conflict as Craig faced off against the rest of them, then the Gruul had struck one of the masons and all of Lord Blessed's allies seemed to be momentarily taken off balance. He took the lull to get up and slowly shift around the wall, as he did Craig unleashed the wave of mental energy, blasting all of those in front of him, knocking back Lord Blessed and the others.

The Nihilist had just made the wall when it struck, the debris scattered throughout the room, he watched for the scabbard of his Japanese sword that he had secreted earlier within the rubbish in the corner where Craig now stood, it had slid across the floor with a broken chair leg, luckily it was coming his way, he reached out and watched as it came toward him and then the candle lights went out, extinguished by the blast, the room was pitched into almost total impenetrable black, aside from the dim light given from the portal in the centre of the room.

He groped around in the darkness, searching; feeling, then he touched the saya, an elegantly lacquered Japanese wooden scabbard, its saya; for holding the long, Japanese curved sword; the katana. He pulled it close by the cord attached to the side of the saya. In near total darkness, slowly and quietly. He then listened.

The Gruul continued to jabber in that croaking, broken voice, throwing its arms out wide toward the widening rip in reality, then the room had been swamped in total darkness. The creature continued, it was almost there, the sounds of people stumbling and the curses of those unprepared for the loss of sight echoed above the Gruul's incantations. Then the portal finally opened, at first the falling away smokiness started to brighten, illuminating, then a brighter light emerged from within the very centre of the widening portal, the smoky clouds fell in toward it and the light grew gradually outwards from within; from somewhere else.

Inside the widening light, movement could be made out within, far off, figures could be seen approaching. A long smoky bridge had opened between the rocky dimensional prison that Ashtoreth and his minions had found themselves imprisoned. Craig could see them approaching clearly. A multitude of different creatures of various shapes and sizes, eager to break free from the prison that they had found themselves captive, anticipating the slaughter that they may reap once more upon the earth.

Sydora slowly stood, she looked about; the room had darkened with the expulsion of the light created by the candles, everything had happened so very fast and now all she could hear was the sound of the Gruul's chanting in the slowly brightening room, people stirred upon the floor, getting back up and turning to face this upstart. Then the portal started to react to the Gruul's summons, the portal abided by the little monsters demands to open, and then it did as it was commanded, she could see clearly into the retreating mists, no planar existence of riches, no gold and plenty could be seen. Instead, all she could see in the distance was the beginning of the advancing demonic legions in their fanatical approach, leering and screaming, onward came the demonic vanguard.

Steve stood, he looked at Sydora, he could see that her attention was no longer upon the lone figure of Craig, but instead she stared into the rip within reality, he struggled to comprehend what exactly she was looking at, then he too saw what view had drawn her.

'What is it Sydora, are they on our side?' He asked.

She did not answer, she just started to back away to the doors that led to safety from the oncoming hordes, Steve followed her, retreating away from the perceived threat.

The Masons were totally unprepared for the magical attack, none of them had ever seen this kind of thing before, magical portals opening; sorcerous blasts of mystical energy and the like, they slowly stood, helping one another, some thought they were in too deep, all were intimidated. Only Lord Blessed's friend alone, David had gathered enough wits to take in his situation. Victoria had been knocked to the side, knocking her head, she lay upon the floor, holding her head, with all of the goings on, she wanted to leave, but with Craig still in the room, her first inclination was to stay down upon the ground. Hopefully Lord Blessed and his son would stop this young man that had already captured her once and now stood in front of them all; facing them off alone.

Hawkins had stood close to his father when Craig had risen in the far corner of the room, he had acted first when Craig sent the wave of magical energy towards Lord Blessed and his allies within the room. His first reaction had been to leap to the left, then he had dropped to one knee, awaiting the attack to finish, then he would launch a counter before Craig had a chance to defend himself.

Chapter 33

The Imps Bargain

Lord Blessed's family lineage had always been very influential, their routes could be traced back directly to a noble family from the Norman invasion, in the eleventh century. Alfred's mother had given him "the touch" and taught him in the intricate magical arts. It was the only thing that he truly enjoyed; it was also the only thing that he truly excelled at. His mother had been a member of the right-hand path, her son would be trained by her when he came home from the private school's he had attended when young.

****

The Gruul had approached the school fence again. Each day for the last three years it had come here, enticing the young Alfred Blessed with a temptation toward true power. The young were always the easiest to lure, a wilful mind to rebel could always be tempted to stray from a straight and pure path. It could always play to the fertile mind with games and gifts, slowly but surely twisting those innocent games into altogether darker, more insidiously motivated ploys, till a virgin mind had been corrupted; completely.

Throughout the years at university, Alfred Blessed had frequently met with the little fiend at the end of the field, beyond the cricket pitch. He initially would advance slowly, with trepidation and excitement in equal measure. To the young Alfred, the Gruul had been his little secret, something to escape the boring lessons and the other arrogant rich children. The Gruul had promised much to Alfred and today the creature had promised to show him something that would change him forever.

When Alfred arrived at the fence the Gruul already sat there cross-legged, patiently waiting; the creature had its long-clawed hands scratching about within the dry dirt, the claws could not only be used as brutally devastating weapons but as very effective digging tools as well.

'You are late Alfred, I thought you would not come.' The Gruul said as the young Alfred neared the fence.

'I was always going to come I just had to finish my work before I could get away,' Alfred said apologetically, 'sorry.'

'Your education here is wasted, I can teach you, I have taught you so much, but there is so much more.' The Gruul said in the croaking and cracked, voice barely over a whisper.

'I'm listening.' Is all he said.

****

Lord Blessed was the last to look toward the portal, it had been continually brightening and now it easily lit the whole underground chamber. All the others attention had been drawn toward it; he now saw what they saw, he was only dimly aware of Sydora and Steve who by now had reached the old wooden door and exit to the chamber. He could see the first demonic creatures approaching from the other side of the portal, though Lord Blessed did not know it, in those first few approaching creatures was Yakk, bestowed with the place of honour as the lead of the vanguard, the little demon was eager to bring misery and despair to the earth again.

Lord Blessed looked over now at the beast upon the other side of the portal, alone lost in the exhilaration of the magics it wielded. The Gruul was deep in concentration, oblivious to the world, holding the portal steady; in place with its warped and evil mind. It was only now when it was too late that the Lord could clearly see the evil trickery that had been presented to him when he was young, all those years ago. He had followed like a blind trusting fool, willingly accepting the help of this creature and furthering his own ends in the process. Now he could also see he had furthered the Gruuls machinations in the process, under-estimating it; at what price had this deception of power truly cost?

All those years that the Gruul had been with his son? Had the creature simply been educating him, or had the creature been tainting his son, twisting his view on the world? Lord Blessed watched as the demons came closer, half in the waking world, half in a dream, he could not help but to think back to where this had all begun, so long ago.

****

When Lord Blessed had finished his lessons he would venture down to the end of the field and see the imp-like creature, they would discuss things; nature, dimensions, time and other worlds, all these things intrigued the young Alfred's mind, and the Gruul knew it, Alfred's alternative education soon moved to being his primary learning. Magic or "the gift, and the touch" as it was always explained to the young. The Gruul soon moved to the darker side of the magical spectrum. The Gruul had mastered the magics of its infernal home dimension over thousands of years, these dark powers the beast taught to Alfred, increasing the powers that his mother had already taught him, deviating from the path of nature and instead nurturing the powers of hate, both were powerful allies in their own way, the yin and the yang, good and evil the Gruul just admonished the young Alfred Blessed never to tell anyone of these powers, but to use them to increase his position in society. By the end of the last year at the prominent English school Alfred did not have any interest in the lessons in his classes, instead he only desired to visit his special secret friend, that had all answers whenever Alfred posed them, the answer was always to deal with it in some permanent manner, to destroy it subtly, from the background, use others until you are ready to strike. Alfred loved this way of looking at the world, a different way to all the rest, he saw all his fellow students were stupid and easily led; sheep, he was the wolf, the alpha and although he didn't like them, he enjoyed manipulating them, and so that is what he increasingly did.

The Gruul encouraged Alfred to use the touch to increase his wealth upon the money markets from early on, the Gruul had always thought it funny that the human race was so preoccupied with wealth and the acquisition of it. The Gruul urged him to manipulate the financial markets to the point that even before he had left Eton, Alfred had bank accounts toiling under the weight of millions of pounds that his parents knew nothing of; the money markets were so easy to manipulate with the touch, it was as if they had purely been created for it.

****

'What have you done Gruul?' Lord Blessed called out, 'your book should have opened the portal to the mines of Solomon?'

The Gruul was lost in its own magics, holding the bridge to the other dimension open. Now Yakk was close and not far behind came more, many more. It was at this point that Lord Blessed realised that the creature who had taught him so much; that he had entrusted his son's protection and tutorship to had betrayed him. It had always had its own agenda, the promise of wealth and power had all been lies and now he saw it, now he wanted revenge. He looked over to his son who knelt on the far side of the room looking at the portal, Hawkins wore a mask of fear, as he gazed into the portal. Lord Alfred looked back to the Gruul his mind made up, he would stop this, he walked towards the broken little fiend that was deep in concentration, he was determined to kill the thing now, like he should have done long ago, but what greed and pride had prevented him from doing then, he would do now.

'Gruul, what about the book, the ritual that we had spent so long trying to find, what is this.' He said as he walked toward the Gruul, but the Gruul did not respond, instead it just kept its arms outstretched deep in concentration.

****

'The book will lead you to riches beyond your wildest imaginations little Alfred.' The Gruul said.

'But why has nobody found it?'

'It's hidden as I keep telling you, but I can help you find it, it leads to the mines foretold of the magus Solomon. It can be yours.'

'But I am already rich, Gruul, what else could I need?' The young Alfred had asked.

'Your money exists only on paper, what I promise you is real, tangible, priceless relics, real gold beyond measure. This wealth cannot be touched by market forces, this wealth will make you the ruler of the world, we just need to find it. Together.' The Gruul trailed off the last words into a broken crackling whisper.

'But what of my plans? Or my families plans?' The young Alfred asked, he knew there was an expectation that he would follow his father's footsteps into politics.

'You can continue with all that, human stuff. I just ask that you help me look for this book, then we both win.'

'Yes, what is in it for you? What do you gain out of all this?' Lord Blessed asked suddenly suspicious.

'I gain the right ear of the ruler of the world, who would not want that?' The Gruul said after a brief pause.

Alfred was not sure if he believed him, but it was plausible.

The offer had proven too much once again, the years of trickled words from the imp had weakened Alfred's resolve and will. He agreed that day and together they would search the earth for this book that the Gruul spoke of; this bronze manual of ancient artifice.

****

He closed the distance quickly firming his resolve, the little beast would put up a fight and the claws were vicious and sharp, but all he had to do was break the concentration, that would be enough, that would break the portal and prevent any of the Gruul's friends from arriving from wherever the portal led. He quickened into a run, Lord Blessed would bowl the unresponsive creature over and then throttle it. He passed the portal, Lord Blessed could feel an unnatural heat from within. But Lord Blessed had not prepared for Yakk and the oncoming horde, the small Yakk, the agile Yakk; the quick Yakk, had made as much ground as fast as its little bony legs could enable, then it had cleared the exit, bursting into the dimly lit subterranean flagstone chamber, Yakk leapt upon the first thing it could see, eager to begin the killing and the slaughtering, that first thing that Yakk had jumped upon was Lord Blessed, the demon plunged its short jagged sword into Lord Alfred's back, in a frenzied flurry of stabs, repeatedly pressing the blade into Lord Blessed.

Lord Blessed's knees collapsed through the sudden pain as Yakk had attacked him, he reached around, awkwardly attempting to grasp the creature and throw it off. But Yakk was small and agile, the creature then sliced at Lord Blessed's hand and arm as he sought to remove it from his back. Yakk hit clean and took off two of Lord Blessed's fingers, he gasped in pain and fell forward, reflexively putting his other hand out to prevent himself from hitting the floor. Yakk took advantage and redoubled the assault into Lord Blessed, jabbing and stabbing; slicing with delight. Then Lord Blessed's strength finally gave, weak from the excessive blood loss, he slumped onto the floor. Yakk did not cease, until finally when Lord Blessed ceased to move the creature took the short sword to Lord Blessed's throat and opened it. Blood spilled from the numerous wounds and his open throat, then Lord Alfred Blessed died.

Hawkins watched as Yakk had hacked his father to death, frozen in fear as his world had come apart at the seams. Then his father had just died, killed by the vile little creature in front of him, Hawkins was not aware of the creature's name or where it had come from, unaware of these things sole aim; unaware that their sole goal was to destroy, kill and ruin, as a praise to their lord and master. But now that his father had died it stirred him slowly into action.

Other creatures had begun to emerge from the billowing smoky bridge to another world, a large beast with two prominent tusks that lent forward, moving in similar fashion to a gorilla, shifting twenty percent of its body weight upon its two foreclaws. Behind this behemoth, more quickly followed.

Ashtoreth's   legions   had   returned   to   the   earth!

Chapter 34

The Hordes Arrive

Craig had prepared for the oncoming assault from all of Lord Blessed's lackey's, none of them had listened, so he prepared to fight them as best he could. As the portal began to collapse, he had hoped it would fail of its own volition, through the inattention of Lord Blessed and his minions, he just needed to stay alive long enough to keep them from stabilising it first. But then the Gruul had acted, Craig then realised that the Gruul had been playing the lot of them, Lord Blessed, the Nihilist and this Sydora? None of them were aware of the Gruul's true purpose for being here.

All of them who now stood against Craig in that room, they had all been tricked; fooled into believing in a promised unicorn. Only that unicorn was really a chimera, a changeable beast that had mutated into everyone's demise. Unless Craig could collapse the portal now.

The Gruul had taken control of the portal, initiating the opening by murdering one of the masons who had been looking toward the intruder, Craig. The Gruul had then stabilised it with its mind, concentrating upon its destination, forcing the bridge between dimensions to materialise, changing its destination and it had begun to open, widening. He watched as they began to realise that something was wrong, slowly, one by one they figured that the portal that they had worked so hard to create had opened to another place, a different place.

Craig witnessed as Lord Blessed had also finally realised the betrayal, he watched as the Lord crossed the space in front of the now fully open portal, with smoky ripples retreating down into the ethereal passage reaching toward another world. Lord Blessed advanced toward the Gruul; advanced until the first creature had leapt out, launching onto his back and attacking with a ferocity that none who stood in that underground chamber had been prepared for.

Hawkins had begun to react, tears had welled within his eyes, he had just watched his father murdered and the little demon now looked for another target, more of the demons came from behind, including a large beast that easily stood over ten feet tall, it leant forward, resting upon its strong bony powerful knuckles, with two vicious tusks protruding from its lower jaw. The giant creature excitedly loped toward the masons. They stood now in terror, fearing for their lives, they had backed away to the side wall, splitting up; separating either way along the wall.

The beast reached out and grasped the closest before he had a chance to escape, catching the mason by the neck. It squeezed, closing its bony knuckled fist with an impossible strength, crushing the hapless mason's throat in a matter of seconds and with little effort. The mason had tried to scream, but he could not, a horrid crunching sound came from within his throat and his body soon went limp, the giant demon then loped further around the wall chasing one of the other masons.

Hawkins backed away slightly, he wanted to hurt the Gruul, but the largest one was in the way. He sidestepped about, focusing his thoughts upon a demonic creature that emerged from the portal, he let himself believe that the creature would ignite, imagining it had already happened, that it was already history; then as the beast placed its first foot in our dimension in over two thousand years, the thing immolated, bursting into flame, its eyes bulged, Hawkins forced the flames to increase their intensity, they obeyed his mental demand, quickly changing colour from orange to blue and then to white. The monster let out an inhuman scream and then slumped forward; motionless, then the flames returned to a dull orange glow as Hawkins released his mental control of the summoned flames.

Craig was stunned by the approach of the creatures, he held his arm out toward the portal thinking to close it; forcing it to obey his demand to close; but it wouldn't seal, he tried again, but he then knew it was useless. He was worried now, he saw another demon burst out, slightly shorter than a man but this one wore black metal plated armour all across its body, a decorated full helm encased its head, the only visible part of the creature was its yellow beady eyes, peering through the eye slit, it brandished a long jagged, spiked mace, swinging it easily with a trained savage grace; it caught the last mason in the thigh, breaking his leg and opening a deep wound, the mason fell upon the floor, the armoured creature then took its spiked mace in both its armoured hands and rose the mace over the fallen mason, it plunged the mace down on to the top of the masons head, with a low pitched thud the mason slumped over, the armoured demon raised the weapon again and slammed it once more onto the masons head, it repeated this again and again; caving the mason's skull in more and more, with each and every gory blow.

Gabby had watched the armoured demon burst from the portal she had also noticed Steve and Sydora exiting from the chamber, she followed, escape was that way, then she saw the sacrificial dagger upon the floor near Lord Blessed's motionless body and headed over to it, hoping that it would offer some protection from these vile creatures. Gabby picked it up, and then started for the exit, running as fast as she could, but Yakk had noticed her, the creature followed, its short sword was red stained with congealed blood in hand. Yakk chased her, gaining easily on her, then with a deft sideways slash caught Gabby across the calf, severing her Achilles tendon, she fell to the ground in agony. She looked down at her leg, her blue jeans had been slashed and they were quickly darkening with blood that flowed from her leg below the knee. The pain she felt rippled up her leg, each time she moved the leg a wave of unbearable pain ran the length of her body. Yakk grasped hold of her collar; then roughly dragged her back toward the Gruul, with each step Yakk took, the excruciating pain wracked her from her leg up to her brain, tears filled her eyes.

Two more creatures burst from the portal, immediately they looked about for things to kill, anything would suffice the maniac urge of demonic madness. The first spotted the grand master of the masons and David stood in a corner, they appeared to be looking for a chance to escape, they had been shocked at what had happened so unexpectedly. Their first instinct had been to retreat into the far corner; away from the exit, now they had realised they needed to escape before they had been spotted. Only the thing was they now they now had been spotted. The other demon had saw Craig, stood in the opposite corner; the demons had moved upon the masons and Lord Blessed's allies first as they were closer, and the chaos caused by their erratic panic had attracted these first creatures like foxes' in the hen house, then the killing had begun.

Craig felt his throat dry as this monster advanced, he gulped, forcing himself to compose and calm down. It held a spear and a shield, its mouth was wide, far wider than any human, with a row of sharp pointed teeth, and its skin was the colour of ochre. It wore a loose tunic over a steel ring jerkin. Craig was unarmed aside from his gift, he wore no armour, he had to think fast.

David slid back along the wall leaving the head of his order, and edging away from this other demon, the grand master just stood there, frozen in terror. He had expected riches, but now could see only death, the aging man had already soiled himself, now this creature approached him, he saw murder within its eyes. It carried a long-hafted axe with wicked spikes upon the back side of the blade head and at the top end. The creature was naked from the waist up; its skin was freckled with pockmarks that were similar in colour to burns. It lifted the axe but could not swing it efficiently with the low ceiling above and so changed its grip, and began to jab, slowly at first, the grand master, pushed the axe head down, keeping any blow from finding its mark.

The pockmarked demon attempted three more times, each time the mason forced the weapon down, then upon the fourth attack, the monster feigned the thrust; the grand master, on cue attempted to force the jab down once more, but this time there was no halberd there, the creature had retracted the thrust; feigned attack and then quickly thrust a second time and this time it found its mark, piercing the old man's stomach. The pock-skinned demon then forced the blade deeper; the grand master grunted, then choked up blood and he fell to the ground. The demon lifted the axe and chopped at the prone grand master, raining blows into his body, the grand master whimpered as he died.

Craig thought only of slowing the spear-armed beast, forcing its movements to falter, he reached a hand out as the creature came forward, forcing his thoughts to settle, forcing himself to believe that this thing would slow. It was harder than at other times, with all the panic and chaos within the room, he found it increasingly difficult to concentrate, almost impossible; the creature came closer and it lifted the spear higher.

Then Craig thought of his Grandfather, this was what he had prepared him for all his life, in case something like this were to happen. His thoughts of his Grandfather gave him strength; purpose. Craig forced through the doubts and fear, determining that this creature would slow, that the very molecules it attempted to walk through would fight its presence, would push back and retaliate against this devilish monster.

It slowed, the very atmosphere had tightened around the creature slowing each movement it made, like an unseen friction that hindered any kind of movement. Craig felt the exhilaration of the gift flow through him, he continued to force those same molecules to action, turning them upon the creature, squeezing the thing, contracting all around it. The beasts grin gradually turned to a frown and then the oversized mouth opened and began to howl, an inhuman howl of savage, bestial pain. Craig watched as he crushed the creature with nothing but the power of his mind, he watched as the creature burst under the pressure as it built up, it split and burst in an imploding shower of blood, gore and flesh, Craig then breathed a sigh of relief.

Dr Humboldt had frozen like so many others, completely unprepared for what was happening, when finally, he had regained enough composure and wit to run it was too late. He made a break for the exit, but his escape was drawn tragically short, a demon armed with a spear, thrust it into his back as it materialised from the portal, skewering him clean in the back, he fell, the creature was quickly on top of him, it produced a dagger and then repeatedly stabbed at the Professor; he never stood a chance.

Yakk continued to drag Gabby over toward the Gruul. She cried in pain with each yard of progress that the demon made. She was close now, the Gruul had come out of the trance like state, with one twisted arm outstretched toward the portal, with the other it had taken the metallic staff from its back. The Gruul faced the portal, the light that emanated from within illuminated the creature clearly, stripping the Gruul's visage of the darkened features and replacing them with a white and yellow glow, so brilliant was the light that it gave off.

'Bring her, she will stabilise the portal.' The Gruul commanded to Yakk, its broken, cracked voice was powerful; filled with a dominance that conveyed the Gruul's true position in the ranks of demon-hood. Yakk continued forcing her closer toward the portal and the Gruul.

'No, please, I don't want to die, please.' Gabby begged.

Yakk was strong for its size, pulling her by her hair ever closer to the awaiting demonic sorcerer. With her freely bleeding leg, her strength had truly escaped her, and now she could not help but be led inexorably to her fate, leaving a dark red trail upon the flagstones all the way from where she had been wounded.

Craig looked about taking in the situation, it looked dire. The large tusked creature had murdered most of the masons, the purple-clad woman had disappeared with the young man, Steve. Hawkins had killed one of the monsters with an impressive attack, he was facing another, the Gruul and another demon were close to the portal entrance, they had drawn a woman close the entrance, Craig feared for her life, but he feared also for what the taking of her life may instigate and what it may signify for the Earth. He then saw in the confusion tucked away on one of the walls the Nihilist, he seemed also to be taking in the situation, he held in his hand the Japanese katana sword; the blade shone a brilliant white with the reflected light from the portal within the centre of the room.

Craig looked back to within the portal, inside, he could now clearly see hundreds more coming far off in the wispy tunnel, maybe thousands of the demonic creatures and they were coming this way fast, the demonic horde was coming, if the portal wasn't closed soon; it would be too late.

Chapter 35

Mad Woman a Power-Hungry Man

David Smith stood surrounded by the chaos that encompassed the whole subterranean chamber, more demonic things came in through the glowing misty portal, one clambered out, it was armed with a halberd and wore a spiked leather corselet, it had a long twisted and pointed nose, its skin was a deep ruddy brown and it stared through yellow beady eyes.

David's eyes locked on this demonic thing, it walked toward him, halberd blade first, David had nowhere to go, he hoped that Hawkins would help; but he was busy. He then looked over towards the Nihilist, but the Nihilist just stood there watching, like the Nihilist knew that David and the masons had sold him out as part of the bargain to gain their support. Then the Halberd bearing demon plunged its deadly weapon into David's chest, he flinched as it penetrated, he felt his life force weaken; ebbing away as wave upon wave of agony rushed through his body with every breath he took. David slipped from the creature's weapon and slipped to the floor, lifeless to rest against the wall.

****

The badger like creature limped still, but it could at least walk, beside the trench-coat clad Dietrich. They had slowly made their way to Heveningham, always walking toward the eye of the storm visible from far away as it was high in the air, now they neared their destination, the Gruul promised reward for all creatures that helped its master return to the earth.

They walked down the long twisting road that snaked through the centre of the Heveningham estate in the driving rain, their goal clear, kill Craig. If a car had went past, they would have been forgiven for thinking that they passed a lone dog walker braving the storm, such was the pairs visage.

Their single goal urged them forth, they could feel the closeness of different realities close to collision, they could now see the stately manor framed by the slowly rotating maelstrom above and to the right. They continued toward it. They paid no heed to anything else, not even the many crows that stood watch upon the fence and all about the fields.

Studies have proved that crows are so intelligent that they can warn each other of a dangerous person, recognising faces and advising each other of a possible danger. Dietrich and the demonic badger-like thing walked through the centre of the large gathering of black feathered birds, they didn't pay any heed to the initial sounds.

'Mwawk, Mwawk.'

They ignored the build-up of cawing from the intelligent creatures, and their warnings to one another.

'Mwawwkk, Mwawwkk, Mwawk.'

The pair also failed to notice the increasing amount of black beady eyes that turned and watched them as they progressed toward the centre of the storm.

Then as one a great murder of crows launched into the air, hundreds of the regal black birds soared into the sky, the two demonic beasts then realised the threat posed, instantly preparing to defend themselves from the impending black winged assault.

****

Jay had watched and waited, he had seen the slaughter begin, he could now also see the Demons charging headlong toward the portal entrance, they would soon be here, he decided quickly that they would be his salvation, he would help them, for a reward they would give; obviously. With his mind made up Jay looked about, he saw Craig in the corner, close to him was the broken and split demon, laying in a wide puddle of its own blood and bodily fluids, its spear lay close by; lain half within the gory puddle, Jay dashed over to it and picked it up. He looked at Craig, who stood directly in front of him, Craig then returned the gaze.

'Gruul I will help you stop these stupid humans.' He said, loudly over his own shoulder.

His gambit was to side with the demons and be rewarded for his service, who knows he may even be made up to the head of the Left-hand path.

'Time to die, you fucking idiot.' Jay said as he raised the spear in both hands to shoulder height, the point aimed straight at Craig.

'Don't be stupid, they will kill you, look at what they have done to your friends.' Craig replied; he gradually rotated his hand around till it was pointing toward Jay.

'they were stupid, and greedy, I can help them, they will reward me.'

'Get out of my way, there is still time to stop that thing from permanently opening the portal.'

Craig stole a glance at the portal; the mainstay of the demonic hordes had not reached the exit to our world yet, but they were getting closer and they were coming quickly, there was also a great darker shadow, further off within the portal. He could see behind Jay, the Gruul stood there still controlling the portal and Yakk; the little monster dragged Gabby by her hair toward the stark figure of Gruul as it stood there.

'No, little man, I'm going to ram this spear where the sun does not shine.' Jay then charged at Craig, spear first, aiming for Craig's heart.

****

Sydora and Steve were the first to leave the subterranean chamber, once they exited the door they quickly ran along the damp corridor, Sydora produced a ball of light from her hand, it sat there like a pet frog, obediently illuminating the way, they arrived at the steps and then headed up, rushing up the stairs and entering the circular room at the top, as they escaped their minds raced with thoughts as to what may emerge from the portal below, the mind would always play mean tricks in any high stress situation, it made their will to escape that much more expedient. And then they were outside, and free.

The rain lashed harder than before, if that was even possible; the morning sky was bathed in a myriad of blotchy light and pastel colours, the clouds swirled directly above, in a multitude of grey and purple shades. The vortex had grown in intensity whilst they had all been underground, it now rotated angrily in an anti-clockwise motion, debris, leaves, twigs and small branches were all picked up in its wild abandoned dance; earth's detritus was all lifted high into the sky.

'Where are we going Sydora?' Steve asked.

'We are getting far away from here, and we are going fast.'

'What about Lord Blessed, and Hawkins, we just left them there.'

'They were fooled by that Gruul, I am not risking my life for Lord Blessed, he can sort it out by himself.'

'But you trusted Gruul.'

'I had my misgivings.'

'You said nothing, why didn't you warn him about the demonic thing?' Steve asked.

'Shut up, we've got to get out of here and quick.'

They headed across the field toward the parked cars by the stable area, the winds whipped up all about and the going was particularly difficult, but at length they forced a way to the stables. Steve pulled out the keys to the BMW and unlocked the car., they both ran over and got in, Steve started the engine with a throaty raw. The power gently shook the vehicle as he pushed the gear stick into first. They pulled away, Steve drove toward the exit, following the slope down toward the back road and off toward Halesworth. Steve had put the wipers to work as soon as the engine had been started and they strained to keep the rain water and leaves from the windscreen.

'Which way, Halesworth, or south?' Steve asked as he looked over to Sydora, she indicated with her head to turn right, towards Halesworth. Steve on instinct hit the indicator and then they sped off toward the nearby town.

They sped through the fluid bends which snaked through the Heveningham estate, then they saw the trench coat clad figure fending off the repeated attacks by hundreds of crows.

'Look, that man is being attacked by those crows.' Steve said.

'That's no man... Stop.' Sydora said.

They pulled up close by underneath the cloud of attacking birds, Sydora got out.

'Need help?' She said.

Several dead birds littered the drenched road, all about the crows surrounded and dived, breaking the trench coat clad Dietrich's concentration. The four-legged creature upon the ground shook a captured crow in its jaws with a savagery that quickly snapped the bird's neck.

'We are here to kill the guardian.' He shouted as he thrust his arms out to fend off yet another birds incoming attack.

'No need, the guardian is finished, the portal is open.' Sydora guessed this creature had been tasked with killing Craig.

'Come with us, quickly. The Gruul has lied, it will trick you!'

Dietrich forced his mind to create an invisible spherical barrier, about him, his pet beast and the two by the blue BMW. Almost instantly, the rain bounced from the unseen barrier that surrounded them and the crows were repulsed from their unending assaults.

Dietrich walked toward the car with the badger-like demon, he looked at the birds that flocked about the protective orb, then slipped into the back of the car, then they all left; retreating away from the hall.

****

Jay ran toward Craig, he was not prepared, there was no magic he could use that would help. The spear was aimed true, Craig attempted to side-step but knew it was hopeless, unarmed he stood no chance, Jay was too close. Then the spear turned at the last instant with a grinding sound, Craig had had nothing to do with it, he looked down, suspended within the air was a shield that had been dropped by one of the demons; floating. Craig looked over; he saw Hawkins nod in acknowledgement of what he had just done. Craig nodded back in response and then quickly stepped to the side, before Jay could regain his balance from the deflected attack. Craig came closer to Hawkins.

'I'll stop him, you stop Gruul.' Hawkins said. Craig ran past Hawkins; as Hawkins prepared to fight Jay.

Craig looked at Hawkins, then turned to the Gruul, he saw that the Gruul with another demon had Gabby, they were laying her at the foot of the portal, she had a blade at her throat, the little demon had dragged her by her hair, it now thrust its sword into her face she obeyed, Craig thought of the gift, focused on pushing the little demon away from Gabby.

The demon that had killed David was eager to kill more, with its vicious halberd, it advanced upon Craig getting in his way, obscuring any chance of using the gift to save Gabby, any real chance of stopping the portal from being permanently opened.

Craig changed his concentration from the little Yakk to the advancing halberd bearing beast, determining the same effect on this one as it was upon the last, forcing the creature back, compelling its motion to reverse. The demon could not fight the gift, it slid backward, helpless, a passenger to Craig's whim.

Craig then released the effect and instead changed his concentration from pushing the creature away, to one of weakness, demanding the creature to strain under the weight of its own weapon, to struggle within its own skin to hold the weapon or its own body weight. The demon could not resist, it struggled, first the blade end of its bloodstained weapon dropped to the flagstone floor with a clang, then its knees bent inward; fighting to stay on its feet. It dropped the halberd and fell to one knee, the demon thrust its arm to the ground as it still struggled with the additional pressure upon it. Craig continued to push down upon the creature with his mind; it was helpless to resist, Craig pushed harder with his mind and the creature's arm gave. The monster then slammed onto the floor, defenceless against Craig's magic, defenceless as Craig continued to force down upon the demon, crushing it slowly, but crushing it none the less.

Jay spun to face Craig and Hawkins, the spear still in his hands.

'Get out of the way Hawkins, we can get a lot out of this, we just need to work together, help the demons.'

'They killed my father Jay, they will kill us, its futile.' Hawkins replied.

'No, they will reward us, they always do bargain, think about it, we could be rulers, not sheep.'

'No, Jay, they won't reward us, I see it now, Gruul never wanted to help us, it was only ever using us to get to this point, Jay, they have tricked us; it's over.'

Jay looked at Hawkins, denial in his eyes, like so many of us humans; we cannot admit to ourselves we are wrong, even at the end when our plans unravel, we cling to different principles of an argument; to allow us to avoid the inevitable admission to ourselves that we have been duped. Jay was at this point now, but the only thing he could do was prove the demon hordes would recognise him as one of theirs, the only way was to help them gain purchase in this world, to help them kill Hawkins and Craig.

'No Hawkins, you are wrong, if you won't help; then, I'm afraid, you will die with the rest of them.'

Jay charged, spear first. But his charge was cut drastically short, from his left side a sword swung low, catching clean into his left leg at the shin, the blow was true and powerful, cleaving deep into the flesh, carving to the bone. Jay slid along the floor, screaming in agony from the terrible wound, his blood flowed freely, he quickly lost consciousness, the demons were not here to parley; they came to slay and to kill. The creature that had hacked Jays leg was pleased with itself; then it looked for its next target, as one kill was not enough. It was still eager to kill.

Chapter 36

Turncoats

Jay lay upon the floor, dead at Hawkins feet; Hawkins felt low, as low as he had when Cliff had died. That seemed like years ago now; though in reality it was only a matter of a few weeks. He forced his anger into an irresistible blast; aimed at the creature that had hacked off Jay's leg. The diminutive demon was caught clean in the head with the explosive force, it screamed as its head took the crushing blow; shattering its skull with an incredible impact force.

He then turned to face the portal, turned to deal with Gruul, the little Imp-like thing that he had regarded as little more than a pet, but had been in reality, a terrible evil, preparing its insidious plans with no thought for others, like a psychopathic killer secretly preparing its murderous spree. Hawkins stepped forward.

Craig saw the giant, monstrously knuckled beast as it swung from behind, a mighty haymaker, aimed for Hawkins head, he never saw it coming. Craig watched as Hawkins head violently bent at the neck with an ugly crunching sound. Hawkins neck snapped like a twig from the power of the awesome blow, he fell silently to the ground; lifeless. Craig was shocked, he shook his head to clear his thoughts, but the monster was already turning in his direction, it lowered its tusked maw, dipping its head slightly then it loped towards Craig.

****

The Nihilist had watched and waited as the halberd bearing demon had finished David Smith, he knew that the freemasons had betrayed him, and Blessed had been only too happy to agree. Deliberating just what was going on, who was on the right side and who was in the wrong, his mind had been made up when a snivelling thing, choking and whining had jumped from the portal, a small axe in each hand, the monster had leapt at the Nihilist, a diabolical beast from the infernal planes intent upon its first kill.

However the thing had leapt at the wrong target, if it was eager for a quick kill, the Nihilist stepped back with a half step then shuffled back with a full step, lifting the katana up, on the half step, then, neat and clean, straight and true; he brought the curved sword down in an elegant elliptical arc, cleaving through the monstrous creatures skull, it slumped down lifeless before it had hit the flagstones. The Nihilist made up his mind to help Craig, he took in just what was happening. Looking over just to see Hawkins neck break from the colossal strike that the giant tusked demon had delivered, from behind to the unsuspecting young man.

It made him sick, all of this had been caused by greed, a greed which had been manipulated into just what the Gruul had wanted; because they wanted to believe in the promises that were given, even himself, he had only accepted the overly generous pay check because of greed. Now he accepted that because it was partly his mess, then he should help clean it up, and so, he slowly lifted the Japanese sword to his right shoulder, point up with his shoulders tucked in, and he advanced toward the large creature; to help Craig before it was too late and to atone in some small way for the jeopardy that he had helped to put the world in.

Craig had seized up, the large monster coming toward him and the Gruul and Yakk preparing to seal open the portal for evermore had shook him. Craig did not know what to do, he panicked and could not concentrate, at this moment when it mattered most, he found that the gift was nowhere in sight. The tusked demon got closer, it reached out, grasping Craig with both of its massive hands, he felt the unearthly strength the creature had, and he could easily see the malice buried deep within, showing in the vile yellow eyes. The tusks protruded from its head, below its mouth, he could smell the foul breath of the creature, it was a scent of decomposing vegetables and ammonia, stifling. Then the creature drew its head back, ready to gore Craig upon its tusks; he was helpless.

Craig saw the curved metal blade slice down, impeccably aimed and impossibly sharp, it removed the mammoth beast's right arm just below the shoulder, blood flowed freely from the straight cut. The arm fell with a heavy thud, the behemoth lifted its head up in the air; roaring in agony as it dropped Craig. It then let out another deafening bellow, a wailing howl of pain. Craig being so close to the demon was left with a ringing inside his head.

Craig fell down onto his knees and crawled away while the beast bellowed in agony, the thing began to thrash wildly, sending bloody droplets in all directions, swinging the one remaining arm like a giant club, it banged into one of the pillars, holding the ceiling, some dust fell but the pillar held fast, it turned on the Nihilist, swinging the arm as it spun, he rose the sword to deflect the attack but the blow was square and knocked him back, removing all air from him, his diaphragm began to spasm and the Nihilist staggered back to the wall gasping for air, each time he tried to take a breath a sharp shooting pain rose from within, he thought that maybe he had broken ribs. The giant beast moved toward him, though now it was leaning upon the ground heavily with its one remaining arm. The beast was beginning to slow from the continued blood loss.

****

The Gruul and Yakk had now gotten Gabby over to the portal, she had passed out long ago, the terror of the situation and blood loss had played a devastating part upon her, robbing her of sense, and then she had fainted, Yakk had dragged her to the portal and now the Gruul pronounced words in the true language of dark magic, the forbidden words of binding, balancing the two worlds, and preparing the sacrifice of Gabby's blood to permanently connect the two worlds by a thread, to bridge them forevermore.

Craig watched as the Gruul lifted the staff high, still babbling in an undefinable tongue, the pointed end was hovering close to her chest. Directly above her.

'Stop!' Craig cried out; his arm outstretched.

The Gruul remembered the skirmish they had had, upon the rooftops. It looked at Craig and lowered the staff slightly.

'What can you do now,' the Gruul said in its broken cracked voice, 'it is too late, I have won!' with a triumphant finality, the Gruul lifted the spear high once more and plunged it towards Gabby's breast. Craig saw the spear tip end of the staff raise, he fixed his mind to the tip that came down, determining that it would stray wide, fixing that it would strike the flagstones, but as his concentration took hold upon the staff, then he saw the fast approaching creature inside the portal on the other side it shook him out of his magical sight, it was an immense winged dragon-like creature and it swept through the misty tunnel at great speed all along the smoky portal that connected the prison realm of the demons to the earth where its wing tips touched the sides small smoky vortices were created. The only feeling Craig had in his head was that they were doomed.

****

As the one armed beast swung for the Nihilist he had lifted his blade to defend, it had cornered him, it had been becoming more and more sluggish, the loss of blood taking its toll, the beast's one remaining fist made contact with the curved sword, the strength of the swing opened the creatures hand, shearing easily through the flesh, the creature yelped once more and retracted its arm, the Nihilist took the opportunity and stepped in, lifting the katana above his head, he then swung clean and fast, taking the sword down in a graceful, majestic arc, cutting into the giant beast's neck, the creatures whines and roars, abruptly subsided, and the giant demon slumped down; dead.

The Nihilist launched himself at the last two remaining demons; Yakk and the Gruul, he saw the staff coming down, he saw Craig stood, dumbly staring into the misty portal, he acted on instinct, three quick steps, rotating the Japanese katana sword clockwise behind himself, then on the third step, following through in an upward cutting motion, Yakk tried to stand in the way but the diminutive creature was just too small to stop the Nihilist's forward motion, the sword contacted the Gruul at the hip and then followed through, shearing into the Gruuls waist, and then its chest, until it exited the demon sorcerer's body between the shoulder and the neck. The Nihilist stopped the cuts motion with trained precision, the metallic staff clattered harmlessly to the flagstones, Gabby was spared. The Gruul fell to the floor in two separate segments.

Craig watched as the dragon flew closer and closer; transfixed, the dark beauty of such a marvellous beast, he was scared now, truly scared, like he had never felt before, would the portal hold long enough for the thing to escape, or would it collapse, he prayed that they had not been too late.

The portal had started to waver, the wispy smoke, trailing into itself had become erratic, fitting and starting, but it had not instantly collapsed upon itself as he had hoped, the creature would escape before the portal collapsed and the dimensions separated.

Yakk fled for the door as fast as it's little feet could carry it, its chances against the swordsmen were nil and Yakk knew it, the demon quickly reached the door and then was gone, leaving the subterranean chamber.

The Nihilist turned to Craig and the wispy portal, he saw Craig still stood transfixed, wondering why the portal had not collapsed.

'Craig, what is it, what's the matter?' He asked.

Craig just stood staring as the flying creature was now within two hundred metres and still coming. The Nihilist looked inside and saw the giant winged beast's approach.

He also felt the fear, but would not succumb to it, forcing himself to action despite terror's icy grip and the sharp stabbing pain in his side.

'Craig snap out of it, SNAP OUT OF IT.' He shouted; Craig looked over dumb from fear.

'How can we close it?'

One hundred and fifty metres.

'I don't know, I don't know.' Craig said slowly.

'We don't have time, try something, quick.' The Nihilist said, turning to face the oncoming horror, he took a stance with the sword level horizontally behind him, ready to strike as the dragon left the portal.

One hundred metres.

Craig looked about, the fear that had grasped him, made all his actions feel slow and forced, time had slowed to a crawl, each thought felt like a slurred slow-motion debate, rather than a quick decisive choice.

The smoky wisps, now erratic, had become unstable, flickering in and out, breaking down, gradually but not nearly fast enough.

Fifty metres. The dragon would be there in but a few more seconds now, behind the legions had been left behind, easily overtaken by the dark prince's dragon.

Craig then spotted the metallic staff laid upon the ground by the Gruul's corpse, he ran over and picked it up, then spun upon his heel and hurled the long staff into the portal, hoping against hope that it would destabilise further.

Twenty metres.

The staff entered the portal as it was visibly collapsing, caving in upon itself, the Nihilist could clearly make out the enormous flared nostrils of the flying lizard-like beast, and then the staff, thrown by Craig, entered the portal, sailing into the mists and smoky trails that were now struggling to find purchase in our dimension.

Ten metres.

The Nihilist could taste the acrid breath of the colossal winged monster, he stepped forward, the sword following in an upward slice, timed to connect immediately as the creature left the portal.

Then as the sword was about to contact with the horrendous beast, the mists engulfed the portal, shrouding the dragon from sight, the katana blade, swished through the mists, harmlessly stroking through the fast disappearing smoke.

Craig looked over at the Nihilist, the Nihilist looked back. Both unsure on whether to fight, walk away or shake one another's hand. There was a long pause, the pair just eyed each other warily.

At length the Nihilist broke the stalemate.

'Well seems as we have not killed each other yet, I am assuming that we are okay.'

Craig looked him up and down, he could see the red stained katana sword, red blotchy patches; spattered all over from the fray.

'I guess so.' Craig said, as he let out an enormous breath of air.

Chapter 37

Blue Skies Above Suffolk

Craig and the Nihilist stood in the underground chamber, corpses both human and demonic, littered the floor, there was large puddles of spilt dark blood all about. Both the Nihilist and Craig breathed heavily, exhausted from the battle, they had both excepted that they were now allies of a sort, but both now wanted to leave. The room had returned to the cold, dankness of before, only the grisly scene and sight of corpses strewn across the floor, told of what had happened here.

'How are we going to get rid of these?' The Nihilist asked, indicating toward the bodies.

'I have an idea, I say we pile the bodies up, burn them, and then I will bring the roof down on top of it all.'

'It sounds like a plan.' The Nihilist said, shrugging his shoulders.

They gradually moved body after body, until the whole sickening scene were piled together at the far end of the chamber.

Craig looked at the gory corpse pile, concentrated and then the corpse pile ignited; slowly the bodies began to burn.

'We had better go.' The Nihilist said.

Outside the subterranean chamber the clouds had swiftly dispersed, breaking up and leaving a bright, clear sky, the rains had stopped falling, ceasing as the clouds broke and leaving the whole area bathed in summer light

They left the Icehouse and then Craig focused on the inner chamber collapsing it within, after a few moments, there was a low rumble and the ground shook slightly.

'It is done, we better get out of here.'

'I'll give you a lift, where do you want to go?' The Nihilist asked as he produced the glass key fob to the Aston Martin.

'I don't suppose you could use your magic to falsify the paperwork on this little gem, could you? Can you?' He asked.

Craig chuckled, concentrated then said just give me some details and it shouldn't be too much of a problem.'

The Nihilist smiled touched the door lock release and they both got in.

'Take me to the James Paget Hospital, I need to check up on my friends.'

The car started with a throaty roar and they drove away, speeding past the fields, Craig could see all of the crows lined up on the fence and walking about in the field, looking for worms after the storm; Craig smiled to himself.

****

Sydora returned with Steve, the trench coat wearing Dietrich and the injured beast, they headed west toward Cambridge after raiding the Manor at Sydora's demand. They took all of the Gruul's library, hoping to gain more knowledge of demon kind, learn more about the Gruul's power. When they got to Cambridge, they consolidated the power of the Left-Hand path, between the four of them they would turn the august organisation into a driving power for their own self-interest. Building upon the lessons they had learnt and with the study they would complete of the Gruul's forbidden texts.

Sydora taught Steve in the ways of blood magic, In the future he would learn how to harness the very potent powers; unlocking many mysteries along the way.

****

Matt had broken his leg and had damaged his right lower lung, the doctors decided to keep him in after stapling surgery to prevent a collapsed lung from occurring in the future. Cairo had stayed with him that first night. She had deliberated heading over to see Craig, to help him, but ultimately, she was not even aware of where he was, she decided ultimately that this was his battle, if she was needed Craig would be in touch. Matt had insisted he would be okay, and she should help, but she was not convinced and felt that leaving him alone in the hospital; that he could very well be in great danger.

They were greatly relieved when the storm subsided, realising correctly that it meant that Craig had been successful. Later that day Craig had walked onto the ward, they held one another in a long embrace that none were eager to leave. They had survived, against all the odds, it had changed all of their outlooks on the world, they would have a bond that none could shake.

****

Victoria had slipped away unnoticed, when the chaos of the subterranean chamber had begun to unfold, she had slipped out quietly after Sydora and Steve, she had then fled to Heveningham Hall and her room. Victoria, fearful of what may have gone wrong; and because she had no experience of the magical world. She was not sure if something had gone wrong or whether this was Lord Blessed's plan all along. Staying in as the storm raged, she had tucked herself between the bed and a chair within the room, when the storms had dissolved, she finally emerged from the room, hoping none would discover her participation within the whole sorry situation.

The police at length found the burnt bodies of Lord Blessed, Hawkins, David, Dr Humboldt and all of the rest of the masons within the buried chamber, the burnt bodies of the demons were sent to, and received by the government, but they were never mentioned in any report.

Victoria went to Lord Blessed's funeral after they had found his body, no matter what had happened, he had always been very kind to her, and she felt she owed him so much for paving the way for her career to flourish in politics. She was also very surprised to receive a very large portion of Lord Blessed's estate in his will.

The Nihilist kept driving, leaving Suffolk; he caught the ferry to Europe, leaving the United Kingdom, he didn't stop for many countries. He went to rediscover himself; he went to determine just how many contracts he had undertaken had been for the worse. The Nihilist retreated from the western world to visit an old friend who would have answers; he went to gain for himself, the clues that could possibly redeem himself; for himself.

****

Two months passed after those terrible nights. Craig had lost his job as he had expected he would, Matt made a full recovery and Cairo went back to university. The Nihilist had left Craig at the hospital, the pair shook hands and agreed that if necessary, they would work together again. The crows returned to the garden where they would be fed two to three times a day by either Craig or his grandmother.

Then someone knocked on the door of the shed where Craig had started to spend more and more time, Craig opened the door. A man in his forties stood there, dressed in an old eighties style shell suit was a man of middle eastern persuasion.

'Hello, can I help you?' Craig asked, confused as to just who this gentleman was.

'I'm glad we finally got to meet; most people call me Wraith. I was a close friend of your Grandfather!'

****

Yakk fled north into the wilderness near Norwich, it was trapped here but unlike the Gruul, Yakk had no magical ability, the creature was miserable at first. Then it realised one important fact, there were many innocent souls on this reality that may be hurt or tortured.

Yakk would be busy.

TO BE CONTINUED.

Printed in Poland
by Amazon Fulfillment
Poland Sp. z o.o., Wrocław